# THE SHADOW KING

## BRYANT JORDAN

BARROWVIEW BOOKS

The Shadow King

Copyright©2022

This book is a work of fiction. The names, characters, places and incidents are the product of the author's imagination or are used fictitiously. Any resemble to actual events, business establishments, locales, or persons, living or dead, is entirely coincidental.

Published in the United States of America.

*For my wife, Linda.*

# ACKNOWLEDGMENTS

Thanks to my wife, Linda, for her encouragement, early edits and later proofing; my author niece, Victoria Pinder, for tips on publishing and even showing me what my novel would look like while it was still a first draft; lifelong friend and super librarian Donna Bryant; former journalism colleagues Debbie Funk, Jim Hand, Don Stewart and Ho Lin; and actor/writer Kevin O'Rourke, a veteran reader of a number of my scribblings. I am grateful for the time and attention they all gave to reading and critiquing The Shadow King. Finally, thank you to book editor Deborah Heimann for her spot-on recommendations and overall edits.

## ACKNOWLEDGMENTS

# CHAPTER
# ONE

I go to Zhang's House of Dragon's most every day from my summer job at Empire Film Exchange, which is on Boylston Street, just a few blocks from Chinatown. Turk, my boss, recommended Zhang's last year when I first landed the summer job. He's got a soft spot for Chinatown. It comes from growing up there when it was still called Little Syria and dominated by Arabs. His people came from somewhere that's now part of Lebanon, so Turk is just a nickname he picked up somewhere along the way and never could shake.

House of Dragons is at the corner of Beach and Oxford streets. It's been in business since the '20s, and Zhang Wei—whose name is now on the sign—started there in the kitchen. Turk said he's been the sole owner for decades, first inheriting it from his wife's family, and afterward owning it jointly with his son, also named Wei, and daughter-in-law, Bao. But then they were killed in a car accident on the

Mass Pike in the late '50s, leaving behind two young children for Zhang and his wife, Li Xiu, to raise, Turk said. If that wasn't sad enough, Zhang's wife fell sick and died six months later. How shitty is that, to lose your son, your daughter-in-law, and your wife all within six months? Zhang didn't have much time to mourn, though, not with looking after his grandchildren, Eu-meh and Li.

Eu-meh is the main reason I go to Zhang's. She works the lunch shift three days a week and some weekend nights when her grandfather needs her. She's drop-dead beautiful, smart-ass funny when she wants to be, and just plain smart. She's also an artist. She just finished up her freshman year at Rhode Island School of Design. She loves to paint—watercolors, especially—but also oils. She's also begun working a lot in clay at RISD with an eye toward sculpting. If that wasn't enough, she also plays the piano "a little" and can juggle.

"You juggle? Why?" I had asked her.

"Why not? Seemed like it would be fun so I taught myself."

"Cool. What'd you start out with?"

"Things that didn't break when they hit the floor."

"That makes sense. What do you use now?"

"Things that don't break when they hit the floor."

In addition to pulling down lunch shifts she has a part-time job at the Museum of Fine Arts gift shop.

She is definitely a class act. Her home, at least for the summer, is an apartment over on Marlborough Street, near the Public Gardens. She shares it with a friend who works for the phone company.

She knows I work at the film exchange and that I have this ambition to make movies, though I'm not sure she takes it as seriously as I'd like her to. But she typically greets me at the restaurant with a *Hey, DeMille,* or *Hey, Kubrick,* or *Hey, Coppola.* It's always good for a laugh.

I asked her out a few weeks after I met her last summer but she said no. She said it in a playful way, a tone that suggested both of us knew it was a silly idea because, well, it just was. A month later I asked again and got the same answer. I haven't asked her out since I started coming back in. Still, I've had this dream a few times. It's summer, and we're sitting at a window table in the restaurant and talking about the most recent college semester—Eu-meh down in Providence and me up here in Boston, where I'm enrolled at Emerson. The problem with the dream is that I'm not in film school yet and I have no idea when I'll be able to start. If ever. Especially at Emerson, which is nearly $5,000 a year. USC's film school is less than $3,000 a year and it's closer to movie mecca, but then there'd be the costs of actually moving to California. Here I am, twenty years old and already feeling like I've missed the boat. I've got a good, if unusual, education, having spent my four years of high school not in school but in libraries, museums and historic places all across the city. That all sounds good, and it was, but it was also the result of a regular classroom education that started going off the rails when I was in the third grade. Up to then I was considered "gifted." I had been reading at a seventh- or eighth-grade level and my parents and teachers expected me to be the next Einstein. But then Dad was killed and I very quickly went from promising student to problem child. I barely spoke in class. I put in minimal effort at schoolwork because I was afraid I'd end up in some kind of special home for dummies if I did nothing at all. My Uncle Barry, Ma's brother, who had done some teaching in the past, came around a lot and prodded me to keep up. Later on, when my classmates were getting ready to start high school, Barry somehow arranged with the school department to let him take over teaching me. That was the end of my formal education. But no public-school education meant no high school diploma. I did routinely ace every test I was required to take so the state could track my learning. And I did snag the GED with ease. That is, when I finally got around to taking the exam at eighteen.

One thing should be clear by now. If Eu-meh and I were characters in a movie I'd be the no-prospects bad-boy and Eu-meh the good girl who has her act together. The difference is that in movies those couples from different sides of the tracks often end up together. We're in the real world, and unless something changes for real, then I have to settle for seeing Eu-meh in the only way possible: as a restaurant customer on good enough terms with her to chat and kid around. Nothing else. And I think that suits her grandfather just fine. The old guy never said a single word to me all last summer. And when I went in earlier this month, on my first day back at the film exchange, he glanced at me once, nodded, and went back to whatever it was he was doing.

Eu-meh's welcome-back was better. When I walked into House of Dragons just two weeks ago, I found it busier than I remembered it. I didn't see her at first and wondered if maybe she'd moved out of Boston, maybe was staying in Providence. Then I heard her voice.

"Look who's here. Long-time no see, Welles. How's the movie biz?"

I'm sure I smiled like a kid, maybe an idiot kid at that, I don't know. But it was a thrill seeing her and feeling like we'd picked up just where we left off. Which was friends, or friendly acquaintances, I guess. Whatever it was, it felt good.

"How you doing, Eu-meh? You look great. College life treating you well?"

"It really is. Have to talk later, though. It's really crazy here today and I feel a bit rusty at this. My brother will be glad to see you again" She dropped her voice to a whisper. "Oh, he spells his name L, E, E now, not L, I."

"Why?"

5

"Let him tell you," she said. With menu in hand, she led me to a table. She placed the menu in front of me, then she said something that made me want to run like hell out of the restaurant. "Fill me in later about film school."

She was gone before I could say a word, which was just as well because I had no idea what word I was going to use and it would have stuck in my throat anyway. I sat there thinking I'd just order a few appetizers to go, when Li—or Lee, I guess—took the chair across from me.

"Hey, you're back!"

"Yes. I just started back at the exchange," I said.

"Cool. So, you're home for the summer. What's film school like?"

So much for dodging that question. "I haven't started yet. There's still the rest of the tuition to come up with." He seemed satisfied with that and asked about movie releases. It was a relief.

"Your sister says you're now spelling your name L, E, E. What's that about?"

I knew Lee was always a big fan of Westerns, but with the popularity of Kung Fu movies and Bruce Lee, it wouldn't have surprised me if that was the reason. I was wrong. Ma always told me not to buy into stereotypes or make assumptions about people based on race.

"Nah, man. Lee Van Cleef," he said. "He's a stone-cold boss and has been forever. Just saw him in the new Magnificent Seven movie. He's taken over Yul Brynner's role."

"Lee Van Cleef?" I said, to be sure I heard right.

"Yeah! You know! Colonel Mortimer in *For a Few Dollars More*. Angel Eyes in *The Good, The Bad and the Ugly*," he said. "I read that the dude was even one of the gunmen in *High Noon* like a hundred years ago."

"Sure, okay. Lee Van Cleef," I said.

He asked what movies I'd seen lately and what I was going to see. It was a conversation we had every time I was there last summer. For some reason, Zhang seems to have no problem letting Lee sit down and talk with me for a while. Maybe he interrogates the kid each time after I talk to him, to find out what I'm up to.

"You and your sister are always pretty friendly when I come in here. How come your grandfather has never said so much as a hello?" As soon as I asked the question, I regretted it. I had no business asking that of a sixteen-year-old kid.

He shrugged.

"I don't know. He's always about business in the restaurant, and he's naturally quiet and cautious." He said his grandfather was like some stern warrior of old keeping a protective eye on those he had vowed to protect.

"He's like this ever ever-vigilant guardian, hovering in the background—

"What? Like Batman?" I joked.

"Actually, my nickname for him is *Yīngzi Wáng* —Shadow King."

Shadow King. Now there's a nickname.


That was nearly two weeks ago. I've been back most days since then but haven't had much conversation with Eu-meh. Lee told her that I wasn't enrolled in school yet. She didn't seem to think it was a big deal, so I made it a point not to talk about it. Very quickly lunch at Zhang's took on the same easy feel of last summer.

Then came last Tuesday. Lee sat with me to talk movies. I said was looking forward to *The Parallax View*, a Warren Beatty film about a reporter who uncovers a plot by powerful corporation to murder a presidential candidate. Beatty usually delivers a good movie.

"Sounds boring," Lee said. "There's a Charles Bronson movie coming out next month I want to see. *Death Wish*. He plays a New York architect whose family is murdered and he becomes a vigilante."

"So it's a Western?" I said.

He laughed, but stopped when he heard his name called. Lee looked startled. His grandfather rarely spoke outside of a whisper while in the restaurant. He turned toward the old man, who waved him over.

"I am summoned," Lee said with a smile. He

walked over and slid into the seat next to his grandfather. I couldn't hear anything they said, but I could see the old man look over at me once. Lee glanced over, too. He looked a bit puzzled. Well, so was I at that point. I was thinking the old man didn't like me. He'd probably seen the way I look at Eu-meh, and I know from what Lee said that he's probably overprotective. Maybe he was telling Lee not to talk with me. Next step would be banning me from the House of Dragons. That would suck.

Lee seemed uncomfortable with whatever he was hearing. He finally got up and headed my way. Yep, he was unhappy, and he also looked worried.

"What's up?"

"Well, umm, I'm not sure how to..." he began but then stopped. He looked back at his grandfather, who stared back at him. Lee turned to me again.

"Don't tell me," I said. "I'm a bad influence and not welcome here anymore."

"What?"

"If that's the case, why doesn't the Shadow King come tell me himself?" I said. I could feel my heartbeat quicken. I was getting a bit hot under the collar, so to speak. That's never good.

"What are you talking about?" Lee said. His face was incredulous and his voice dropped even lower as he whispered: "Why are you talking like that? You crazy?"

"Well, what is it then?"

Lee seemed uneasy. He continued to speak in a whisper.

"He asked me to ask you if you know anything about a white van with New York plates that broke down in Boston a few nights ago. When the driver went off to find a payphone to call for help the van was stolen. He heard it ended up in Charlestown."

I stared at him. Whatever relief I felt that the old man wasn't barring me because he didn't want me around Eu-meh instantly disappeared. He thought I might know something about a hot van in Charlestown. That's the first fucking thing the guy wants to talk to me about? And not even talk to me, but send his frigging grandson over?

"What makes him think I'd know?" I said. I kept my voice down and tried to act like I wasn't taking it seriously. I chuckled. "What? I look like a criminal? Like I'm mobbed up?" But even as I made my hopefully comical protest, I was doing a 54-frames-per-second playback in my head of the times I'd broken the law. Small stuff like robbing parking meters, stealing comic books and 45-rpm records when I was thirteen and fourteen, to that time when I thought I was a hot shit and tried my hand at selling drugs. I had just turned seventeen and thought I was really something. Luckily, I wasn't busted by the cops for any of that shit, though Uncle Barry put a stop to my dealing days with a serious caution (It'll kill your mother if she finds out), sound advice (you've already got too much going against you and a drug dealing rap will fuck you up for good), and a punch in the head to help me reflect more on the caution and advice. As for the stuff I was caught at: public intoxication and disturbing the peace charges when I was what, maybe sixteen? But it was Bunker Hill Day and shit like that happens on Bunker Hill Day. I got off with a warning. More serious was the pot bust last year. Yep, even though my dealer days were years ago and short lived, I remained a consumer. It was just a roach, really. Barely anything left to it. Yet enough that the cop, a detective no less, got me on possession. Ma cried a lot, which made me feel like an asshole and a loser. And all I could do was thank God I never got busted for the dealing. I don't know how it happened but the judge continued my case without finding for a year. That ends in November. But it means that if I stay out of trouble the charge goes away.

Okay, so I have done some shit in the past. But why shouldn't I protest? Did they assume that I would know about a heist just because I'm a Townie?

Apparently, it worked.

"Okay, I'm sorry," Lee said. "Don't get all pissed off! He just wanted me to ask is all." Lee shook his head. He tugged at his shirt collar like Rodney Dangerfield. "Just askin', is all. And he wonders if you wouldn't mind, you know, asking around about it."

"Why me?"

"Because you're from Charlestown. No one from Chinatown can go over there and ask about it."

I nodded.

"Okay, yeah, I get it," I said. "I guess it would be like a Townie coming over here and asking where he can buy some opium."

"Not really," he laughed. "You people do that all the time. Every weekend there's some *ègùn* from Charlestown, Southie, Brookline or other White neighborhood coming into Chinatown to eat and drink, then try to score some opium or cocaine or even heroin before heading home. It's been like that forever. Who knows? Maybe your grandfather bought opium from mine fifty years ago."

Man, that really threw me.

"How does that work? You say White guys can come into your neighborhood and ask about a crime but no one from Chinatown can go into a White neighborhood and do the same. That sounds pretty racist."

"It's two different things," he said. "The guys coming into Chinatown are asking to buy something that is illegal. But they're not asking where it came from, how it was transported, and who is handling it now. Those kinds of questions can buy you something you're not looking for and don't want."

I had to admit, the kid had a point.

"So come over and ask as a customer? Say you're willing to pay to get the van."

He shook his head.

"Look, I don't know what is going on with this. I don't know where the van came from or what it was carrying. I'm like Sergeant Schultz: *I know nothing!* I'm only passing along a request from my grandfather."

We both looked across the restaurant at the old man, who stared back silently. Then he raised a hand.

"Me?" I mouthed silently, hoping he'd shake his head no. He nodded yes. I started to get up. "Hey, Lee," I said, "what's an *ègùn*?"

"Huh?"

"*Ègùn*. What is it?"

"It's Chinese for *guest*." He smiled.

"*Ègùn*," I said, trying out the word.

I headed over to the old man's table. I was nervous. I hoped I didn't look it.

Zhang gestured for me to take a seat. I nodded, sat down, and said "Hello, Mr. Zhang."

"Relax, Mr. Lyons," he said, so of course I didn't but nodded anyway as if I was immediately relaxed. I couldn't get over the fact, after all the times I'd been in, when I finally had a conversation with old Zhang it was to talk about whether I could help him find a hijacked truck. I was more at ease when I was arrested.

"I could tell even from over here that you are reluctant to make the inquiry," the old man said. "I can understand that. Doubtless some would wonder at your interest in the van."

"Wondering, I don't mind. People thinking I'm

asking around in order to snitch is what I worry about," I said.

He nodded.

I was kind of surprised by how he spoke. I always saw him at his table, statue like. I guess I already had ideas in my head of what he would sound like, talk like. I thought he'd be aloof, even mysterious and magisterial. In other words, the stereotype I knew from movies and TV shows. Of course, Lee's nickname for his grandfather didn't help much either. Shadow King. Even if Lee intended it as a joke, it did sound kind of Fu Manchu-ey.

"I am not looking for trouble. I am not looking to get you into trouble," he said. "I only ask that if you learn the whereabouts of this van—or, more importantly, of its contents—that you would let me know."

"What was in the van?" I asked. I figured it would be only natural to show some curiosity, so I did.

He nodded and smiled. "Old film," he said. "I gather from your work at the film exchange you have an interest in such things."

I smiled back. I couldn't help myself. I said, "What kind of films?"

He shook his head.

"That's not important. I will tell you that I paid for them and I paid to have them brought here from New York."

"So you're the owner?"

"I am the owner, yes."

When he said that I did relax. Not because I thought everything was on the up and up. Far from it. Something still seemed off. But now I was genuinely more interested in what was going on. The phone he kept by the table rang.

"Excuse me one moment," he said and picked up. I couldn't hear the caller. I could barely hear Zhang, his voice dropped so low. He placed the receiver to his chest. "Please stay a little longer, Mr. Lyons. I have to take this in my office. I will be back directly." He put the caller on hold and left with the light blinking. A moment later the light was solid again and I knew he'd picked up.

I turned to Lee, who mouthed, *What?* I shrugged. I saw Eu-meh watching intently from across the room, her brow knitted in a way that could mean concern, or suspicion. So I turned away to look at the walls around Zhang's table. There were dozens of photos. Up until this point I had seen them only from a distance. I scanned the pictures quickly because Zhang could be back any moment. Some were quite old, images of China that could have come right out of *National Geographic* before the days of color film. There were also family photos. I recognized a much-younger Zhang with his wife in what was obviously their wedding photo. He looked pretty dapper in a suit. She was dressed in a traditional Chinese wedding dress. There was a photo of a group of soldiers, all Chinese, posing with their rifles in front of some ancient temple. Next to it was one of a Chinese woman standing next to a military aircraft. And from the way she was dressed it seemed she must have been the pilot. There were also photos of the Zhangs with their son and his very young family, including one taken out on a boat in Boston Harbor. This was no dinky little boat, but a really good-looking and doubtless expensive bridgedeck cruiser at least forty feet long. In the family photo the younger Wei is crouched down, his arm around Eumeh, who looks to be about four years old. Bao is standing next to them holding Lee, who is just a baby. Neither could have any real memory of their parents. Only these photos let them know they once held them in their arms.

I was surprised as hell to see old Zhang and his wife with various Hollywood stars and politicians. Some were at World War II war bond drives and others at fundraisers to support China in its fight against Japan. Lee had told me his grandfather had raised money for the war effort, and even sent money and supplies to Chinese fighters before the U.S. got into the war. Until that point, though, I'd had no idea the old guy was rubbing elbows with Hollywood royalty and politicians back then. I have to admit, I particularly liked the photos with the stars. There he was, only feet away from Cagney, whose face revealed a tough optimism, with Bob Hope mugging for the camera, and a laughing Groucho Marx, minus the paint mustache. In one photo, a banner in the background read "1942 Hollywood Caravan." The venue looked like Boston Garden. In others, taken downtown, Dorothy Lamour, Bette Davis and other stars and big-wigs were hawking bonds from a patriotically decorated flatbed. Bette was from Lowell, but Boston liked to claim her as its own. And there was Zhang in 1944 posing with a stylishly-dressed Jackie Gleason in front of the Shubert Theatre, the marquis read *Follow The Girls.*

Elsewhere, Zhang and another Chinese guy were standing next to two of the biggest local pols of the day: Gov. Leverett Saltonstall and Boston Mayor Maurice Tobin. I wouldn't have recognized either of them except their names were written on the photo. But I did know the other Chinese guy. It was a very young Keye Luke, who back in the '40s was playing roles like Number One Son in the Charlie Chan movies. Now he's world famous as Master Po, the blind Shaolin priest on the *Kung Fu* TV show. Weird, I thought: Almost thirty years between roles and Luke is still playing a support role to a White guy made-up to look Chinese. I turned to another photo. Zhang and his wife were wearing bright, beaming smiles and standing alongside two beautiful and elegantly dressed women, one Chinese and one White. The women looked vaguely familiar. *Butterfly* was written, signed maybe, just under the picture of the Chinese woman, and beneath the blonde was written *Edith*. Edith also turned up in another photo, this one among a group of some eight people sitting around a large table at the restaurant. It looked like the '50s and the gang was having quite a party. And there was Gleason again, the biggest guy in the group, no surprise there. I was still trying to figure out who they all could be when Zhang returned.

"My apologies, Mr. Lyons. I had to take that call."

"No problem, Mr. Zhang." I wanted to ask about the photos but he got right back to business.

"As I was saying. I am the owner of the films. I hope that makes you feel more comfortable."

"So why not go to the cops? They won't mind going into Charlestown to ask questions. They might already know who has them."

He looked at me like I was naive.

"I did not say I bought them from the original owner."

"Okay, they're hot," I said.

He shrugged. "Let's say they are warm. The owner did not want them, but also did not wish to sell them. I had an opportunity to acquire them and so I did. As I see it, they belong to me."

"So you're already out the money on this. A lot?"

"Who I paid and how much has nothing to do with our conversation here, Mr. Lyons," he said.

He was right. I just nodded.

"I do not expect you to make the inquiry for nothing. If you turn up information that helps me recover these films, I will pay you a finder's fee of two thousand dollars."

I'm sure my mouth dropped open. I've never seen $2,000. I don't think I've ever seen more than a couple of hundred dollars at any one time, and it was never mine. I just nodded again. I was starting to feel like a dashboard bobblehead. He picked up a pen and wrote something down on a piece of paper. He handed it to me.

"This is my home telephone number. Should you learn anything that can help me, call. Anytime, day or night."

I made a real effort not to nod, but just said, "Okay."

"Thank you, Mr. Lyons," he said. "Let Eu-meh know your lunch today is on the house."

Eu-meh looked gobsmacked when I approached her.

"What was that about?"

"Nothing. Look, your grandfather said my lunch is covered today."

"Jimmy, you and my grandfather have never even been within twenty feet of each other, let alone talked," she said. "All of a sudden you're deep in conversation with him? What's going on?"

"We were talking about movies. I gotta get back to work." Both things were true.

I waved to Lee and headed out the door.

Jesus, who is this Zhang? Is he a Chinatown mob boss? If so, big time or small time? Will he deliver on the money if I help? Or just tell me to piss off? Maybe worse. My imagination was running away with me. *Shadow King*. Lee's nickname for the old guy no longer sounded like a joke. Not at all. Still, two grand is two grand. That's college tuition right there, at least some of it. Jesus! Film school! I just had to live to get there.

I was grateful for one thing though. I got through the strange meeting without letting on that I already knew about the van, the movies and who had them.

# CHAPTER
## TWO

Back at the film exchange after lunch at Zhang's I zombied through work. Pick up, carry, put down, repeat. I barely said a word to Turk. Stolen films— God knows what's on them—and the quiet, distant restaurant owner I had only seen but never spoken to suddenly reveals a gangster side. And asks me to help him find these stolen mystery movies by putting my nose into Charlestown gangster business. And I was stupid enough to say yes. *What were you thinking, Lyons? You're no Wise Guy. You do step-and-fetch-it work at a Boston film exchange. Tough, you bought it.* True, I did, but I was having buyer's remorse. I was wishing I never saw Zhang's House of Dragons. Or Empire Film Exchange. What do I care about movies anyway? I haul reel-filled film cases bound for the theaters and drive-ins from the storage shelves out to elevators, where they go down to the loading dock to be put on a truck. When they're returned, I haul them from the elevator and bring them to Turk and another guy, Ralph, who rewinds them on a film editor and checks for damage before I lug them back to the storage room until next time.

And that's what I was doing as I berated myself for saying yes to Zhang. I dragged four film cases off the elevator and placed them aside, then lifted two of them and trudged them over to Turk's station. I could feel his eyes on me but I ignored him. I turned and went back for the other two.

Fucking movies! Maybe I could get a job with the T.

But even as that thought came to me, I knew I'd be miserable. The T is a great job in terms of money and benefits, I understand, but I know it's not for me. Between last summer and this one I'd tried a number of jobs. I spent a few months working an admin job at the Charlestown Navy Yard, which is just blocks from where I live in the projects. Then, thanks to a tip from my Uncle Barry, I landed a job that I did like. I ran the projector and did other jobs at The Arte House, a theater for serious film lovers near Harvard Square, Cambridge. What was missing? Eu-meh. She was back at RISD, though living in my head all the same. Man, I missed her. I told myself I'd see her again, sometime. In the meantime, I had a job I enjoyed.

The job lasted six months.

Toward the end of May the manager, Stefan, called me in to say my six months was up, and that his cousin needed the job. That the job had only been temporary came as news, though he insisted he told me. I was furious, but didn't think it would do me any good to call him a fucking liar and make a scene, so I just walked out.

Fortunately, I hadn't burned any bridges at Empire. I went into the office the same day I left the Arte, not really expecting to find a job available, but to find out if anything might be opening up. My luck had turned. The manager, Jack DelloRusso, same man who hired me before, told me that two people were retiring in October and I should apply for one of those jobs. In the meantime, he said, the same summer job I did previously was available.

"If you want it, it's yours," he said.

That made my day. I was back downtown, at Empire, and looking at the possibility of a full-time job there in about four months. And in the immediate term, I'd get to see Eu-meh again.

I started back on Monday, June 3. I felt great. I was happy. Then, just eight days later, I'm telling myself the whole movie thing is crap, and that I never should have gone into Zhang's restaurant in the first place. But I wasn't buying my bullshit. Even as a kid I wanted to make movies. At first it was films like *The Seventh Voyage of Sinbad* and *Jason and the Argonauts* firing up my imagination. It was the idea of bringing clay figures and monsters to life through stop-motion animation, like the great Ray Harryhausen. But soon it was all kinds of movies. Well, not musicals. So, well before I landed the summer job at the film exchange, I knew that making movies is what I wanted to do. Which was good, because if I hadn't been certain of that, the ambition would have been killed cold by the monotony. Not to mention the workout. I'm not afraid of exercise, including a bit of lifting, but not all lifting makes for an enjoyable workout. A two-thousand-foot reel of film that runs twenty-four minutes weighs just over ten pounds. So a two-hour feature, say *Magnum Force* or *The Exorcist*, is going to run about five reels. Then factor in the heavy-duty, metal cases the films are stored and shipped in, and before you know it you're up to about sixty pounds. I'd have hated doing this job for Warner Brothers when it released *Woodstock* a few years ago. It was three hours long.

And then there's Eu-meh. If I didn't have this passion for film, I never would have landed at Empire. I never would have met her.

"What's wrong?" Turk finally said. I realized I was wearing my mind's chaos on my face. I kept my mouth shut. I didn't feel like talking. Unfortunately, he did.

"Either the pork strips ain't settling right in your stomach or Zhang's granddaughter shot you down," he said.

That got my attention. "Maybe a bit of both," I offered as a way to deflect. "What makes you think I'm interested in Eu-meh? I never said that?"

Turk chuckled. "No, but you've told me any

number of times that she's an artist. You've repeatedly told me how she calls you DeMille, Coppola, Ford, Hawks and—"

"No, she's never called me Ford or Hawks."

"Whatever. You bring her up all the time for no good reason. Oh, and you find her 'interesting.'"

"Well, she is."

"Hmm. Okay."

"Okay what? What are you saying?"

"Jimmy, the girl is beautiful as well as 'interesting,' and you'd be a fool, blind or hanging out at the Punch Bowl at Park Square not to be interested in her. So what happened? Did she say no or did ole' Zhang wheel-kick you out the door?"

I looked over to Ralph's station. Seat empty, no reels in the editing machine.

"Where's Ralph?"

Turk looked at the empty station.

"He punched out early. He's been doing that a lot lately." Turk mimed taking a drink. "You stick around you could get his job."

"How well do you know Zhang? I know you go back a ways in Chinatown but just how well do you know him?"

"Jesus, Jimmy. What are you asking? Did something happen? Tell me you didn't touch Eu-meh."

"Fuck no! I have, literally, never touched her. And I've never said anything remotely rude or off-color to her."

"Then why the question about Zhang?"

So I told Turk what Zhang wanted me to do. I left out most of the details, just told him that a van with New York tags was hijacked in Boston and brought to Charlestown. That Zhang was interested in it and offered me a reward if I learned anything that helped him find it.

Turk rubbed his chin like he was thinking about what he should say. We were both doing some dancing here.

"Zhang has something of a past," he finally said, the understatement speaking volumes.

"I saw some pretty snazzy photos of him back in the day," I said. "He was some kind of big deal during the war, I guess."

"Well, yeah, there's that. But I'm talking about things that don't show up in family or party photos." I had a feeling we were about to get into the interesting stuff. "I lived in Chinatown right up until the late '40s, and I did have Chinese friends—good friends. But the Chinese kept a lot of things to themselves. Shit! When it was Little Syria, we Arabs did the same."

"Sounds a lot like Charlestown," I said.

"You got it, kid. It's the same thing. Look, I'll tell you what I know. At least what I remember, or remember hearing."

So Turk painted me a picture of Zhang from his recollections of decades ago. As the story goes, Zhang was sent to Boston from L.A.'s Chinatown by his father in the 1920s, an angry teenager with a broken heart and a chip on his shoulder. Here he was to marry the daughter of his parents' friends. That he wanted to stay in L.A., where he had a girlfriend he hoped to marry, carried no weight with his family and tradition. As far as his father was concerned, Zhang was lucky to be marrying at all. Chinese had been barred from entering the U.S. since the 1880s. And since most of those who had reached the U.S. before or since were men, Chinatowns across the country were basically bachelor neighborhoods. Some women still got smuggled in, but most Chinese women in America were native-born. Bottom line, though, there weren't many of them. Turk said a lot of Americans had expected, if not hoped, that banning Chinese immigration, in particular of women, would eventually result in all Chinese in the country dying out. I found that hard to believe, but then I thought about what we'd already done to the Indians.

In Boston Zhang worked in the family friend's restaurant, then just called House of Dragons, and lived with them in their cramped upstairs apartment. He shared a room with his future brother-in-law, Yow, a timid kid who supposedly took an immediate dislike to Zhang, seeing in him a rival for the family business. Zhang couldn't have cared less about the restaurant. He wanted to get back to California, away from the cold, snowy city where the Irish-dominated police force hated the Chinese even more than cops did in warm Los Angeles. His intended wife, Li Xiu, meanwhile, slept just down that hall in a room right next to her parents. She was pretty, quiet and obedient to her parents—as you'd expect —but she also had a better head for business than her brother. Zhang was amused that Yow's actual rival might very well be the sister he ignored daily.

Zhang may have been angry about being in frigid Boston, but he had no trouble fitting into the family's restaurant, where he'd worked seven days a week.

"He'd arrived knowing the business because he'd been working at his own family's restaurant since he began eating solid food," Turk said. "In the restaurant and under the family's roof, Zhang was above reproach. That's what everyone said anyway. He was sharp, and everyone thought he'd be a great match for Li Xiu."

That's not to say Zhang was happy, though. Turk said it was around this time that he met Zhang. The two got on well because neither one was happy with their families. Turk said his parents didn't like the crowd he ran with or the fact he was so determined to put his own Arab culture behind him. Some of his friends were guys back from the war— that would be World War I—and "full of piss, vinegar and some of them maybe shell-shocked," he said. They got into all kinds of shit, and what wasn't illegal was no less frustrating to the community because it still brought unwanted attention from the Boston cops, who seemed to hate everyone who wasn't Irish, or at least White.

"What kind of shit were you getting into?" I asked Turk.

"We're talking about Zhang," he said in a way that made it clear his own bad old days were not up for discussion. "Zhang played nice at the restaurant and with his intended family, but he had a plan. He was biding his time and saving what money he could so that he could head back to L.A. before the marriage was forced on him. He wasn't paid much, though, because his father-in-law to-be felt that marrying Li Xiu, and eventually helping Yow run the business, was reward enough."

So Zhang looked for opportunities outside of legal businesses. Within six months of arriving in Boston he was part of a Tong. He took to the life like a natural, including the violence. He wasn't afraid to use it. Like everywhere else, Chinatown had a lucrative underworld that included protection rackets, opium, prostitution and gambling. And people smuggling. Politicians could order Chinese excluded from immigrating to the U.S., but it wasn't stopping them from coming. The Tong helped move the arrivals into Chinatown and beyond, and Zhang was happy to earn the cash. As for the rest—shaking down merchants for protection money, dealing opium, or helping to run whores—that's just the way it was. Still, more than once he had to kick the shit out of some asshole who started beating on a girl. That part of the job was more than okay.

"Holy fuck," I said when Turk was finished.

"That's unbelievable. That's just—"

"Unbelievable. I know," Turk said. "So Zhang never did get back to California, but he did well for himself in Chinatown. He put away a lot of dollars. In the '50s he bought this great boat. It wasn't brand new, but it was a beauty. A 1947 bridge-cruiser designed by Ed Monk out in Washington State. He bought it from some muckety-muck on Martha's Vineyard. Back then he took the family out on it a lot. Now, not so much, if ever."

"Do you think any of it's true?" I asked.

At first, he was quiet.

"I'll tell you, kid. I got to know Zhang better in the '30s. He was, or he became, a different man. He went from this Tong heavy to, I don't know, Sun Yat-sen."

"Who the fuck is Sun Yat-sen?"

Turk shook his head.

"Think Michael Collins, but in China," he said. "After the Japs invaded China in 1931, Zhang all of a sudden got really protective of Chinatown. Not just protective of his own Tong or the merchants who paid for protection, but of everyone who wanted Chinatown and the Chinese to matter. He wasn't the only one. His brother-in-law, Yow, went back to China to fight. He's buried over there somewhere. And when we finally got into the war one of Zhang's sisters, who had a pilot's license, became a WASP. She flew military planes like the B-29 fresh from the factory to military bases all over the country. She even flew the planes towing targets that air gunners shot at for training."

"I think I saw their photos on the wall at the restaurant," I said.

"Yeah, that would be them. I'm sure what they did, especially Yow—who Zhang found really annoying—played a part in Zhang putting his gangster days behind him. Or, rather, using his gangster skills in a positive way. He pulled together enough muscle to clean up some of the worst elements around those blocks. Muggers and burglars who preyed on teachers, ministers, priests, healers of any kind—they'd get one warning, then..." Turk drew a hand across his throat. "He made contacts in the mayor's office, the city council. Even the governor's office and beyond. Far beyond. He—"

"Wait a minute! Japan invades China, where Zhang's never been, and he's suddenly a born-again patriot?"

"I'm just telling you the things I know about him from back in the old days. And no, his 'change of character,' let us call it, and his new role in Chinatown didn't happen overnight and it didn't happen without bloodshed. But it happened. Shit! By the time the Japs hit us at Pearl Harbor. Zhang already had contacts with both China's nationalist government and the commies, sending them money, medicine and guns."

I believed Turk and was ready to say so, but he kept on going.

31

"To tell the truth, kid, all the other shit about him? A lot of it's true and might not even be the half of it. He was never someone to screw with. There are still some very tough people around who will go to the wall for Zhang. Some are family. Others are not, but what he's done for this community has earned him real loyalty. If you'll take my advice, you'll tell him next time you see him that you asked around about his movies but couldn't find out a thing. There are some pretty tough and mean people who are loyal to Zhang, including Ping On."

I don't know shit about this Ping On gang beyond the fact they exist and supposedly have ties to a Chinese mob in New York City. Zhang obviously knew some shit, though.

Turk was still talking. "Maybe this will all blow over. Maybe Zhang'll just croak. And if that happens, who knows? Maybe you'll even score with Eu-meh."

"For fuck's sake, Turk!"

"Oh, I hit a nerve there. Look, just stay outta Chinatown trouble like you're staying outta Charlestown trouble, kid."

"I told you about shit I did in Charlestown?" That threw me for a loop.

"Obviously," he said.

"Fuck. I talk too much."

"So keep quiet and stay out of Zhang's business. Live to be a really old fart like me."

"Old fart is right," I said.

# CHAPTER
# THREE

It's not like I was really mad at Turk. I was just shaken by what he'd told me and what I might have gotten myself into. And even if he did piss me off, I couldn't stay pissed at him. He's a good guy. Shortly after I started at Empire last summer I told him that I hoped to make movies someday. He walked off to another part of the building and came back with an old Bell & Howell 202 projector that had languished, broken, in a back room for three years. He said he couldn't help me with a camera, but that if I wanted to lug the projector home and try to repair it, it was mine. Man, I lugged that motherfucker home like it was a lost treasure—to the T stop at Boylston Street, down the stairs to the train, then downstairs again at City Square in Charlestown to catch the Bunker Hill bus. While I was waiting, with sore arms and banged knees, a drunk ambled over from The Morning Glory, one of the smoke-filled bars where I plied the shoeshine trade when I was thirteen or so. He smelled of booze and trouble.

"That a movie projector?"

"Yeah," I said.

"Shit. I'd love to have that."

"Yeah."

"Give it to me."

"Fuck, no."

"Hand it over or I kick your ass and take it."

I looked him over real quick. He was a good half-foot taller than me and heavier, and not in a fat kind of way. Still.

"Okay," I said and put it down in front of him. He snickered. He bent to lift it and I hit him twice in the face. Not hard enough to put him down, but enough to send him three steps backward with a bloody mouth and nose.

"Fuck! Fuck!" he yelled, actually looking surprised when he took his hand from his mouth to see blood on it. "You fuckin' ath-o!"

"Fuckin' puthy," I said.

He walked away with his hands over his embarrassment. A few minutes later I hauled my treasure, now one that I'd defended from a wanna-be pirate, onto the bus, which delivered me to my stop on Bunker Hill Street. It was directly across from the Lexie, where I'd taken those boxing lessons. I had a nice, warm feeling for the old brick building in that moment. I walked into the projects, crossed O'Reilly Way and through O'Meara Court to my building on

Walford Way, where I dragged the projector up the three flights to the apartment where I lived with my mother and my sister, Helen.

"What's that?" Helen asked.

"The stuff dreams are made of," I told her, in my best Bogart voice.

"You're so weird," she said.

Thanks to Frank, the guy who ran weekend movies at the Boys Club, I got the projector working. After looking it over he told me what was wrong, what I needed, and where I could probably buy or scrounge parts. I spent a few months and a good portion of a few paychecks to get it running, though the only movies I could get were a couple of Army training films from World War II. I got these with the help of George Gloss, the owner of the Brattle Book Shop, who I met when I was in my early teens and discovered his store had boxes filled with 1950's science fiction and adventure pulp magazines and old, hardcover editions of the Tarzan novels. George's forte is books, but if there's anything old and collectible to be found, he can find it. It was another few months before I got my camera and editor/splicer. Uncle Barry came over with them one night. He did a lot of things for me after my father died, though at times I wasn't certain the things he gave me were legally purchased. In those early days he was always coming by with baseball cards and comic books. And when I decided at thirteen to be a comic book artist, he bought me sketch books, various pencils, a kneaded eraser, and one of those wooden, adjustable mannequins. Hell, he even took me over to the Museum of Fine Arts once a week all summer long because he thought I should see "real" art. I became a fan of John Singer Sargent, Edmund Tarbell, William Rimmer, and Childe Hassam. Something about them being from Boston, I guess.

I also became a fan of the nudes of women, regardless of the artist, and the busts and statues in the Greek and Roman collections. The Ancient Egypt Collection was cool, as you'd expect when there are mummies. And the display of Chinese art. The one thing that always grabbed my attention was the regal-looking statue of what, at first, I thought was some ancient emperor. Turns out the statue, which is actually a wood carving, represents Guanyin, a Buddhist who achieved enlightenment but chose to stay on Earth to help others trough her example. A museum security guard told me she's also known as the Goddess of Mercy, but that label was given to her by Jesuit missionaries, another example of the Catholic Church re-purposing other people's religious icons. In any event, it's a beautiful statue.

My Uncle Barry was complicated. For someone with a college degree and teacher certification he never seemed to have done much except bartending, these days at The Brigantine, better known as The Brig, a long-time dive off a nothing street between City Square and the Navy Yard.

He also liked to play the ponies or the dogs, but

usually he lost. He liked to say that instead of getting his head filled with Melville, Hawthorne and Shakespeare he should have been a plumber or an electrician, or just gotten a job with the Post Office. Better money, he'd say. I don't know if he was trying to exorcise all he learned in college or what, but he sure did his best to push all that stuff into my brain. He got me to read Shakespeare's *The Tempest* by telling me it was the basis of the movie *Forbidden Planet*. Turns out it was good, so I read more of the plays even without a science fiction tie-in.

The camera and film editor were gifts that seemed too expensive for Barry to have bought. Even I thought they must have fallen off the back of a truck. Ma told me I couldn't have them, but then Barry swore to God that they weren't hot. That was enough for Ma, who didn't think Barry would risk the wrath of God by swearing to a lie. Me, I had no idea where he got them and decided I didn't care. Since getting the camera I've put about six hours of film in the can. It's mostly scenes of Charlestown. A good thirty minutes is footage taken from the rooftops of the projects where I live, and another half-hour of last year's Bunker Hill Day parade. There's also footage of the town from the top of the Bunker Hill Monument and the three T stations— Sullivan Square, Thompson Square and City Square —with the trains arriving and leaving and people coming and going. The papers say the Thompson and City Square stops will not be replaced when the elevated trains running along Main Street are pulled down in the next year or two. Instead, the line will be moved away from Main Street altogether. The times they are a-changing, so I figured I should capture what's here now. I've also got some good—I think—footage of the Tobin Bridge that links Charlestown and Chelsea over the Mystic River. That's another change. Up until five years ago or so it was the Mystic River Bridge, then it was renamed for the one-time mayor I saw in the photo with Zhang.

I took a lot of kidding from friends when I filmed close-ups of the bridge stanchions and cross-beams to get the peeling and blistered paint. Can't believe it now but we used to climb the two levels of crossbeams running from the ground to the under-belly of the bridge's first level. I'll admit, I only climbed up the first level. A few daredevils went all the way up. Anyway, my pals thought it weird that I'd film peeling paint.

On the other hand, no one thought it was weird last year when I grabbed my camera and rushed over to the Tobin Bridge after a huge truck smacked into an upright and caused the upper deck to collapse onto the lower. That was a grisly accident. Took a while to get the driver's body extricated from the cabin. A couple of people asked me if I was going to hawk the footage to a local TV station. Can't say I wouldn't have tried that, but the stations had news crews on the scene and they were rolling tape. I figured I'd use my footage as part of the vaguely conceived documentary I want to make about the town. Feature films may be my ambition, but a small doc about Charlestown makes sense to me right now. I know the town, it's right outside my window and I have a camera. My dream picture will have to wait until, I don't know, Hell freezes over or something. We'll see.

Turk is not the only one able to read a face. My mother's even better at it. She has that radar mothers develop so they know when shit's going on with their kids. Not to mention the kind they develop if they have a husband who's tight with, or part of, the town's gangster starting line-up. But since Ray Lyons went off and got himself killed a dozen years ago, Ma's redirected that power, putting it into monitoring me and Helen. She's fourteen chomping at the bit to be eighteen, so I try to stay out of trouble, figuring it's better if Ma is free to focus on her without worrying about me.

Still, she knew something was bugging me and was waiting for me to say something. No way I was going to tell her.

"What's going on, Jimmy?" she asked at last as she put supper on the table. It was skirt steak with mashed potatoes and mixed vegetables—peas and carrots. If for any reason I ever came home on a Tuesday and somehow forgot what day it was, skirt steak and potatoes and carrots and peas would tell me it's Tuesday. I'm not complaining, mind you. Just pointing out that some things in our lives are fixed, repeating events. Also, even though the Catholic Church no longer requires eating fish on Fridays, Ma still considers that an important part of the faith. That's cool with me because I like it. Can't say I'm much of a Catholic, though.

"Well?" she said when I didn't answer.

"Nothing, Ma. Nothin's going on."

She stared a hole through my forehead and turned her mouth down in a not-smile.

"Is it Sheila? You two break up again?" She suddenly looked panicked. She darted a quick look at Helen and then back to me. "Oh, God! She's not ... Sheila's not—"

I quickly chewed and swallowed the bit of steak in my mouth and gulped down some milk.

"No! Of course not! We broke up three months ago and never got back together, Ma! C'mon! Nothin's wrong. Nothin's goin' on. Can we just eat?"

"Is it work? You don't like the job anymore? You in trouble? They're not gonna fire you, are they?"

"Ma, suppa's gonna get cold. But the answer is everything's great with work. No problems."

She took up some potato on her fork but paused before eating it. "Okay, don't tell me."

Across from me, Helen was balancing her fork on her right index finger and her butter knife on her left. Without taking her eyes off the silverware dangling over her plate she said: "Maybe you should take up with Mary Connor. I think she has the hots for you. Of course, her dad'll probably kill you—"

40

"Don't you talk like that," Ma said.

I stopped eating. Mid-bite. Not because Helen mentioned Mary Connor. Yeah, she seemed to like me, but given that she's ten years older than me and used to babysit me when I was a little kid, I never took her too-friendly greetings seriously. These days I run into her in the street and she just waves, says hi, have a nice day. But for a while about two years ago she would kind of follow me with her eyes when she saw me. And she seemed to see me a lot, as if she was stalking me. Pretty creepy. On one occasion she came over to talk with me and I didn't know what to think. As she got closer I saw she had this anxious expression. If that was scary, what happened next was terrifying. Out of nowhere her father appeared and grabbed her by the arm.

"No, Mary! Stay away from him," he said, then turned to me. "And you keep away from Mary."

Yeah, Mary is a bit weird, but it's her father who really worries me. I know he worries Ma, too. Brendan Connor's name is not supposed to be mentioned in our home, but when it has been, she becomes the Sphinx, her face blank, indecipherable. Connor, according to just about everyone, is a killer. His own father, a longshoreman and union boss, raised the boy to be a fighter, hoping he'd turn pro so that the old man could bask in his son's glory. Brendan fought all right, but most of it outside the ring. By the time he was fifteen he'd probably fought half of Charlestown and a good number of the cops working out of Station 15. At last, the court gave him a choice: join the Army or go to jail. Instead, he joined the Marine Corps. Given his penchant for violence, lots of people figured he'd found his calling —that is, if his fists didn't get him sent to Leavenworth. Instead, war broke out in Korea—not his fault—and that's where he went. No one in town was surprised he survived the fighting. They were surprised when he came back with a Silver Star, an Honorable Discharge and a reputation as a stellar Marine. So, what was next for him? He became a cop. Even made detective. It seemed the world had turned upside down.

That lasted a few years. Then he was an ex-cop, for reasons unknown or not talked about. From there it was the long shore, something people considered a fall from grace. Maybe God punishing him by making him repeat the labor of his father. I doubt Connor cared what anyone thought. Like his father, he ended up a union rep, and supposedly a good one, respected and likely feared by both his union brothers and company management. All that sounds perfectly respectable, but there were whispers he occasionally moonlighted as a leg-breaker and worse for people so powerful and connected their names don't even slip into the papers.

Why would any of that scare me? Or scare my mother? Because dad's end was violent. Because he was involved in Wise Guy shit. And because he and Brendan Connor had been longtime friends, supposedly best friends. But I was always sure that Connor was involved in Dad's killing. I believed Ma knew something, but was too frightened to say anything to anyone. This being Charlestown, the fear made sense.

Dad was killed in 1961, when I was seven. Those were some bad old days, worse than now in some ways. There was a gang war between Charlestown's own McLaughlin mob and the Winter Hill gang in Somerville. Depending on who's talking, my old man was either a day laborer at construction sites who occasionally did small jobs and errands for Punchy McLaughlin or he was into the criminal shit up to his goofy, shamrock green porkpie hat and went locked and loaded on more serious business. He was found dead near the sea wall on the other side of Little Mystic Channel—better known as the Oilies—a polluted waterway of sickly, dark-rain-bowed ribbons of oil and god knows what else that swirled and coiled with the tides and comings and goings of barges. It's pretty disgusting, for sure, though that never stopped us from swimming in it when we were kids.

I never got a satisfactory answer as to who killed my dad and why. One story is that he turned rat. Some people said the phone number to the FBI's Boston office was found stuffed in his mouth. Another is that he was killed for stealing from Punchy. That didn't sound like Ray Lyons, but you never know. As fucked up as this is going to sound, there is one version that I'd rather believe. In that one he was killed when a business-as-usual cash delivery to a couple of bent detectives went bad. Supposedly, he gets to the meeting place and sees them, still in their unmarked car. One's in the front seat. The other's in the back, where he's forcing some girl to give him a blowjob. Dad picks up a brick and smashes it through a passenger-side window. Unlocks and opens the door and starts pulling the girl out. The detective in the front seat jumps out and my dad punches him in the face, knocking him back against the car. The cop draws his gun on my old man. Meanwhile, the girl's out and running as fast as she can to get away. By now the other asshole detective is out of the car and he's also got his gun on Dad. That was it. Either one or both the fuckers shot him dead. So, if one these stories is true, I'd rather it be that one. Maybe there was some good in him after all. But I have to admit, it was all so long ago and I was so fucked up from what I heard that I sometimes think I made up the last story. I just don't know anymore.

So how did Connor fit into any of these stories? Whether Dad's murder was gang-related or a case of cops killing him, Connor was on the force at the time and even then it was said he did contract work. Either scenario made it possible he was Dad's killer. Then there was Connor's visit to Ma a day or two after Dad was found. Sure, I was just a kid, but I remember it. Ma was crying and Connor was telling her that something went bad but that it wouldn't do any good to go talking to the cops. He held out a thick roll of bills, leaned in close and whispered something. I don't know what it was, but her head jerked back. Her eyes were wide. She nodded, reached out, and without another word took the money. Connor never stepped foot in our apartment again.

So when Helen joked about him killing me it didn't strike me as funny at all.

"C'mon, Ma. I was just joking," Helen was saying. "Mary just seems to really like my big *brudder*. Every time she goes by, she waves and gives Jimmy a big hello when he's out there with his friends. And she has the biggest smile."

Ma changed the subject.

"What are you doing with the silverware?"

"Practicing," Helen said. "I'm going out for cheerleader when school opens so I'm practicing balancing things."

Ma put her own silverware down on the table like a juvenile court judge setting down his gavel and gearing up to lecture.

"The table is not the field or the place to play cheerleader."

"But, Ma—"

"Don't 'but, Ma' me. Use the silverware to eat. Now. Or you're gonna get it, young lady."

Helen surrendered and began eating. It was quiet

for a minute, then Ma took the conversation in another direction.

"Besides, you don't even know if you'll be in Charlestown High in the fall. You could get bused someplace else."

"I'm not goin' ta school if I hafta go outside Charlestown," Helen said. "Especially not Roxbury with all the ni—"

Helen stopped mid-word as Ma's silverware hit the table. Hard. Busing had already been ordered by a federal judge, and it was supposed to start in September with a couple of towns, Southie and Roxbury. It's next year that Helen will have to worry, when the desegregation plan is extended across the city, including Charlestown. But already Townies were worried and pissed off about it.

"Don't you use that dirty filthy awful word in this house. Not ever!"

"What's the big deal? Everyone uses it," Helen said.

"'Everyone' doesn't live here," Ma declared. "How a bunch of prejudiced people talk outside is one thing. It doesn't mean those words get said here. And you shouldn't be talking like that outside either."

Helen moped. "I don't know what the big deal is."

I didn't say anything to Helen. I learned what the big deal was a couple of years back. And I knew that

Ma was now going to let her know what the big deal was while she ate her supper.

Though Ma was born in Charlestown, her family had moved away for a while, maybe six years, and lived in Dorchester. She had lived there until her mid-teens. Not right on the Dorchester-Roxbury line or anything, but close enough that her neighborhood had a good number of Black people. Sometimes the kids fought. Sometimes the grown-ups argued. And it's not like there wasn't prejudice. People used racial insults, including "the N word." But Ma said she had good friends over there, Black friends as well as White. For a long time I thought maybe she was recalling things as rosier than they were. Then, about six or seven years ago, some Black families moved into Charlestown, into the projects. Turned out the mother in one of the families was someone Ma had known in Dorchester. Her name was Lily.

When they saw each other that first time after so many years you'd have thought they were family. I'd never seen anything like it, and I don't think any of our neighbors had either. Ma and Lily were hugging and crying and it was a real scene. Everyone who saw it was surprised, and a lot of them clapped. Some of the ladies cried and said it was so beautiful.

It was the '60s, so no one seemed too surprised at a few Black families moving into town. Had to happen, right? And they were genuinely nice people. Everyone seemed to like them, and they got on well with everyone. And Lily's husband, Eugene, was a really good guy. The new families made friends quickly. If there was any badmouthing going on it wasn't falling on my ears. Like I said, it was the '60s and things seemed to be changing. Ma was happy to have linked up with her childhood friend and to talk about old times. Likely skipping over the bad times that, I'm sure, there had to have been. It was something to see. Pretty fucking remarkable, really.

It didn't last. One night there was a fight. Some people said a Black gang came into town and started beating up White people. Next thing you know it was torches and pitchforks time. A mob formed. They wanted revenge. So they targeted the local Black families, including Eugene and Lily's, who had nothing to do with any of the supposed attacks. They were under siege as rocks, bottles and threats were hurled through their windows. Police arrived, lights flashing and sirens wailing, and held off the mob, threatening the loudest of them with arrest if they didn't "get the fuck back."

The siege broke, and the crowd was gone in less than an hour. Then came the moving trucks. Before the sun came up next morning all three families were gone. Ma was heartbroken. She barely spoke to anyone except me and Helen for nearly two weeks. She didn't know, she told me, if any of her neighbors were part of the attack on Lily's family and the others. She said she was ashamed.

"Why? You didn't do anything," I had said.

"None of this would have happened if those Black people from outside didn't come in and start it. Right?"

She had looked at me as if she didn't know who I was.

"You are so wrong, Jimmy. What matters is that people here went after Lily and the other families, who had nothing to do with any of it. Why do you suppose that was?"

When she said that it was like a light went on. I got it.

As Ma retold the story I wondered if the light would go on for Helen. I hoped so.

We finished supper and Ma gave Helen a few bucks for the carnival. Used to be one held just down the street, with all the game booths set up in the schoolyard behind St. Catherine's church and the rides in the parking lot adjacent to it, behind the court known as Tuna Park. Why Tuna Park? Who knows? Something about Charlie the Tuna in some old StarKist commercials. Anyway, the church-sponsored carnival folded a few years ago. So now we go to the one that comes in each year to the Ryan Playground down at the Neck, a wide-open recreation area near Sullivan Square. There is a hell of a lot more space down there, meaning more games, more rides and more people. Especially since it's close to the border with Everett and Somerville. Still, I liked it better when it was just down the street. But things change, don't they? Helen was

49

going to meet up with her friends and then head off.

"Are you going, Jimmy?" Ma asked. "If you do, maybe you can bring Helen back with you."

"I don't want to come back with him," Helen protested. "I'll come back with the girls."

I could understand Helen wanting to be with her friends, and not be seen as needing a brother chaperone to get home. But Ma wanted to make sure she got home safely and that meant me.

"You'll meet your brother and come home with him," Ma said. The judge had spoken, but she threw Helen a break. "You can stay out until ten. But be home by ten."

Sis, surprised, quickly stifled her protest.

"Oh, okay."

"I'll meet you about nine-thirty by the Hurricane ride and we can walk back," I said.

# CHAPTER
# FOUR

I headed to the carnival with Billy Jumper and Red Whelan in Red's old, beat-up Bonneville, nicknamed Hell Trap II. It's a mystery how he keeps the thing going. Give him credit, though—he spends as much time under the hood as he does driving it. The original Hell Trap, a '69 Chevy Nomad Wagon he bought for $150 just over a year ago, lasted only six weeks. He splurged and spent $400 for this one. He's become a pretty good shade-tree mechanic, but some jobs require the skilled kind. For now he's driving around in a car with no state inspection sticker because he can't find and fix a problem with the electrical system that's periodically skewing his taillights. And rather than pay a pro he's waiting on a friend who works at a garage near Sullivan Square to get him a sticker.

We drove down Medford Street, me in shotgun and Jump in the back. With the mood I was in after thinking about my dad, driving down Medford Street wasn't the best route. A long stretch of it along one side are shuttered businesses and long-empty warehouses. Then there's Terminal Street, which runs off Medford and hooks back in the direction we were coming from, on the side of the Oilies where my dad died. Everyone calls that area Montego Bay because it's anything but a resort. It's a place of abandoned buildings and litter-strewn, weed-covered lots. I had learned to shut out my childhood's nightmarish image—of Dad lying dead among all the trash—whenever I had to pass Terminal Street. But it was difficult that day. Maybe I was spooked by my deal with Zhang, especially after what I'd learned of his past. I should have suggested using Bunker Hill Street. Too late now. Terminal Street—Christ! So aptly named.

Jump moved into the projects only a few years ago. Before that he lived up near the top of Bunker Hill in one of the old three-story brick townhouses. Nice, but he's in the projects now. He doesn't seem to mind. It may be public housing with a bad rep—not entirely deserved—but plenty of Townies from outside like it. People in the projects generally don't care if you're just hanging out. Get too noisy and they tell you to move off the stoop. So you just cross the street and sit on another one, or maybe go around the back or into another court. Even if you decide to play some half-ball no one bothers you.

Well, unless you hit their windows maybe. Then they might tell you to get the hell away. It's rare anyone calls the cops for that kind of shit. Or any kind of shit, really. Sometimes the cops do show up. When they do it's usually on a weekend night because underage drinkers are out hoisting a few. Even that doesn't amount to much. Just got to keep an eye out and be ready to run with your beers or wine. Some of the cops will take it from you. I lost a few beers to the badges when I was hanging out. Drugs are another matter, as I found out. Some cops will bust you for even a smallest amount of pot.

And Jump wants, of all things, to be a cop. He's pretty strait-laced, tries not to get into trouble. He doesn't even smoke pot. He does like to hang out and drink, though. Ma thinks he's a good influence on me. If she knew Jump's views on crime in Boston she'd think differently. He says crime is a big problem in the city. Not so much in Charlestown but in other parts of Boston, especially Roxbury, with all its drugs and the violent crimes done by pushers and junkies. He knows that Charlestown has all the same problems, and that things are getting worse, but he says it's different in Roxbury.

"Why's that?" I asked him once.

"O, man! Whataya think? The fuckin' niggers," he laughed. "They're just different. More dangerous."

Now I might be Charlestown born and raised

but even I knew that Jump had the wrong attitude for someone wanting to carry a badge and a gun. I told him to never let my mother hear him use "that word" or he'd be the victim of a violent crime.

"Your mother's a liberal?"

"I guess she is."

"That's fucked up," he said. "How'd she get like that?"

"Reading, I think. Shit, man, you sound like a fuckin' redneck."

That was the last time we talked policing. I thought of Eu-meh and Lee and wondered how an Officer Jump would treat them. Not well, I bet.

Red I've known since we were little kids. His real name is Lenny, but he's called Red for the same reason most people are called Red. He's a year older than me and has a small apartment up on Cook Street. His widowed Aunt Lucy owns the three-story house and she let him have the upstairs flat rent-free two years ago in exchange for doing minor work around the house and driving her to appointments. Until then he'd been living at home. His parents were all in favor of the move, since he otherwise seemed slow to be moving out on his own. That, and the fact they worried about Lucy living alone, what with break-ins becoming more frequent. His father, Colm, even brought Red out to a gun range, where he taught him to shoot a handgun, then bought him one. Then he got himself two more, though not from any legit retailer. I'm guessing his ma, Mary, is in the dark about any of the guns. Or even the lapsed inspection sticker. Anyway, Red and I still hang out together, and I often spend weekend nights up at his place if I'm too tired or drunk to walk back down the hill.

We went to the same schools—the Kent, then the Warren-Prescott, then the Eddies for junior high. For reasons I already explained I never got to go to Charlestown High with him. In our early teens he was usually my partner in those minor crimes I committed, as well as some other dumb misadventures. We once built a twelve-foot-tall robot out of silver-painted cardboard and a flashlight, tying the arms on with wire so they'd hang loose and move. After dark we stood it up on the corner of the roof and waited for someone to see it. A crowd gathered down below and we could hear the chatter and the shouts of "What's that?" "This gotta be bullshit!" and "That's fake."

But no one came up onto the roof to see it. Well, not until someone called the cops. We knew they'd make the climb. As soon as we saw the blue lights coming up Walford Way, we pulled the robot back from the edge, lowered it down to the ground on the other side of the building, then ran down three flights to grab and run with it. Still, we didn't get far. Some cop spotted us and caught up. They actually thought it was funny, though. They simply told us not to do it again and, better yet, get rid of the thing. Cops can surprise you sometimes.

We carried out a more sophisticated prank a few months later. We went into Boston to scope out the historic markers along the Freedom Trail. Red measured the signs and I made some sketches and even copied down the inscriptions, paying close attention to the what the letters looked like. We then spent almost two weeks making a sign. Red did the sawing and planing. Then I went to work on the inscription. What a motherfucker that was to do. Since the letters were supposed to be raised, I ended up doing a bunch of them—but not all, certainly— out of gum. I chewed the gum and crafted it into the letters we used for the words. It didn't matter that they looked a bit off, because we painted the sign to look weather-beaten and old.

We placed it on the side of an old, abandoned home on Main Street, several blocks from the Warren Tavern, a resurrected eighteenth-century tavern where Paul Revere supposedly bent his elbow on a regular basis. Our marker read:

*Bar Maid, and Esteemed and Enthusiastic Friend to Many a Patriot. On April 18, 1775, Mistress Molly could be*
*heard through her window, exhorting Paul Revere to "Ride! Ride Hard, Paul Revere!"*
*And from this spot Revere later that night rode as well to*
*Lexington to warn that "the British are coming!"*

The sign was up less than a week before the cops came and took it down. But in that week we spent a bunch of time down around there, watching people stop to read the thing. Cracked up a lot of people. Tourists looked confused. It seemed too crazy to be true, but the damn sign did look authentic. Of course, we hung it high enough that no one could inspect it too closely. The best part was watching people take photos of the thing, or taking down notes on it, usually looking for street signs so they could tell friends exactly where to find it.

Tell the truth, I found the prank funnier and more worth the effort than Red did. He wanted more of a rush when it came to being a public nuisance. He was always kind of crazy wild. Like a lot of kids—yeah, me too—he tried his lungs at smoking and snatched the occasional beer from an inattentive parent. And like a lot of us, he would climb the spans holding up the Mystic Bridge, play on the logs at the lumberyard when it was closed, and, in winter, "bump" cars—crouch down, grab hold of their rear bumpers as they passed and be pulled along the snow-covered streets.

But by fifteen Red wanted to be the guy behind the wheel, so he decided to steal a car. He didn't know how to drive, but he thought he'd figure it out by doing. He did. And he was doing okay for about a year. At least once a month he'd hot-wire some car and speed through the town as if he was paying homage to the Loopers of long ago—crazy shits whose high-speed freewheeling made them, now decades later, legends. Red would race along Main Street under the elevated train tracks to Sullivan Square, where he'd zip all the way around the rotary before hanging a right—sometimes shooting up over Bunker Hill Street, other times barreling down the length of Medford Street. It was mad. No other word for it. He finally quit after crashing into a steel upright on Main Street.

The only thing that saved him from a conviction and a likely sentence to Lyman School, a hell-hole for teenage offenders, was that he was so banged up no one thought he'd make it. He was in the hospital for two months, during which time the police and prosecutor's office seemed to lose interest in him. By the time he was released, walking on crutches, his head wrapped in a bandage, nose taped, and neck accessorized with a brace, the charges had been dropped from grand-theft auto and damaging city property to reckless endangerment.

He pleaded guilty to the reduced charge. He knew a bargain when he saw one. And even if he didn't, his father insisted he take the plea deal. He felt his son couldn't be allowed to get away entirely with what he did. Fortunately, because it was a juvie conviction, Red won't have to worry about it in the future. Well, as long as he stayed out of trouble, or at least didn't get caught.

The experience changed Red. When I went to see

him a few days after he got out of the hospital, he said he was going to stop stealing cars.

"That's probably a good idea," I said.

"I think I'm also gonna quit drinking and getting high, except maybe on holidays."

"You think you can do that?"

He smiled, and his blackened eyes, bordered by the head bandage and nose tape, lit up. "Not really, but a guy should have aspirations."

He never again mentioned those aspirations. And he and I went on to see any number of holidays and regular old weekends through the glow or fog of one thing or another. But he did stop stealing cars. Some change did come a few years later, shortly after he turned 18 and his aunt offered him the apartment deal. Maybe it had to do with driving his aunt around, but he vowed he'd never drive drunk or high —ever. Not long after that he quit smoking dope, saying a drug conviction, now that he was legally an adult, would screw him up in the future. For a long time, he didn't know what he wanted for a future. Then a few weeks ago that changed. He decided he was getting out of Charlestown. He went over to the Army recruiting office near South Station and joined up under some delayed entry deal. He'll be leaving at the end of the summer. He says it sucks that Vietnam is almost over because he won't get a chance to fight.

"So what are you gonna do in the Army? Something that'll get you a job later on, when you get out? Like car mechanic?" I asked him.

"Fuck no! My recruiter says I can be airborne. Man, I'll be jumping out of airplanes," he said. "How fucking cool is that?"

Still a wild man. Fearless.

His decision made me reflect more often on what Ma suggested, that I go into the Army for the education benefits. But Red's impending move was also further evidence that the world was changing around me while I seemed stuck. Worse than stuck. Stuck would mean I'm not moving forward. I feel at times like I'm slipping backwards.

Change. Everything is change, and sometimes it's hard to tell whether the change is good or bad.

These days there's a new housing development built across from the old projects where I live. It's called CharlesNewTown, which sounds pretty lame, but there's no doubting that the apartments look better and offer more space than those in the old projects. The NewTown development backs against the Oilies, though not the far side where my old man died. NewTown displaced the decrepit pier off which we used to dive or jump, as well as a lumber yard where many of us sometimes snuck into on weekends to play on the mountain of debarked logs awaiting the buzzsaws.

These days, the Oilies is means waterfront living for many NewTown residents, with a paved, fenced-in walkway to walk or jog along. The water still looks like something out of a horror movie, but with the shipping gone maybe it will clear up in a few decades.

Things don't look so good for the old projects. It's sad, really. The place was built in the early 1940s and was one of the first public housing projects in the country. It replaced block after block of run-down three-deckers and even some old, long-vacant wagon-houses. It's funny. Lots of Townies these days hate Democrats because they blame them for the school busing that's coming. That's quite a turn-about for Charlestown. The projects owed their construction to Democrats led by Franklin Roosevelt. It was his Depression Era legislation that made them possible. By the time they were completed, World War II was over and lots of guys coming back from the war were happy to move their families into the three-story brick-and-concrete fortress apartments that boasted hot-and-cold running water, gas stoves, refrigerators, heat, good plumbing, and windows with removable screens. There were even clothes yards set up throughout the project for hanging laundry. And for the kids there were jungle gyms, swings and at least one ankle-deep, sprinkler-fed pool for cooling off on summer days.

When people first come into the project it's like a maze, what with so many buildings looking exactly alike. But there is order to it. From above, say from a plane or even from atop the Bunker Hill Monument, you can see it's a series of T-, L- and bracket-shaped buildings. It's roughly three good-sized blocks wide and stretches about a half-mile from Decatur Street at one end to Polk Street on the other. But most of the project is made up of row after row of bracket-shaped buildings, which form courtyards—abbreviated to courts, as in O'Meara Court, Starr King Court, Carney Court—where there are trees and good-sized fenced-in grassy areas. Buildings that abut the streets also originally had garden areas running alongside.

The housing authority cut the grass and kept the courts, sidewalks and streets clean. Problems with an apartment? There were maintenance people for that. Each court had an incinerator attached to one building and that's where household trash went. And in the cellar beneath that building a maintenance guy would shovel the ashes, blackened tin cans and shattered glass bottles into trash cans and place them on the curb to be picked up by the city.

The projects filled up quickly. That's not to say it was a paradise. It was like any place where you'd have more than a thousand families living in close quarters. But people seemed to think it was a good deal.

Well, fast-forward a few decades. In the '60s the city came through and tore down many of the trees that had been there since before the place was built. Walford Way, which ran the length of the projects, was a hotter place in summer. Before long the little amenities put in for the kids were no longer repaired when worn or damaged and were finally removed. The city made tried to make up for the disimprovements by putting in a number of small, colorful, child-friendly static concrete displays of dolphins, horses and whatnot in some of the courts. Total failure. Even the little kids they were intended for grew bored with them quickly, so that soon they were pathetic, broken, abandoned testaments to a bad idea.

Housing authority oversight slackened and regular maintenance became not so regular. And within each building, where residents were responsible for keeping the stairs and hallways clean and clear, standards also slipped. Some families no longer took a turn at cleaning their part of the stairs or halls. As a result, even within a single building, some areas might be spic-and-span and others look like crap..

Then there were the gangs. These were not hardened criminal gangs, just teens and twenty-somethings who sometimes got too loud and, at times, when they got someone to buy for them, too rowdy and drunk. None of this was new or unique to the projects or to Charlestown or — hell! — anywhere. Also, the gang that hung out in one court or another typically included those who lived there. Even if obnoxious, they also served as watchdogs for their court. Then, too, their own parents were just a shout or complaint away. Were there fights among these kids? Or between them and kids from another street or court? Are you kidding? Where doesn't that happen? Still, these corner gangs were not a big problem. Notwithstanding the physical appearance of some buildings and the waning services, there was a different feel to the town only a few short years ago. The long-haired-hippie-freak look once relegated to the Hippies on the Common downtown became common in Charlestown, along with pot, hashish, mescaline, acid, and recreational use of uppers and downers. And for a time—a very brief time—it seemed to actually mellow out some of the same people who a few years earlier were hot to drink and fight. Yet, the drugs got harder, more dangerous, and the vibe changed again. Marijuana laced with something called PCP, or Angel Dust, turned simple weed highs into a nightmares of paranoia, delusion and even convulsions. People became hopelessly strung out on speed, cocaine, even heroin. Overdoses are a thing now. Most every street-corner, project court, or town park hangout in Charlestown has lost someone, some more than one. And it's not like all these people were bad. A few devils? Maybe. But most were just stumbling their way through wild teens and twenties and fell into a hole they couldn't climb out of.

It's not getting better. Whether it's junkies needing cash for drugs or your everyday thieves wanting to make a quick buck, break-ins and robberies are becoming more frequent. Even the copper siding encasing the project rooftop entryways is starting to disappear. And then there's the spike in bank robberies. It's said that when a bank is hit anywhere in Boston, Somerville, Cambridge or

Everett, the first thing the cops do is rush to the bridges leading to Charlestown. Especially if the crooks seemed to like jumping the teller counters. Supposedly that's a signature move for Townie bank robbers. I don't know if that's true, but that's what they say.

Don't get me wrong. Like in any town, most people mind their business and try to stay out of trouble. And there's still the Townie pride we all like to talk up. And there's this kind of buzz in the air as the city gears up to celebrate the country's 200th birthday in 1976, though for us in Charlestown the party really gets underway next year, on the bicentennial of the Battle of Bunker Hill.

The more optimistic Townies say NewTown proves that things are getting better. Maybe that's true. Another new housing development has gone up on the other side of town, on Main Street. It's called Mishawam, which is what the Indians called the area before the first Townies came from England and moved them along. Don't get me wrong—I'd love to see things improve, but it's hard to believe it when much of what used to be industrial Medford Street is so run down and getting worse.

Then there's the coming busing disaster. My sister not wanting to go to school if it means being bused across the city, maybe to Roxbury, reflects only half the problem. The other half is Townies not wanting kids from out of town, like Roxbury, being bused into Charlestown. They say it's not about color, that it's not about Black kids going to school in Charlestown. I'd say that's a really big part of it. Yet, it's hard not to see the basic craziness of busing poor and working-class kids from one part of the city to another, and busing poor and working-class kids from that neighborhood to this one. The courts say that's justice. Maybe, but it's sure not fucking fair.

# CHAPTER
# FIVE

Helen was holding a large, stuffed Panda under one arm and a Coke in her other hand when I met her at the Hurricane ride. She and her friends were gabbing away and laughing. When she saw me she immediately split from her girlfriends and headed my way.

"Look what I won," she said. "Pretty cool, huh?"

"A can of Coke isn't much of a prize," I said.

She immediately looked serious.

"No. The bear. What—you didn't notice the Panda? I mean, I didn't win it, but Potato Head won it for me at one of the pitching stalls. He knocked down ten of the friggin' targets without missing. He's got a good arm. I told him he can be a pitcher for the Red Sox someday. He told me—"

"Are you high?" I said. She stopped talking and looked around to see who might be listening. She shrugged. I didn't need her to answer. It was in her eyes.

"Where'd you get the pot? Who gave it to you?

Was it Potato Head?"

She shrugged again. "Why are you in a bad mood. I'm okay. It's no big deal. You smoke pot," she said, then added with a smart-ass tone, "Or did you forget that?"

"I didn't forget shit," I said, angry that she dredged up my pot bust last year. Helen moved to step past me but I grabbed her by the arm and held on, looking past her, past her girlfriends, into the crowd, searching for Potato Head—real name Kevin Leary. His nickname was born of a Little League ground-ball hit down the first base line, where Kevin was waiting for it. As he bent to scoop the ball up it hit a rock and flew over the glove, striking his forehead. The first base coach, kneeling over him as he lay on the ground howling in pain, offered these comforting words. "You'll be okay. You'll be fine. But you're gonna have a fuckin' potato on your head for a while."

I saw him over at one of the food stands with a few friends.

"Hey, Potato Head," I said, stepping up to him. I was still holding Helen by the arm. "You give my sister some dope? You give her the pot?"

He looked at me like I was crazy, then his face turned to a mask of innocence.

"Oh, Jimmy, hey, no man, I—"

"Did you give her pot? I asked you if you gave her the fuckin' pot."

He stuck his thumbs in his back pocket, looked

at the ground, then up into my face with that sincere look of concern.

"Don't worry, man. It wasn't laced with Angel Dust or anything. It's cool."

I let go of Helen, made a fist, and punched him just below his left eye. He stumbled back a few steps and hit the ground.

"How cool is that, asshole," I said. "Don't let me see you anywhere near Helen again. I'll take your fuckin' teeth out next time." I didn't wait for an answer, but took Helen by the arm again and headed home. Behind me I heard Potato Head's friends laughing. "Shit, man, looks like you're growing another potato," one said.

I expected the walk back to be one long argument with Helen. It wasn't. We walked back over Bunker Hill Street, which looks a hell of a lot better than Medford Street and also is better lit.

I started to feel bad about punching Potato Head. Another time I might have just yelled at him and told him to stay away. I guess I was keyed up thinking about my dad. That's what I was thinking when Helen broke the silence.

"Don't tell Ma, okay?" she said after a few blocks.

"I won't. But you can't get into that shit, Helen. I hate sounding like a teacher or guidance counsellor, but I do know you shouldn't be smoking pot—or doing any drugs for that matter. I don't even want to find out you're drinking."

"You drink. You drink, and you were drinking even before you were legal," she said.

"That's different. I'm a guy. Worst thing that'll happen to me is I'll get my ass kicked by someone I might piss off. You could get raped. Don't be stupid."

She stopped walking.

"Potato Head would never do something like that," she said.

I stopped walking, too. I didn't think he would, either, but you never know.

"I'm not saying he would, but some of the guys he hangs out with? I wouldn't trust them around the neighbor's dog."

She laughed. I laughed with her.

"Don't tell Ma," she said again.

I nodded. "That's the other thing. Ma would freak out if she found out you were doing drugs or drinking. She's already had her share of problems. My getting busted last year. Hell, I'm still on probation for that. And then there's Dad and all. Last thing she needs is to see you doping or drinking or getting into trouble with the law. Or hurt in any way."

We were passing the Bunker Hill pool. I nodded hellos to the gang that made the park area there its own patch. I've known them all for years, went to elementary and junior high school with a lot of them back in the day. One of the guys, Tommy, called over and asked if I wanted a beer.

"Nah, man. Gotta get my baby sister home," I said. Helen punched me in the arm and said I was embarrassing her. The Parkies all laughed and let out a steady stream of "ooooohs" and "woahs." Some of the girls hanging out told Helen not to listen to the guys, that they were all assholes.

"Yeah, and my brother can be one of the worst," Helen said.

Everyone laughed and we kept walking.

In that one mundane moment it hit me, just how much I really liked my town. It was fucked up on so many levels: the drugs, the gangsters, the common bullies, the pride people took in the town's reputation for being tough. But it was a place where everyone seemed to know everyone else. Sometimes too much. On most days you could walk from one end of the town to the other, see people and families you'd known your whole life, and whose people your parents—if they were from Charlestown—probably knew their entire lives. There was something comforting in that. I know some people think of Charlestown as one square mile of terror. Maybe we're all screwed up. Go figure.

Helen nodded her head back toward the pool.

"If it's nice tomorrow I'm going swimming. Then maybe back to the carnival if I can get Ma to give me a few dollars."

"Don't ask Ma for more money. I got paid today. I'll give you a fiver. That reminds me, I gotta give Ma ten bucks."

She hugged my arm. "It's nice to have a rich brother. You really give Ma money every week?"

I nodded. "Yeah. You think I'm a bum or something? I make about eighty bucks a week and take home just over seventy, so even after I give Ma a sawbuck I've got about sixty. But I'll give you five if you don't ask Ma for money."

"A week? Five a week?"

"What are you? Crazy?"

"Figured I'd ask. I thought they paid you more than that at the movie place," she said.

"You figured wrong. It's just a minimum wage job."

She made a face. "Really? Kevin said he might be getting a job making really good money working on some movie they're making on Cape Cod. Harry's already down there working on it."

I knew the movie. I'd read the book last year. It's about a giant shark terrorizing the shit out of a beach community off Long Island, N.Y., but it's being filmed on Martha's Vineyard.

"Potato Head again," I said.

"Can we forget about that? I won't do any more pot. Or anything. Okay?"

"Okay. As for Potato Head, he's only fifteen, he's never punched a clock or even had any job where you got paid by check. And even to get a gopher job on a film set like his brother Harry did, he'd have to be in a union. Potato Head is not in any union."

"Kevin said a movie lawyer down there owes Harry a favor, and that's how he's getting the job."

It sounded like Potato Head was trying to impress Helen. Harry—aka Harry Hollywood—is Potato Head's brother. He got the name after landing some minor roles in couple of movies filmed in Boston. The first was one was *The Boston Strangler*, the Tony Curtis movie filmed about seven years ago. He was one of an army of Teamsters' Union guys who got jobs on the picture. Everything from constructing sets to hauling gear, but Harry actually snagged an on-screen part as an extra. He's tall, well built, dark hair and dark eyes. Black Irish handsome, he claims the casting guy told him. He didn't have any lines in the movie, but he appeared in several scenes as a cop. That got a laugh around town considering that, in addition to his legit job, his background included burglaries and minor league debt collection. The year after *Strangler* he landed another part as an extra, this time in *The Thomas Crown Affair*, with Steve McQueen and Faye Dunaway. That solidified his reputation, at least in his own mind, as a star. After those brushes with movie glamour he began dressing a bit fancier. He started getting stylish haircuts and wore sunglasses regardless of the weather. Thus, Harry Hollywood was born. A year ago he landed a part in *The Friends of Eddie Coyle*, the Robert Mitchum mob movie. This time around he got the part his background prepared him for, as muscle for a loan shark. He's also done other films and TV shows filmed in Boston, often just a passer-by or "man reading newspaper." Now he's on the Cape. Gotta give the guy credit.

Helen wasn't buying my arguments about Potato Head. As far as she was concerned he was Cape-bound to work on a movie.

"A movie company lawyer? You believe that? The only lawyers Townies talk to are public defenders."

"We'll see," Helen said. "How about this? If Kevin does get a job on the movie down there you give me twenty-five dollars."

I laughed but told her it was a deal. Why not? The whole thing was ludicrous.

Before long the pool and then St. Francis Church, built atop the highest point of Charlestown, were behind us and we were walking down Bunker Hill, passing the well-appointed wood-frame homes and the stately looking townhouses, past small convenience stores, a pool hall that used to be a supermarket, the funeral parlor that saw lots of business, a fish shop, the nineteenth-century ceme-tery that included dead from the Revolutionary War and, finally, the projects. Home.

"Where you going?" Helen asked when we got to our building.

"Just out someplace. Maybe walk around and see who's hanging out. Tell Ma I'll be home later."

"Yeah, okay. Hey, thanks for not saying anything to Ma about the pot. And I'm sorry for saying that stuff about Mary Connor at supper. I didn't mean anything. I only thought about her because I saw her at the Red Store this morning."

I fought the urge to roll my eyes and say *'Pleaaaaze, not Mary Connor again!'*

"She still works there?"

"Yeah, she said her dad was just dropping her off, then he was going to the Cape."

"Great. That's what the movie industry needs. Another Townie thug trying to make it onto the Hollywood Walk of Fame."

"Cut it out, Jimmy," Helen laughed. "He can't be that bad. Besides, Mary is sweet. She told me to say hi to you."

"To tell the truth, I don't know why she's always so nice to me. I know her father used to be a friend of Dad's. But that's it. She seems nice. Her father doesn't." I've never shared with Helen what I witnessed between Ma and Connor, nor my belief that he pulled the trigger on our father. I wasn't about to now.

"Pretty, too, don't you think?" Helen said through a smile.

"Pretty old. She must be like thirty." I laughed. "Okay, go inside. I'll see you in the morning. And remember. No more pot. Or anything else."

"Wait! My eyes, Jimmy. Do they look okay? If Ma sees—"

I looked at them.

"Your eyes are fine, sis. They're gorgeous."

75

# CHAPTER
## SIX

Mickey Ryan was the guy who I'd heard ended up with the van and the movies. Mickey's a big lump of a guy, maybe 99 percent lard, but with a cruel, bullying nature that no laugh he ever gave up or smile he attempted could hide. He's a drug dealer and fence with a bunch of artful dodger-types lined up to peddle his pot, pills and smack and supply him with stolen goods. Some of these are also regular customers for the drugs, though a small but reliable crew of enforcers keeps his sidewalk labor in line. I know these things firsthand because he's the guy I briefly sold for a few years back.

Every guy running a crew has a bar where they hold court. For Mickey, it was The Brig. Why? He'd tell you it was because it was local and near the Navy Yard, which has been associated with patriots for almost two hundred years. The real reason is because all the better places were taken.

The shipyard has been around almost from the

beginning of the country, building ships and sending them off to fight pirates in the Barbary Wars in the early 1800s, the English in the War of 1812, all the way up through World War II. It may seem ironic that The Brig has long been off limits to the sailors and Marines stationed a stone's throw away, but it makes sense. Servicemen from out of town wouldn't mix well with locals after a few drinks, even if the town genuinely lionizes "the troops." And it does. It's supplied enough of them over the years and wars. But none of that stops wrong words being said or wrong looks given at the wrong times to the wrong people. No. The Brig is a place for locals. That includes underage locals if you have a passable ID that says otherwise. I had one of those, and would still if the drinking age hadn't been lowered to 18. Now my twenty years on Earth is good enough.

Inside smelled of cigarette smoke and too many spilled beers. The jukebox was blaring the Rolling Stones. But as loud as the music was, Townies are louder. The house was raucous. Beers and shots moved fast from bar to tables, then nearly as quickly were drunk and refills called for. Nursing drinks was not a concept understood by many people at The Brig. If any place in Boston deserved to be called a saloon, it's The Brig. Sure it's seedy and dangerous, but that's part of the allure, isn't it? Can't say I ever saw anyone stabbed or shot there. Punches thrown, some blood spilled, yeah, but fights were quickly brought under control and those responsible told to take it outside. Preferably far away outside, where durations or degrees of beatings were not management concerns.

At times The Brig was like Rick's place in *Casablanca*. One night a few weeks back I was in there downing a beer when the detective who had busted me for the roach strolled into the bar, chatted with one of the bartenders, and was quickly—and not at all sneakily—handed a roll of bills that went right into his pocket. As he turned from the bar he saw me and smiled. I was halfway tempted to go over and say "I'm shocked—shocked to find graft going on here!" but figured even if he got the joke he'd drag me outside and knock me around a bit for being a smart-ass. And I still have the court's sword of Damocles over my head, so if the asshole wanted to really fuck me up, he could bring me in on some trumped up charge and I'd probably end up at the Charles Street Jail.

I stood next to the waitress station and caught Uncle Barry's eye. He brought me a Miller long-neck and I forked over a buck and a half.

"Thanks, Unck."

"Sure thing. How's the family? Everyone okay?"

I nodded. "Yep, everyone's great. How you doing?"

He put his palms up toward the ceiling and scanned the room.

"Fuck, Jimmy. I'm living the dream." He sounded like he meant it, though that was hardly the case. He lived pretty much hand to mouth, or hand to track is more like it since most of what he earns ends up at Suffolk Downs. Still, I laughed and pointed the bottle toward the ceiling. "Here's to dreaming."

"Maybe I should be California Dreaming," he said in a dryer tone as he walked away. "Be good and be cool."

I saw Mickey where I expected he'd be—sitting in the far corner with some of his crew. I stayed at the bar, in no hurry to talk with him. He was not someone I ever sought out for conversation or anything else, so heading on over now for small talk would be more than a little out of character for me. Also, I hadn't figured out yet how to open a conversation with him that would somehow get around to asking about the hijacked van. So I took a stool at the bar, tapped my hand or nodded my head to the music while keeping an eye on him. Every so often someone would go up and say hello, shake his hand —that is, pass him some cash. Mickey would nod to Juicer, one of his guys, who was sitting at another table. Juicer would get up and head out the back door to the parking lot, followed shortly after by the guy who put the cash into Mickey's hand. Brig bosses didn't want drugs being dealt anywhere in the bar. They didn't need the hassle of cops coming in, disrupting everything, and maybe being pissed enough to try and shut the place down. I mean, it *could* happen, notwithstanding some of their own pulled down a few bucks there. Even Mickey respected Brig rules.

The place was even busier than usual because Bunker Hill Day was coming up and that had everyone pumped for the parade. After Christmas, or maybe before, Bunker Hill Day is the most wonderful time of the year in Charlestown. To my right there were suddenly cheers, and then Barry shouting "*Get the fuck off!*" I turned to see Billy Turner, a mechanic at Tully's Garage on Medford Street, up on the bar dancing to *Brown Sugar*. Barry had a small bat in his hand, ready to take Billy out at the knees, while the drunk's cheering squad shouted. "*No, no, man!*" and "*The dude's off to the Marine Corps on Monday!*" and "*Let him be, Barry!*"

"Then get him the fuck off the bar!" Barry ordered, and Billy's buddies pulled him down and put him on a stool. Billy seemed unfazed.

"Where's my beer, man?" he asked.

At a nearby booth Mike Carbery, a cousin so distant I have no idea the family connection, was with friends who were buying him rounds and welcoming him back from his Vegas honeymoon. His wife, Emily, was nowhere around. That didn't surprise me. It was supposed to be a two-week love-fest and here he was back in Charlestown after just four days. He was partying like he didn't have a care in the world. If Emily's still in Vegas she'd be smart to stay there. But, if Emily was smart, she never would have gotten involved with Mike in the first place, let alone marry him.

I was about to signal for another beer when Deb, who graduated from high school last year and works at Schrafft's down at Sullivan Square, asked me to dance with her. She's was looking gorgeous in tight jeans and black halter top. Even with the shiner. I was going to say yes, put my beer on the bar, and head to the floor with her. But then I realized what a stupid decision that would be. Her boyfriend, Crazy Pug—no one calls him Crazy to his face—had to be around there somewhere. Pug's a muscle-head of the first order. Pumps iron like it's the true faith and takes steroids for communion. I shook my head and said I'd pass. Seconds later she coaxed another guy up onto the floor and the room temperature must have spiked about twenty degrees as she danced. The magic moment was broken when a beer bottle flew past her partner's head—far enough away so that he would know the miss was deliberate but close enough to deliver a message. He stopped dancing, turned and headed back to the bar for his drink. An instant later Crazy Pug walked onto the floor from the same direction the bottle flew. He wore a Red Sox cap on his buzz-cut head, a tank-top bearing Elvis in his "Jail House Rock" outfit, jeans and black Jack Purcell sneakers. He put his arm around Deb. She was good with that. I thought about the black eye she was wearing and wondered what it would take before she decided to be free of the guy.

"You're lookin' pretty interested in Deb there, Lyons," Muggles, one of Mickey's crew—the smart one, I've always believed—was next to me. "Shoulda gone and danced with her."

"You fuckin' nuts? Risk the wrath of Pug for a dance? I was happy enough with the view."

Both of us looked back to the dance floor. Deb was moving beautifully, and Pug was pumping his arms up and down while taking one step to the right, then to the left.

"What's he doing?" I said.

Muggles laughed. "Yeah, he might dance like a goof but he'll be goin' home with her."

"What do you want?" I asked Muggles.

He pointed toward Mickey.

"Okay," I said. "What's he want?"

"You should ask him that," Muggles said.

I took a chair at Mickey's table and he signaled a waitress named Suzie as she was walking past. In no time she placed a coaster in front of me and a bottle of Miller. Suzie's been at The Brig for years. She's about forty, quite pretty and with a flippant humor that reminded me of Barbara Stanwyck in *Meet John Doe*. Suzie has a kind of confidence and invisible armor that most guys would like to have. I thought of Uncle Barry. He may be unlucky at the track but he's lucky in love. Suzie lives with him in an apartment up on Auburn Street.

"How you doing, Jimmy? Okay?"

"I'm great, Suzie. How about you?"

She just rolled her eyes, smiled and headed back to the waitress station at the bar.

Mickey wasn't a Wise Guy. He was a criminal, sure, but he didn't get into things that were, let's say, above his pay grade. And I had nothing against him or his guys. Back when I told him I didn't want to sell anymore I thought he'd try to make me. He's done it to other guys. I've seen him beat his sellers bloody to keep them on the streets. He just looked at me, said I was a dumb shit and to get the fuck away from him. I don't know why I was so lucky, but I suspected that Barry may have had a talk with him. Nothing else made sense. It gave me a newfound respect for my uncle, that he could convince a thug like Mickey to let me walk away. I'm just glad I've been able to reach twenty without having to worry about any felonies or jail time on my still-unwritten resume.

But since we did have some history I made it a point to avoid him. If we did speak it was usually to say hi and not much else. So I was surprised he wanted to talk to me, but I also was lucky. Now I didn't have to make up some lame excuse to see him. Whatever he wanted to talk about, maybe I could bring the conversation around to a hijacked van and hot movies.

"Thanks for the beer, Mickey." I took a swig from the bottle. "What's up?"

"Lyons! How you doin'?"

"Just working and hanging out. All set for Bunker Hill Day?"

"Oh, yeah. Gonna barbecue in the yard and then watch the parade down by the Trainin' Field," he said. The Training Field is a small park down off the Bunker Hill Monument. The Colonial militia once trained there.

"Sounds good," I said. "I'll probably watch it across from the Lexy."

"That sounds good, too," he said in a tone that indicated he didn't give a shit and that the small talk was over. "Listen, Lyons. I need ya ta do somethin' for me. I mean, if ya can."

If you can. Yeah, right, I thought.

"I need to borrow your projector," he said.

I thought I misheard him. "What?"

"Your fuckin' projector! You know? For movies? I wouldn't ask but I got some movies and they don't run on mine," he said.

Well, at least I don't have to figure out a way to casually bring up movies, I thought. I was surprised, too, that he owned a projector.

"You have one?" I said.

"Yeah, and it's practically new. You'd think a new projector would be able to run some old fuckin' movies, wouldn'cha?"

I didn't answer the question because that's not something I'd have thought.

"What kinda movies you trying to watch?" I

asked him, playing for time and trying to think my way out of this.

"Movie movies. Whatta ya think?"

"Like something you'd see at a regular movie theater?"

"Yeah, like that, but probably no theater you're old enough to get into," he said and laughed. His guys laughed with him, but I didn't mind. He gave me my way out of doing him a favor.

"Okay, that explains it," I told him. "What do you have? A Super-eight? You need a thirty-five-millimeter projector."

"No shit, Sherlock. That I already know. Isn't that what you have?"

"No, man. Mine's a sixteen-millimeter. It won't work for your movies."

"What the fuck is with all this millimeter shit? A fuckin' projector should be a fuckin' projector."

"You can get a thirty-five-millimeter," I said. "There are probably places right downtown that sell them."

"Why the fuck would I wanna pay for one?" he said.

I didn't like where this was going.

"What about Harry Hollywood? Can't he get one for you?"

Mickey shook his head.

"He was the first one I called. I told him days ago that I had these movies and he's the one who told me about this thirty-five-millimeter shit. He's got another make-believe job courtesy of the union. Fuck. This time he's down the Cape doing some movie about a shark."

Okay, so Harry really is at the Cape for a film.

Mickey kept talking.

"He said he'd see what he could find out, see if they have any down there that could be, you know, borrowed. But I haven't heard from him in like three days."

"Probably keeping him busy," I suggested.

"Right. Big fuckin' star is probably sitting around the beach most of the day doing jack shit," Mickey said, sounding more than a little jealous. "So, can you get one for me?"

"You want me to get you a thirty-five-millimeter projector. How am I supposed to do that?"

"I'm not sayin' ya gotta steal it. Just borrow it is all I'm askin'. You keep movies over at your work. You gotta have projectors for them, right?"

"No. We don't stock projectors. Only the movies." I told him how it worked and what I did there.

"Jesus, Lyons, that sounds like a shitty job."

I didn't argue that. One of his guys, Walter, said I must be dumb to keep a job like that. There are some people you take shit from and then there's Walter, who hated being called Wally.

"You still selling papers off of milk crates down at City Square, Wally? You're what now, twenty-five, twenty-six?"

"What are you saying, Lyons?"

"Oh, sorry, Wally. I thought I was speaking English. I'm saying you're a loser."

He made a grab for me but I was up from the chair and out of his reach in a heartbeat. He stepped toward me and swung, but I blocked his punch and just managed to clip him in the jaw when both of us were grabbed by Mickey's other guys and pulled apart. My heart was racing and I didn't give a shit what happened. Now that's the definition of stupid.

Muggles voice, low and clipped, was in my ear. "You want to end up all busted up in the fuckin' street, Jimmy? Cool it. Now."

I nodded, shrugged him off me. I could feel eyes on my back. I turned to see Uncle Barry looking my way, the hand holding a liquor bottle paused, frozen, over a glass on the bar. An instant later he continued pouring. He wasn't going to interfere with this. I wouldn't expect him to.

"Both you assholes sit the fuck down," Mickey said, then, to Walter. "Who the fuck asked you to butt in?"

Walter looked embarrassed. "Sorry, Mickey. I didn't mean nothin'."

Mickey turned back to me. "Look, help me out here, Lyons. If you don't have one at work—fine. You know where I can get one?"

I thought about it. Barring them breaking into a movie theater, where there was bound to be alarms, there was only one place I could think of nearby that would have one. Leastways, I thought there might be one. Did I really want to tell him? No. But would I? Sure, especially because he had about seven guys with him and maybe one of them might feel badly enough to want to stop it from happening. It was a local place after all, and one that nearly every guy in Charlestown felt some loyalty to.

"I think the Boys Club has one."

"The Boys Club? You shittin' me?" Mickey said.

"No. Don't they still run movies every Saturday? They get them from the different exchanges downtown, so I figure their projector must be a thirty-five-millimeter."

Muggles piped in. "He's right, Mickey. We used to go there to see lots of movies. Like Captain Marvel —remember? And I think we saw one'a the Three Stooges' movies there."

"Yeah, the one where they go into space!" Walter added. "That was funny!"

"But Curly wasn't in it, so it kinda sucked," Muggles said. "I liked the Captain Marvel movie."

"It wasn't a movie," Walter lectured. "It was a serial, with chapters. Remember? They'd run a new chapter every Saturday."

"What? You suddenly Gene Shalit?" Muggles said.

Mickey had enough.

"Quiet, for Chissakes! Okay, Lyons, I'll find out about the Boys Club. I hate havin' to take theirs, but I gotta see what's on the film, so I got no choice.

Fuck. I'll make sure they get it back. It's a good place."

"Yeah, 'cept I never liked havin' to swim there all ballicky-bare-ass," Walter added. Every head nodded and there was laughter. Only members of the club's swim team could wear bathing suits in the pool. Everyone else went into the pool as they came into the world: naked. The only other exception was if there was a "Splash Party" scheduled, because then the pool was also opened to girls.

I thought it was a good time to ask a question about the movies, since Mickey brought them up.

"What's the deal on these movies? They just regular porn films or is there something special about them?"

He studied my face for what seemed like a minute, though it probably was a matter of seconds.

"I dunno, Lyons. Someone wanted 'em bad enough ta steal 'em and bring 'em here from New York, so maybe there's stuff on 'em that important people might find embarrassin' enough to pay good money to get 'em back."

I nodded and said okay. He seemed to read something in my expression.

"What's up, Lyons? You heard something already about these movies?"

"I heard something at work, but I don't know how good the information is."

He splayed his fingers on the table in a way that said, *tell me more.*

89

"Here's the thing," I said, "Some guys who truck the movies between the exchange and the theaters were talking at lunch about some van filled with movies. One of them seemed to think they were supposed to go to a guy in Chinatown."

"Chinatown? The Chinks are involved in this?" Mickey asked. I shrugged an I don't know as Mickey looked to the guys around him. "What's that Chink gang over there now? Anyone know?" It was their turn to shrug. Mickey turned back to me.

"Is that it? You got any more?"

I had an idea and I thought I'd go with it.

"Could be bullshit, but one guy I heard talking to his friends on the loading dock said the Chinese guy is called the Shadow King."

They all looked at me in silence and I thought I'd fucked up, overplayed it, and that they were going to laugh me out of The Brig. Instead, they looked uneasy.

"Can you find out more?" Mickey asked in a way that was more than asking. It's what I expected, but I can't say I was happy. I already regretted what I said.

"I can try," I told him.

"Good. You do that, Lyons. If the Chinks are somehow involved there must be more to it than some fuck films. Has to be."

"Were they all in film cases?" I asked. I just couldn't stop myself. "Did you open all of them to see if there was, I don't know, maybe drugs in any of them?"

Mickey nodded. "Yeah, they're all in fuckin' cases. About ten or twelve of them. And they all have movies in them. Nothin' else."

No one said anything.

"Okay, we're good here," Mickey declared. "You can split, Lyons. Tell Suzie to give you another beer on me."

"Okay. Thanks, Mickey."

I wanted to leave, but that might look bad, so I took a stool at the bar and waited to catch Suzie's eye.

"Having a good time, Jimmy?" she asked.

"Always. It's The Brig, right? I'll have a Miller. Mickey's picking up the tab on this one, too."

She threw a coaster on the bar and signaled Barry to bring me another beer.

"What's your business with Mickey and the Mouse Club over there?"

I didn't say anything right away. It wasn't her problem.

"Nothing much. He was asking me about movies and shit. Seems to think I'm Stanley Kubrick."

"Really. I had you pegged for a Billy Wilder."

I laughed. I was surprised by her quip.

"Right, you're wondering how a Townie chick slinging drinks at The Brig would know who Billy Wilder is."

"I guess."

"Well, I'll tell you, Jimmy. I had a real life before

all this. It was bright lights, glitz and wine nearly every night. Doors opened for me. I saw more stars than the guys at NASA."

"Wait a minute! Are you seriously telling me you once worked out in Hollywood?"

"No. I used to date a guy who ran the projector over at the Paramount. We'd always bring a bottle of wine and glasses into the booth."

Had I taken a swig from my beer it would have shot out my nose then. Good for both of us that I hadn't. She suddenly leaned in to me, her face all serious. "You should keep the fuck away from Mickey and his bunch. They ain't the fuckin' Mafia and they ain't connected with the big guys, but they can be dangerous if for no other reason than they're fuckin' stupid as well as criminal."

"Got it," I said. Something in the way I left the words hanging out there bothered her.

"What is it?"

"Nothing. Everything's cool."

She looked skeptical. "Listen to Suzie, Jimmy Lyons. Some people don't," she said, cocking her head toward Barry. I smiled. "Good thing he has a good heart, because the head—for all the education he's had—sometimes leaves a bit to be desired."

She walked away as Barry headed down with my beer.

"What are you smiling about?"

"Nothing. Suzie is pretty funny."

He made as if he was going to snap a bar rag at me. "Yeah, she is."

Looking back, I should have followed my first instinct and left without that second free beer. No sooner had Barry stepped away than Mickey was next to me.

"Fuck it, Lyons. I don't like the idea of stealin' the Boys Club's projector. I'm just gonna see if I can sell the movies. Just put out a price—maybe ten grand—and see if anyone bites. Let someone else screw around with blackmail if that's what goin' on."

I wondered if Mickey was scared off by having to deal with a Chinese gang led by "the Shadow King."

"Yeah, I think you're right, Mickey. Let someone else screw around with that shit."

He stayed sitting on the stool, not saying anything.

"When you opened up the film cases, did you try looking at any of the films to see what's on them?" I said.

He turned to me like I'd insulted him.

"I look like some kind of pussy nerd? I'm gonna hold up some fucking film to a light to see if I can tell what's on it? The movies are hot. That tells me all I need to know that someone will pay to get them."

He looked left and right, to see if anyone had gotten close enough to hear him. As if anyone could with the music cranked up. "Listen, if anybody at that place where you work knows someone you can call, like soon, to see if they wanna buy these movies, you call 'em. I got a bad feelin' about this."

Mickey turned and went back to his table before I could say "what do you mean *you* call them?"

I downed the rest of my beer in quick-time and left.

# CHAPTER SEVEN

The projects are an easy walk from the bar. I passed the basketball court at Decatur Street, waved hello to the guys there polishing off a six-pack, then passed Hayes Square, where Ma and Helen went to church at Saint Catherine's and Ma worked part time at McCarthy's grocery store. I made a quick right at the church rectory and then a left onto O'Reilly Way. A short distance up I crossed right, through McNulty Court, and entered my building, which fronts on Walford Way. I don't know if my building is the geographic center of this red-brick labyrinth called home but it feels like it. Up three flights, a turn of the key and the heavy metal door opened. Only the living room light was on. I hoped I didn't wake Ma and Helen coming in. I sat down in an armchair and turned the TV on, with the volume real low. Some old gangster movie was on. Unfortunately, it wasn't a Bogart, Cagney or Robinson film. It was George Raft, who I think was a crap actor. I'll take a bad

Bogart movie—that's a joke because there isn't one —over the best Raft movie—also no such thing— any time.

Still, this was not a night I wanted to watch gangster movies, not when I was dealing with real life gangsters. I shut off the TV. I looked at the family photos on the wall by the chair. My dad is in only a few. There he is with my mother on their wedding day outside Saint Catherine's. There he is holding me at the hospital on the night I was born. There he is a few years later with my sister. This was two days after she was born because he had to be out of town on business. So the story goes. Then there's me in my white suit for First Communion. Next to me, in her own frame, my sister in her First Communion dress and veil. It occurred to me that I shared with Eu-meh and Lee the fact I lost my father while still young. Their father seems to have been a good family man who was in line to inherit the family business when he died. Mine was not that. As far as I knew, neither of those things applied to my old man. My mother never talks about him, and always dismisses any attempts to do so with "the dead are dead. Leave them that way."

It also occurred to me that, beyond the wall photos, I have few actual memories of my father. I remember being with both parents up at the Bunker Hill pool. And I remember them once taking me and my sister over to the Public Gardens to ride on the Swan Boats. But he didn't get on them. He suddenly remembered he had to be somewhere else. Ma was furious. She demanded money so she could get us on the boats and then buy us a treat somewhere. He handed her some money and slipped off.

Helen and I had a good time just floating along, taking in the view. Ma didn't say much at first, but by the time we got off she seemed happy again. Looking back, I think she was acting that way for me and Helen. We walked a few blocks to Brigham's. It was like going to ice cream heaven. Helen and I got sundaes. Mine was chocolate ice cream with hot fudge and whipped cream. Helen went for vanilla ice cream with strawberries and whipped cream. Ma got a frappe.

I also remember being with Dad at a Red Sox game and one or two Bruins games. We got into Fenway and the Garden by meeting up with someone who let us in through a door where there were no crowds, hot dog vendors or program hawkers. I don't recall any ticket takers either. I had hot dogs and Cokes. Dad drank beers. It's hard to believe how things ended up. Ma wants only to make sure I don't follow in Dad's footsteps. Considering where they led, I'm not eager to do that either.

We don't have much money. Besides her shifts at McCarthy's, Ma also babysits for a few neighbors. That work is under the table. And then there's the ten bucks I give her each week. Luckily it doesn't cost much to live in the projects. She's also hoping I can somehow get into college. Worse comes to worst, she says, I can join the Army, like Red. I'm not too keen on that idea but there is an argument to be made for it, what with the GI Bill and all. I'd just have to hope Vietnam doesn't stretch out or another war doesn't pop up to ruin things.

I thought of the Shadow King's $2,000 finder's fee. That refocused me. I put aside the risk that went with being Mickey's messenger and thought of the money. Hell, that's almost half a year's tuition at Emerson. Maybe Mickey would throw something my way too. No. That's not on. Taking something from Mickey means you're back on the payroll. Don't want that. Don't need that. If he offers money, I'm just going to say I was happy to help. That's all. Funny, though, I don't feel that taking money from Zhang would lead me into any future trouble. I only hope I'm right. I looked at my watch. It was just after midnight. Well, the old man said to call anytime. I picked up the phone.

Eu-meh answered.

"*Nǐ hǎo,*" she said.

*Shit!* I thought. Suddenly midnight didn't seem like a good time to call after all. Hell, why was she even there? She has her own place!

"*Nǐ hǎo?*" she said again. I assumed she was saying hello. I should have hung up. I didn't.

"Hi. Is this Eu-meh?" I realized that sounded dumb as soon as I said it, and I half expected her to come back with *No. You're Jimmy.*

Instead, there was a long silence at her end. Then: "Jimmy? Jimmy Lyons?"

She sounded surprised—not like *Wow! Jimmy Lyons! This is great!* surprised. But also not the *Who the hell are you to call here?* kind. Just surprised.

"Hi," I said. "Is, umm, is your grandfather in?"

The silence again.

"You want to speak with my grandfather?" Suspicion flavored every word.

"Yeah. Is he there?"

"No. He's still at the restaurant. What's this about?"

I didn't know what to say so I said nothing.

"Jimmy? You still there?"

"Yeah, yeah, sorry. Umm, okay. I can try him there. At the restaurant."

"What's going on? Why would you contact my grandfather? And late at night."

"He asked me to. He thought I could help him with something."

"Really? Like what? My grandfather doesn't have any interests outside the restaurant anymore."

I didn't want to be rude to Eu-meh, God knows. But I also had no business telling her about my conversation with her grandfather.

"I got the impression it's some kind of project he's working on. Or thinking about working on. I don't know for sure."

"Uh-huh. Right," she said, then let silence float across the phone line like a question I was not supposed to hear, but was supposed to answer anyway. "You're a Townie, aren't you, Jimmy. You're from Charlestown?"

"Yeah," I said, drawing out that small word slowly and feeling like I was confessing to something.

"I don't want you getting my grandfather into any shit!" she said. "You understand?"

The words hit me like a brick. At first I wanted to apologize into the phone, tell her I'm sorry and that I won't call him again. Then I was mad. I'm thinking: *Why am I the fucking bad guy here?* I wanted to say, *Look, Eu-meh, your grandfather asked me for a favor. He asked me to help him get information about some secret goddam porno movies with God knows who in them, which I did by having a conversation with a gangster. Someone I'd have been better off not talking to at all. And now I'm into some criminal shit I don't need.* Yep, that's how mad I was. That's what I felt.

"Don't worry. I'm just helping him with something. I wouldn't let anything happen to your grandfather." *Lyons, you're such a wimp,* I told myself.

"You promise?" she said, her voice, fierce a moment ago, cracked. I imagined tears in her eyes and I almost couldn't speak.

"I promise."

"Okay. Okay, good," she said. I could barely hear her. There was another brief silence. Finally, she said "bye" and hung up. I felt like shit. Me, a go-between for gangsters in a deal involving stolen movies—

possibly porn—and blackmail, promising Eu-meh I wouldn't let anything happen to her grandfather. I was suddenly imagining my obit appearing on the pages of the *Charlestown Patriot*. What the hell. I opened the phone book and found the number for the restaurant.

Lee picked up, saying, "House of Dragons. May I help you?"

"Hey, Lee, it's me, Jimmy."

"Who? Jimmy?" he asked.

"Yeah, Jimmy from Charlestown. Damn, Lee, Eu-meh recognized me at hello."

"You called my sister? Why?"

"Don't get all panicky. I called the apartment first, like your grandfather said to, but she answered. I wasn't expecting that."

"Oh, right. She's helping go over the books, but it's loud here so she's working in grandfather's library," Lee said. "It's kind of late, you know."

"He told me to call any time. Is he free?"

Lee put me on hold. In what had to be less than a half minute he was back on with me.

"He's here, yeah, but he's helping out in the kitchen. One of the cooks went home sick. He says you can call him here tomorrow or just drop by. We open at ten, though he's always here by seven."

I was annoyed. *The old man asks me to get into all this stuff and to call anytime, and now when I call he's too busy to come to the phone? What kind of gangster shit is this?* But I didn't say that to Lee. I said that was fine and I'd come by tomorrow.

I turned on the TV again without even thinking about it. George Raft was still there. I switched the channel to catch the rest of *The Tonight Show with Johnny Carson.* Trouble is, it wasn't with Johnny. Rat Pack back-bencher Joey Bishop was sitting in with a guest list that didn't interest me in the least. I turned off the TV and thought of Eu-meh again. Remembered her voice on the phone. I was still thinking about her when I closed my eyes, just for a minute. That was it. Goodnight.

# CHAPTER
# EIGHT

I woke up to a test pattern on the TV and the earliest morning light creeping through the window. I turned off the television and made for the shower, the sound of which woke Ma, who of course got out of bed so she could call through the bathroom door to ask me why I was up so early. I told her Turk asked me to come in especially early because there was a backlog. She accepted the answer without asking a backlog of what. That was good, because there's never a backlog of movies going out or coming in. Doesn't work that way. I dressed, wolfed down some toast and coffee and was out the door, footing it to City Square. I grabbed the train to the Essex stop and walked the several blocks to House of Dragons.

I walked up the three steps between the colorful Foo dogs and through the large red door decorated with Chinese symbols. Inside I found Zhang at his usual place. He was wearing blue jeans and a white tee. He nodded and waved me over as if I worked for him. It was unsettling.

"Good morning, Mr. Lyons. Would you like some tea?" he asked and poured for both of us into small, beautifully adorned cups. I said thank you and he indicated the chair opposite him. We sat in silence and he lifted his cup, which I took as a signal to raise mine. He sipped. I sipped. We placed the cups on the table.

"Thank you for coming in," he said. "It was very busy here last night and I could not take your call. Frankly, I am surprised you called so soon after we spoke yesterday. I take it you have some information for me?"

"Yes, I do, Mr. Zhang," I don't know why, but I was conscious of what I sounded like, how I spoke. I forged ahead. "The guy who has the movies does want to sell them."

"That is good. Did he say what condition they are in? Have they been damaged?"

"He didn't say. From what he did tell me he tried to watch one on a Super eight projector—"

"A Super-eight?" he laughed. "I take it he does not know how this works." Zhang brightened up so much in that instant that I laughed along with him.

"You've got that right," I said. "Sounds like he gave up after the one try. He did open each case to take a look, but that's it. He couldn't be bothered trying to eyeball the actual film. Also, he said there's about ten or twelve cases. Is that what you were expecting?"

The old man nodded. "Yes, that sounds right."

"Good. If he handled them just the way he said, it sounds like they're probably in the same condition they were when they were stolen."

"Acquired," the old man corrected.

"Right, acquired," I agreed. "At first he asked me to get him a projector he could use. He knew I had one, but I explained mine was just sixteen-millimeter and he needed a thirty-five. He just didn't want to go to the trouble of locating one."

Zhang was lifting the cup to his lips again and smiled into it as he paused, saying "Yes, thirty-five is the industry standard." He sipped, then continued. "Mr. Lyons, you are giving me far better news than I could have hoped for so soon after our discussion."

"I was surprised myself to find out this shi—find out this stuff so fast."

He smiled again. Then he got down to business, asking how he could contact the man holding the movies. I was still nervous about all this. I had no great love for Mickey, but I was not about to just give up his name and possibly get him whacked. Sure, Zhang said he wanted a simple deal, but for all I knew that could be bullshit and maybe he'd send someone in to collect the movies in the most efficient, old Tong way. After all, Mickey did steal them from him. And though Mickey didn't tell me not to give his name out, common sense told me not do that.

"The guy who has them? He doesn't want me to give you his name just yet," I lied. "What he did say is that he wants ten grand for them. And he doesn't want to haggle. He said he just wants ten thousand. That's it."

The old man nodded. He didn't look pleased or disappointed. He must be good at poker.

"I agree to that," he said. "A simple transaction. No complications."

I realized I was holding my breath and quietly exhaled. I actually felt pretty good. It seemed like this whole thing was going to wrap up quick and easy.

"If you are willing, and you have been authorized to accept it, I will give you the money now. But you should also be certain, if you accept the ten thousand dollars, that this man actually has the movies and will hand them over to you."

My heart began beating faster. No way I wanted to walk out of there with ten thousand dollars in cash, stroll through Chinatown, downtown Boston, and back into Charlestown. And in that same instant it occurred to me that Mickey might be lying about having the movies. I mean, he seemed to be talking straight, and what I heard in his voice and saw on his face at the bar seemed to be coming from an honest-to-God scared place in his gut. But I never saw the movies myself, not on the reels and not even in the film cases. And at the end of the day, Mickey is a scumbag. The Shadow King was right.

"You and him should do it. Or whoever you both want to send. I'd rather not be in the middle of that."

"That is a wise decision, Mr. Lyons," he said. He wrote down a phone number on a napkin. "Please pass along this number. It rings here but is separate from the business line. Tell your employer to call so that we may arrange things."

"He's not my employer," I said quickly and in a tone that made it clear I felt insulted. "I'm only doing this because you asked me to, and because I like Eu-meh. And Lee."

"Forgive me, Mr. Lyons. I meant no offense," he said.

He may have been sincere. It sounded like it, but I wasn't sure. I thought of Eu-meh.

"It's okay, Mr. Zhang," I said. After a brief silence and no tea sipping I figured we were done. I got up from my chair and walked toward the door.

"Mr. Lyons?" he said, and I looked at him. He took a pack of cigarettes from his shirt pocket and shook one loose from the pack. He paused before putting it to his lips. "I want this to go well. It would be painful to me if something went amiss and I did not get these films."

"I understand, Mr. Zhang," I said. I turned to leave. In the silence I heard the match-strike and a hissing burn. I didn't realize he was a smoker. I'd never seen him smoke in the restaurant. I'll also admit that I didn't really understand what he meant by his last comment. Was he maybe suggesting it would also be painful for me? Screw it. I'll tell Mickey he's got a deal for the ten grand and that the old man is serious about it going down without any problems. Let them work out the time and place. I wanted nothing to do with making the arrangements, and definitely nothing to do with handling the cash or the movies. I couldn't wait for this to be over. As I started for the door Eu-meh came out from the kitchen carrying a blue work shirt, the kind a janitor might wear. She offered a nod as hello as she passed me on her way to her grandfather's table. At the door I paused to look back. They exchanged some words in Chinese as he put the shirt on. So he was also the head janitor, I thought. I didn't find it funny or demeaning. Far from it. It made me think: The Shadow King is not afraid to get his hands dirty.

Just around the block was one of the colorful, pagoda-topped payphones found on Chinatown streets. I threw a dime in and called Mickey. He sounded like he'd just woken up. Pissed off, too.

"Lyons!" he said. Yep, he was pissed. So I quickly gave him Zhang's name and **number** and told him the old man was expecting his call.

"Really?" he said. He still sounded pissed, and I thought, *this guy is never satisfied.* "The price has gone up."

I choke-laughed into the phone. It wasn't a haha

funny laugh but the I'm-so-fucked-now laugh you do when the only other option is crying.

"Are you kidding me? No way! I don't know this guy, not really. I delivered your message saying ten grand. He said fine, and now you wanna go back on it and say he needs to pay more? And you think he's gonna be okay with that?"

"I don't give a shit. It's what it has ta be," he snapped.

"You offered a deal, Mickey. And he said yes to it. How can you change it now?"

"Because everything has changed," he shouted. "Everything! Let me ask you, Lyons. Did you tell anyone else about these movies?"

I hadn't. I wouldn't. And that's what I told him.

"Well, somebody dropped a dime, and now everything is changed. It's early in the mornin' and I've already been threatened by some Southie asshole and a fuckin' lawyah."

"Well, I didn't say shit to anyone."

"I don't like this, Lyons. Not one fuckin' bit."

"I don't blame you. I didn't like being dragged into this shit in the first place."

Mickey swore and then got quiet for a moment.

"Fuck! I don't know what's goin' on here!" he said.

I didn't want to get any more involved than I was already, but I asked him about the threat.

"This Southie guy calls me at three fuckin'

o'clock this mornin' to say the movies were stolen from him! That he was supposed ta steal 'em first."

"Steal them first? What's that even mean? They were already stolen in New York, right?"

"Yeah, but this guy says he was suppos'ta to grab 'em when they got to Boston, before they got to the Chink—the guy you're talking to, this Shadow King."

"Fuck," I said.

"Damn right. And then this mornin' I get a call from some scumbag lawyah who says he represents the ownahs, the real ownahs. Jesus! Who the fuck sics a lawyah on a gangsta' fencin' shit he stole from ya? You call the cops, right?"

"Right," I said, thinking this was one crazy conversation. But Mickey was right. The lawyer sounded connected. That is, if he really was a lawyer. "So if the lawyer isn't threatening you with the cops, what's he saying?"

"That's the thing. He's offerin' me fifteen grand for the movies. He says I gotta give him an answer in the next forty-eight hours. If I say no, then he'll go t'the cops, he says."

"That sounds fucked up," I said, but remembered what Zhang had said. The owner didn't want them, but also didn't want to sell them.

"You sure you didn't say anything to anyone about this?" Mickey pressed again.

"No. Fucking. Way." I was so pissed I didn't care if I came on too strong. I thought about Dad. I

110

didn't want Mickey or anyone to think for an instant I would run my mouth off. "How about your guys? You sure of all them?" I could almost hear the clockworks turning in his brain as he wondered.

"They wouldn't. I'm sure," he said at last. I thought about his crew. Some were pretty dim bulbs but that didn't make them backstabbers. But it's possible one of them let something slip. Possibly Harry Hollywood?

"Mickey, you have any luck finding a projector?"

"What? A projector? No, dontcha remember? I said I didn't care what was on the fucking movies, I just want to unload 'em."

"Oh, right. I forgot. I just thought Harry Hollywood might have found one for you. Unless you told him to forget about it."

"Fuckin' Harry. I don't know where he is. I've still not heard from him. And he's supposed to be getting me tickets for the Melody Tent. Jerry Lewis is gonna be there in August and I wanna see him. But Harry's never in his room when I call. Big man, ya know? Movie star. Or so he thinks."

That was that. I'd floated Harry's name and his connection to movies but Mickey gave no sign he thought Harry's lips were loose. I was glad of that.

"Okay," I said, "the lawyer is saying you can get fifteen grand from his boss. So if the Shadow King doesn't meet that price you give them to the lawyer, is that it?"

"No fuckin' way! I ain't scared of some shystah!"

Mickey said. "There's no way he's gonna go to the cops. Use your brain, Lyons. These movies must have some pretty hot stuff on 'em for the ownah to have his fuckin' lawyah pay me for them instead of draggin' my ass off to jail. The tits, pussies and cocks in these movies could belong to some of today's big names, you know. You think the studios want these out? But if you bring in the cops there's no tellin' that, maybe, you know, these movies could go missin' from some evidence room or copies made of them, and pretty soon it gets out that Academy Award winner so-and-so did fuck films before making it big. Maybe even homo films. So, no, I ain't givin' the lawyah jack shit."

I had to admit, Mickey made a good argument for ignoring the lawyer, but he'd be missing out on the extra $5,000 if Zhang won't agree to the new price.

"Okay, so you do want to sell them to the Chinatown guy, but you want me to tell him the price is now fifteen thousand."

"Don't you listen, Lyons? You forget about the Southie guy? He wants me to give him the movies plus five grand for his trouble."

"Wait a minute. What trouble?"

"Me! My guys heistin' the fuckin' van before he got to it!"

I got a sick feeling in my gut.

"Let me see if I got this right. You're gonna hit the Shadow King up for fifteen grand for these movies so you can keep your original ten grand, but then turn over the movies, plus five thousand, to some asshole from Southie. Am I missing something of this crazy plan that involves ripping off the Shadow King?"

"Yeah, you're missin' the fact that the asking price is twenty thousand now because I'm adding an extra five grand for *my* trouble."

"Fuck your trouble, Mickey. And fuck this Southie guy and his trouble," I blurted into the phone. "Do the right fucking thing here. This Shadow King will come after you."

"Comes after *us*, asshole. You think he doesn't see you as my guy in all this?" he said in a mocking tone. "Look, I ain't saying the Chink don't sound dangerous, but I'm more afraid of the devil I know than the one I don't. And the Southie asshole? It's Whitey Bulger. He's Satan with a fuckin' capital D. There's no negotiat'n' with that sick fuck and I don't wanna end up bleedin' out in a chair while he's jerkin' off to some skin flicks that I tried to keep from him."

The sick in my stomach worsened and for a moment I thought I would throw up. I didn't.

"How did Whitey even get onto this? From what I was told the movies were stolen under orders of the Chinatown boss, this Shadow King. How the fuck would Whitey know—"

"Does that even matter?" Mickey said. "Maybe he had a contact in New York who caught wind of the Chink's deal and made a phone call. What the fuck difference does it make?"

"Oh, Jesus," I said. It wasn't a prayer so much as resignation.

"There's nothin' I can do except give him the movies," Mickey said. "He's even insistin' on bein' there when I meet with the Chink."

"Why? Why the hell would Whitey want to be there? And possibly get into a shooting war once the Shadow King realizes you've ripped him off? Why would Whitey risk a fight he doesn't need?"

"You think I asked that? It's Whitey fuckin' Bulger for chrissakes!"

"Fuck!"

"That's right. Now you go back to the Chink and tell 'im the price is now twenty grand. If he agrees, I'll call him later with the meeting details. And keep your fuckin' mouth shut about how I'm playin' this. And about Whitey too,. You understand? You don't wanna end up like your old man."


I didn't have a chance to open the door. Eu-meh was just coming out, a broom in her hand. We looked at each other but said nothing. Inside there was no one in the dining room. I could hear people talking in the kitchen and what sounded like pots and pans being moved around. I called out and the metallic din stopped. Zhang came out from the kitchen. Only for an instant did he look surprised. Then he looked annoyed. He wiped his hands with a towel as he walked toward me.

"Mr. Lyons. Back so soon."

"The thing is, Mr. Zhang ... I spoke to the guy who has the movies, and, umm..."

I felt like I was ten years old.

Zhang was in my face. He didn't shout and he didn't pick up anything to hit me with but I'd be lying if I said I wasn't expecting to be thrown against the wall, notwithstanding he had to have at least five decades on me.

"You are back here to tell me the arrangement has changed. And I am certain the change is an increase in the price? Am I correct, Mr. Lyons?"

I nodded yes, and before I knew it I blurted out "I'm sorry, Mr. Zhang. It's not my fault. I just—"

"Be quiet! Do not offer an excuse," he said. He stepped over to the bar, tossing down the towel and taking a coaster from atop a stack next to the beer taps. He slid it down the bar in my direction, took a pen from his shirt pocket and sent it after the coaster. Behind me I could hear someone open and then close the door to the street, but I didn't turn to see who it was. "Write down the amount this man is demanding," Zhang ordered.

I did. He walked down and looked at the coaster but didn't touch it.

"Was there anything else?"

"No. Nothing," I lied.

"You gave him my number?"

"Yes. I did,"

"Very well. Tell him to call with the arrangements, Mr. Lyons."

I opened my mouth to say something. I wanted him to know that I had nothing to do with changing the amount.

"We are finished here, Mr. Lyons," he said.

I turned and headed for the door.

Eu-meh was sweeping the sidewalk out front. Her long black hair was in a ponytail. The sun was right on that perfect face and dark eyes. She was in jeans and a white T-shirt bearing the image of a statue of an Indian on horseback, his eyes and hands raised to the sky. I couldn't make out the words underneath but I didn't need to. I recognized the statue as the one out front of the Museum of Fine Arts. And notwithstanding everything else going on and me feeling like I was headed for a fatal accident, all I could think in that moment, looking at her, was, *Jesus, she's beautiful.*

"Everything okay, Jimmy?"

It was a question, but her look told me she knew already that things were not good.

"Yeah, everything's fine. How are you?"

She stopped sweeping and held the broom slightly away from her, reminding me of a soldier at ease.

"Don't try to bullshit me. You said you'd make sure my grandfather would be okay. Right now, I certainly don't believe things are okay."

She had me there. I wasn't going to try and deny there was a problem, but I also wasn't about to lay it all out for her either. I didn't like it. In fact, I hated it. But for better or worse it was not something I could tell her.

"It's not my place to say anything, Eu-meh. Ask your grandfather. It's up to him," I said. The simplicity and honesty of those three sentences made me feel better. But only for an instant, because they didn't do a thing for Eu-meh.

"Screw you, Jimmy," she said, then stopped, as if she suddenly forgot what she wanted to say. Maybe she knows I'm right, I thought. She looked me up and down, that beautiful face now showing disdain.

"You should forget about being a filmmaker. Or maybe just accept the fact you'll only make shitty movies," she said.

I had no idea what she was talking about.

"What's that got to do with any of this ... other stuff?"

"Because good movies, like good books and art, should tell some kind of truth. And I don't see any truth in you. All I see in you is deceit and Townie bullshit. And now you've got my grandfather in it."

The words hit me hard. I really wanted to tell her. I might have, in fact, but she turned away and went back to sweeping. "Goodbye, Jimmy," she said.

I felt lower than the dirt, bits of paper and cigarette butts she swept off the curb into the sewer grate.

I made my way back to the pagoda payphone and called Mickey again. He answered on the first ring with a curt "Yeah."

"You're all set. The guy said he'll pay you what you want. Twenty grand."

"Holy shit!" he shouted into the phone. "That's great. That's fuckin' great!" He laughed, then asked me if "the Chink" said anything else.

"He said for you to call with the arrangements. I can tell you this, though. He's pissed. He is really pissed."

Mickey stopped laughing then. "Pissed like he's gonna do something?"

"He's pissed that you changed the price but he still wants to deal," I said, absolutely hating Mickey in that moment. "As for being pissed enough to do something, I think that'll be after you double-cross him."

"Fuck you, Lyons!" he said. I hung up.

I looked at the time. It was just after 8:30. I had a half hour to kill before I had to be at work. I walked out of Chinatown onto Washington Street and hung a right. In an instant Chinatown was gone and I was in the Combat Zone, several blocks of X-rated cinemas, strip joints, peep shows and hookers. Being early morning, the porn-houses and titty-bars weren't open and the street walkers hadn't yet hit the sidewalks. That would change in a few hours and go on through the day into the night, when the seamy and the criminal played out in a neon glow.

It wasn't always like this here. This part of Washington Street used to be known as theater row and the entertainment fare was respectable. The neighborhood abutting the theater district, whether called Chinatown or Little Syria or whatever other ethnic minority established a community there, was always pretty poor.

Turk once said. "It's been a hand-me-down neighborhood since the upper-class Brahmins who first settled it decided the neighborhood was turning to shit 'cuz the train yards were expanding from South Station and more people and noise was coming through," adding with a laugh, "especially you Irish."

Turk's grandparents arrived in the neighborhood around 1880 or so. There were some Chinese in Boston at the time, he says, but not many. They began arriving in larger numbers, mostly from Chinatowns in San Francisco, Chicago, and New York, in the early '20s, as the Arabs were moving out.

"So when were the Irish there?" I asked. It bothered me that I didn't know Irish immigrants had settled into the place I always knew as Chinatown.

"That's going back a ways," he said. "The posh Bostonians were living in the area in the mid-1800 or so. They moved on because of the development and expansion of a railway hub that's now South Station, and as they left you Irish began moving in. Made sense, too. There were plenty of you doing the work there on the railway. Later on, lots of Italians settled there, then Jews from Eastern Europe, which gave Boston its garment district, and then Arabs from Syria, Palestine and Lebanon. The neighborhood picked up the name Little Syria then. Now there were some Chinese here as early as 1870s, but they were very few. One large group arrived in the middle of the 1870s from San Francisco. Their first destination was out in Western Massachusetts, where some company paid to bring them in to break a strike. Naturally, when the strike ended they weren't wanted there, so they came to Boston. And that, kid, is how Chinatown was born. Like I said, it's a hand-me-down neighborhood."

I shook my head. "I never knew any of that."

He laughed.

"That's because Boston Irish think the city was always Irish and Catholic, and that their ancestors sailed here on the Mayflower right from Galway Bay."

Turk could really bust your balls. He seemed to know a lot of history, though. He stayed on in Chinatown until the late '40s, when he moved to the West End. He said the West End was a great place to live, kind of like a United Nation's community because there were so many different groups. West Enders loved their working class, working poor neighborhood, but the city didn't. Too run down, the pols decided. West Enders tried to organize and save their homes, but the city had other plans, which they executed under the banner of "Urban Renewal."

"They and their developer friends had a new vision for the city," Turk said, his words dripping with contempt.

Turned out their vision not only made history of the West End, but nearby Scollay Square, too, a once thriving entertainment district that was already going downhill back in the 1930s. It did enjoy an eleventh-hour boon thanks to World War II, when it suddenly became the entertainment mecca for tens of thousands of soldiers, sailors and marines assigned to or passing through the Navy Yard, Boston Army Base, and other installations and offices in and around the city. If war was Scollay's last hurrah, peace was its fatal hangover. The military demobilized, which meant all those troops went home to Kentucky, Indiana and wherever else they were from, leaving behind struggling theaters and movie houses, but also saloons, tattoo parlors, drug dealers, whorehouses and streetwalkers.

When I was about six I heard my grandmother raging at my grandfather about going to "that awful Scollay Square." Thing is, that scandalous trip had to be twenty years earlier. Talk about long memories! He was saying something about a musical comedy show but she wasn't buying it. Just what he did and how she knew he did it I have no clue, but she told him he'd burn in Hell for patronizing "that Devil's own Babylon." I was just a little kid and didn't quite grasp what was being said, but I thought even then, without knowing why, that something particularly interesting and naughty was going on at Scollay Square. I really wanted to find out what.

That wouldn't happen though. The bulldozers went to work, beginning in the mid-1950s with the West End and then in the 1960s with Scollay Square. Turk said he moved to Quincy just two weeks before his West End home was torn down. As bad as he felt about that, he said it was worse when Scollay was demolished. Not because he had any great feeling for or connection to the Square, he said. But because Chinatown inherited its old vices, as the pimps, prostitutes, dealers and others decamped to lower Washington Street on the border with Chinatown.

"That was the second hit Chinatown took. The first is when a chunk of it was taken by eminent domain to build the expressway," he said. Turk doesn't believe the city is out to get Chinatown. He thinks the city just doesn't give a shit about it, no more than it gave a shit about West Enders.

"Won't happen again, though, kid. This ain't Chinatown of old," he told me. "The community won't take shit like that anymore. The last straw was letting the strip joints and whores move in."

"Didn't you tell me that Chinatown had some of those things back when Zhang was in Tong business?"

Turk grimaced. "Yeah, well... Different time back then, too."

I let it go. It made sense that the neighborhood would change over the years, that the residents—Zhang among them—would demand better. I could only imagine what Chinatown residents felt like when the Scollay Square refugees landed on their doorstep. Lower Washington Street was soon dubbed the Combat Zone for all the violence that came with the new, seedy economy. The cinemas didn't disappear; they just changed the fare. The Stuart is now The Pussycat Cinema. The State and the Pilgrim kept their names but, like the Pussycat, show only skin flicks. Nearby clubs and restaurants morphed into strip joints with names like Naked i Cabaret and Teddy Bare Lounge.

As for Scollay Square, all that's left of it is an oversized, perpetually steaming brass tea kettle that hangs on Court Street outside what was once the Oriental Tea Company. On the bones of old Scollay arose new commercial developments and a kind of grand central station of city, state and federal office buildings called Government Center. The most prominent building there, at the heart of a brick-paved desert passed off as a plaza, is Boston City Hall, which looks like the Lincoln Memorial turned upside down. It's one ugly building, a concrete monster. I'm told the architectural design is called brutalist. And, yeah, I can fucking believe that.

A few more blocks along Washington Street and I was out of the Combat Zone and at Downtown Crossing, where two department stores, Jordan

Marsh and Filene's, dominated what was still a very vibrant commercial area. Filene's was certainly upscale, but it's mostly famous for its basement, where everyone's mother said you could find great clothing bargains.

I looked at my watch. I turned and headed back. Time to go to work. And that's all I did was work. I barely said a word to Turk. Ralph was in but we never talked. Lunchtime came but I skipped it. There's no way I'd go into Chinatown, but I had no appetite anyway. How could I? Zhang, Mickey, and now Whitey Bulger.

And then, out of nowhere, I had another unsettling thought. Mickey said he still hadn't heard from Harry Hollywood, who was supposed to call him last night. And according to Helen, Brendan Connor went to the Cape yesterday morning.

I felt sick to my stomach.

By two o'clock I'd had it. I told Turk I was sick and had to leave early. He just waved me off.

"See you tomorrow, kid."

# CHAPTER
## NINE

I felt better the next morning but that didn't stop me from calling in sick. Turk sounded pissed but let me go with a simple "Hope you're better tomorrow."

In the course of two days my entire world had turned to shit. When I went to work on Tuesday there were really only two things I wanted: to go to college and, more immediately, to be with Eu-meh. A guy can dream, right? But trying to make those dreams a reality by getting involved in this gangster shit made my life a nightmare.

I've got Mickey running me and threatening me like I'm some flunky, Zhang cold-talking me like I'm a disappointing, low-level servant, and Eu-meh taking me for a career hood out to hurt her beloved grandfather. And now Whitey's in the mix. The prince of fucking darkness himself. Whitey's interest I could understand, though. The guy always has something going on—wherever and however he can make an illegal buck. But Brendan Connor? What's he getting out of this? He never seemed the hijacking or blackmailing type.

The thing is, the more I thought of Whitey and Connor the more relaxed I felt. They might be wolves circling a campfire, but the camper was Mickey, or maybe Zhang, but not me. I just had to be far away from the campfire when the wolves decided to attack.

I reached over and pulled the curtain aside to see a bright morning. It was already warm and looked to be a scorcher by noon. In other words, a perfect day for the beach. A few years ago I'd be with Red, Jump and a dozen other Townies lined up on the bridge entryway by now, thumbing rides to Revere. I'd love to be able to do that right now, but those days are gone. I figured I'd stay in bed and play sick a while longer. I could hear Ma in the kitchen making breakfast and talking to Helen, who was getting ready to go to the pool with her friends. A little after 8:00 they were out the door, and only minutes after that I was up having a bowl of cereal and a cup of coffee. By 8:30 I was trying to enjoy the morning sun on Pebble-Dash Beach—that is, the rooftop. It's where you go on beautiful days when the beach or the pool are not options.

I stretched back in the chaise, sipping a Coke and wondering what to do next. That was easy. I put down the Coke, pushed PLAY on the cassette player and listened to Black Sabbath because, well, why not? Then I pulled a small baggie and papers out of my pocket and rolled a neat if slightly blimped-out joint. Fire it up, I told myself, and did so. I took a good hit, held it, let it out. I looked over to my right and could see the steel-girdered Mystic Bridge and thought about the beach again. The Townie patch at Revere Beach was along the seawall across from the Cyclone roller coaster. Somehow or other, at some point in the past, we seem to have settled into that section. Other neighborhoods, Eastie—East Boston, that is—Chelsea, and Revere, of course, occupied other sections. Southie and Dorchester had Carson Beach. I tried to remember if I ever saw or heard of any part of the beach where people from Chinatown hung out. I didn't think so. I thought it strange, and then I thought it strange that I never thought of it before. Why wouldn't they come to Revere Beach? Come to think of it, I've always known that there was no part of the beach where Black people hung out, leastways not in any big numbers. I never even imagined there was a Roxbury section, you know? You'd see some Blacks here and there, but not many. It was just assumed that Charlestown had this part of the beach and other towns had other parts. But all the parts were White. I tried to picture Roxbury on a map. It was next to Dorchester, so maybe they go to Carson Beach? I don't know. I took another hit. Does Eu-meh go to the beach? She must. But where? I took another hit and looked over at the bridge again, making a deliberate effort to change the subject in my head. The bridge, right. I thought about the crash that I filmed, but then remembered one, a few years before that, but almost in the same spot. Another trucker barreling onto the bridge from the expressway, also losing control and smacking into an upright. The bridge wasn't fazed, the driver lived and, luckily, no one was standing there hitching at the time of the crash. The only casualties were the hundreds of lobsters the truck was transporting. These were scattered across the lanes, some dead but a lot of them crawling around. Once the ambulance cleared out a bunch of us were out there grabbing every lobster we could. I smiled at the memory of everyone making off with their haul in whatever we could find to carry them in. No one I know thought of it as stealing. I mean, the lobsters would have been picked up by the public works department anyway, and those guys would be taking home everything they could carry. So this just seemed like traditional salvaging to me. It's not like those old stories of people lighting beacons on the shore to lure cargo ships into treacherous, rocky waters, then steal the goods when the ship crashed. Taking the lobsters wasn't like that. It wasn't criminal.

And then I remembered: Eu-meh considers me a criminal. Jesus! She's really in my head and it's exhausting trying to figure out how to maneuver through this maze of crap. I reminded myself that I'd decided to wash my hands of the whole thing. *Remember, Lyons? You're free. Stay away from the campfire and the wolves. You've met whatever stupid obligation you had to both Mickey and the Shadow King. Hell, they're both gangsters, aren't they? So fuck it. I'm done with them. Let them work out whatever deal they want to make—porn films, blackmail, whatever. It has nothing to do with me.* I took a hit from the joint and congratulated myself that I was out of the whole mess.

Yeah, that lasted all of a minute. The brief wave of relief crashed on the rocks of Mickey's taunt: *"Comes after us, asshole."* He was probably right. I might have no obligation to Zhang, but that doesn't mean he'll see it that it way. Zhang might decide he needs to fuck me up.

I should never have taken up Zhang's offer. Turk was right about staying clear of him. Or when Mickey asked me about projectors, I could have just left it at telling him he needed a 35-millimeter, and that the film exchange doesn't have them, either to steal or to borrow. I felt stupid. I felt used. I was early morning litter being swept into the sewer grate. *What a loser you are, Lyons! How could you let these fuckers talk you into mixing into shit you swore you'd never be part of? A Chinese gangster asks you for a favor and when you do it a Townie gangster asks you for a favor. Information is all you were supposed to get and give. That's it! But no. Suddenly you're a lackey for both sides, not even remotely respected by either.*

My hand shook as I reached down to turn off the cassette player. All of a sudden, I didn't need Ozzy Osborne's dark visions adding to my own real nightmare. It was possible that I could still end up like my father, after all. And possibly on the orders of Eu-meh's grandfather, of all people.

*Unless Whitey takes him out first.* That thought came to me out of nowhere and repulsed me. *Fucking coward! What are you thinking? That's Eu-meh's grandfather! You'd let him die? You told her you'd look out for him.*

*I knew then that whatever Zhang thought of me, no matter that it was his—let's face it—theft of the movies that started all this, and in spite of what he might do to me if Mickey's double-cross succeeded, I'd try to help him out. I owed that to Eu-meh, who likely despises me.*

So there I was. Back in the mess again. I could almost hear the wolves circling.

"Everything's coming up shit," I said out loud, startled at the sound of my own voice. I looked to see if anyone was around to hear. No one. "Jesus, Jimmy," I muttered, "being stoned really ain't helping."

It was noon when I went downstairs. Ma and Helen were still out. I made a sandwich and was heading to the shower when the phone rang. I picked it up.

What the fuck is going on?" someone asked in whisper. "Eu-meh told me you had an argument with my grandfather."

"Lee? How did you get my number?

"The phone book. How'd ya think, man?"

"Yeah, right," I said. "It was hardly an argument. I—"

"So what is all this? Eu-meh says you've got my grandfather involved in some criminal shit."

I wasn't ready for that. Not from Lee. It was one thing to feel like shit in front of Eu-meh, or to offer her an apology that I couldn't even explain to her. But Lee? He knew this was his grandfather's mess. And he knew damn well that his grandfather dragged me into it.

"I'm not the one who had a bunch of a skin flicks stolen in New York and hauled ta Boston, then lost them to Charlestown gangsters. I didn't ask to get in the middle of all this shit."

There was dead silence on the other end of the phone. And in an instant I realized I had said too much. Yeah, he knew his grandfather had an interest in finding the contents of a white van that made off with some stuff from a New York van that broke down in Boston, but Lee obviously didn't know the details.

"You're a fucking liar!" he hissed into the phone. "A fucking liar! And if I see you again I'm gonna clean the fucking streets up with you! Don't you ever come over here again! In fact, stay outta Chinatown you fuckin' asshole. I'll kill you, I swear!"

I didn't doubt him. Not for an instant. That was a lot of crap to hear about your grandfather. I was sorry for spilling what he didn't know. What he didn't need to know.

"I'm sorry, Lee. I shouldn't have said anything." He was silent again. Just for a minute. Then, still in a whisper, he told me to prove what I said.

"How the hell can I do that? You're the one who came to me and said he needed a favor, to find out about stuff stolen from a broke-down van and brought to Charlestown. Then he told me they were movies. I even asked him what kind of movies. He wouldn't say."

"I don't care. *Yeye* would never get involved in stuff like that. Jesus! Are you shittin' me? Porn movies? No way!"

I didn't say anything. Then Lee asked about Eu-meh. "Did you say anything to my sister about these movies?"

"Hell no!" I said. "No way would I tell her. I should not have told you but you pissed me off. I really am sorry."

"Yeah," he said, a verbal shrug.

"Lee, what did you think was in the van? You had to know there was something illegal going on."

"Yeah," he said. "I figured he was buying some stuff under the table from a restaurant in New York. A restaurant closes up, and sometimes decorations, furniture, kitchen fixtures go out the back door and end up for sale cheap. I never figured my grandfather for a saint. He had a tough life and did some stuff, I know. But that was a long, long time ago. And I

132

don't think he'd ever get into the kind of shit you're talking about, man."

I nodded as if he could see me.

"I'm sorry. And maybe it's not what it seems like," I told him, though I couldn't figure it to be anything else.

"Yeah, right," Lee said.

I don't think he was counting on another explanation either.

I was about to hang up when the shit hit the fan on the other end of the line. I heard a voice shouting at Lee in Chinese. I knew it was Eu-meh. And though I wouldn't recognize anything in Chinese that I didn't see on a menu. I knew she was saying she'd heard everything on Lee's end and wanted to know what was happening.

She was furious. She was screaming and there was panic in her voice. Lee was also shouting, but from his tone it sounded like he was asking her to calm down.

"Lee! What's happening there?" I said. There was no reply, so I just held the phone to my ear and kept my mouth shut. The shouting diminished and then only Lee was talking. Then it was silent. I was about to speak up again when Eu-meh was on the phone. Her voice was shaky and she stumbled on a few words, but she sounded determined.

"You bastard, Jimmy," she said. "You ha—you have to tell us everything. We want to- to- to talk to you. Now. And answers. We want answers. I—"

She stopped talking then. The last thing I wanted to do was go back into Chinatown to talk about this. It was close to 1:00 now and I had no idea how long this talk would go on, let alone how it might end. I told myself I had already decided I was out of it. It was just proving impossible to tell that to Eu-meh. I couldn't say no to her.

"Okay, I'll be over later on. Give me an hour or so. I've gotta get a shower

change and then grab the T. But I'll be there. Should I meet you at the restaurant?"

"No. No way. We'll come to see you. Where are you?"

"Jesus! I'm in Charlestown," I told her. "I live in the projects. You don't want to come over here. Are you out of your mind?" It's not as if there are no Asian people in Charlestown. There are a couple of Chinese families, I think. Used to be one that lived here in the projects, though they moved away. And there used to be a bunch of Chinese laundries in the town, but that was a while back. I assumed at least some of the owners lived here, but I don't know if any still did. Most of the Asian people in town are Filipinos. Still, Charlestown being so small, Eu-meh and Lee would stand out right away, especially in the projects. Most people wouldn't care. Some would just be curious. But with this gangster business in the air right now it would only take a whisper that some Chinese people were in the projects to meet with me and that would be it. "It's just not a good idea," I told her.

"I don't give a damn what you think right now," she said. "We are coming over there. I want to see this crazy town that thinks it's God's gift to the city."

I wanted to say not just the city, but Eu-meh was in no mood for jokes.

"Where shall we meet you?" she said.

"Take the train and I'll meet you at Government Center."

"Jimmy!" she said.

"What?"

"We're driving. Where should we pick you up?"

"Fine," I said, "you should be able to find the Bunker Hill Monument. Drive around the square until you get to the flight of stairs leading to the statue of a guy in a long coat and wide-brimmed hat. He'll be holding a sword. I'll be there."

"The Prescott statue. Right," she said.

"You know the Colonel Prescott statue? I thought you'd never been over here."

"I know it from my history books. But mostly when I look at it I remember seeing it on a rerun of some old television show, *Route 66*."

"Really? I saw that, too. It was pretty good," I said, hoping to lower the tension I could still hear in her tone.

"I couldn't tell you. All I remember is some Townie assholes were writing shit on the base of the statue. We'll see you in an hour."

I didn't know whether to be angry or embarrassed by her take-no-prisoners reply. I didn't shout the word *fuck* as I put down the phone but I said it loud enough that Ma heard as she was coming in the door. She drilled me with her eyes. If she was a Gorgon, I'd be a bird-shit-covered statue someplace right now.

"Okay, mister. Tell me what is going on with you and tell me right now," she said.

"Nothin's going on," I said.

"Are you wrapped up in something? Are you?"

There was no way I was going to tell her what was going on. She didn't need to know, and it's not like she could do anything about it.

"Forget it, Ma. Don't worry. I'm not going to turn out like Dad. I'll take care of things. I'm not going to be a bum."

I never saw it coming. All I knew was my left cheek burned and my ear was ringing.

"You little shit!" she said. "Don't you ever talk like that about your father! He doesn't deserve that."

Now I was confused. I knew he failed her and the family in any number of ways. Hell! She wouldn't even talk about the man. But suddenly I'm slapped sideways for calling him a bum?

"For God's sake, Ma! That was work on the phone," I lied. "They need me to come in right now. There's a problem."

Work was a powerful word to Ma. You'd have thought I told her I was joining the priesthood she was so thrilled. Even more amazing, she bought it. I can only figure I said something she badly wanted or needed to hear. With tears in her eyes, she hugged me.

"Go. Go get your shower. Hurry now," she said.

It had to be the fastest shower I ever took. I got out, dried off, and quickly slipped into a pair of jeans, a Pink Floyd T-shirt, and sneakers. I put my wallet, cash and key into my pockets and headed to the door. I think Ma was thanking Jesus as I left.

# CHAPTER
## TEN

I was looking at the statue of Col. William Prescott and thinking about how much it sucked that of all things about Charlestown, Eu-meh knew this statue, and that she associated it with Townies acting like jerks. Sure, the sword has been broken off and stolen on a few occasions. And kids have long liked to climb up onto the statue and maybe dangle for a few minutes from the colonel's left hand. But mostly the statue is left alone. Townies consider the Bunker Hill Monument sacred. It does, after all, commemorate the first pitched battle between colonists and English soldiers. Sure they beat us, but it took the fuckers three assaults on the bunker-defended hill before our guys were routed, and we killed more of them than they did of us. But, yeah, we did finally retreat. I say "we" and "us" like I was there, I know, which might sound stupid, but it's how we feel. Turk said it's another example of Townies of today re-imagining the colonist defenders as period versions of themselves.

"Do you think they were all good Irish Catholics just off the boat from Killarney?" he teased.

That's ridiculous, I told him, but I felt kind of embarrassed because I did sort of think about the colonists as being, well, like me. Turk laughed and said it was okay, that it's only natural to say "we" and "us" when talking about "the home team." No different than saying "we" when you talk about the Sox, the Celts, the Bruins—even the Pats, he said, laughing, and swearing that "someday we will have a winning football team."

I looked past Prescott to the actual monument, which is like a smaller version of the Washington Monument, but predating it by several decades. Ours —there I go again—had one of the first steam-powered elevators in the country when it opened up. And some of those who made the ride on the day it opened to the public were a handful of veterans of the battle. The elevator didn't last. I don't know when it was uninstalled but it had to be a long time ago. The only way up and down is the 294-step spiral stone stairwell. I must have made the trip to the top dozens of times. At the top is a circular room and four windows looking north, south, east and west. Except for some metal bars the windows are open to the sun, wind, rain or snow. You can see well into Boston, to the old Customs House and the Pru beyond it, and of course Boston

Harbor. From the other windows you can see Chelsea, Everett, Somerville and Cambridge. Pretty cool, and remembering the times I was up there made me forget for a moment why I was standing next to the colonel.

But only for a moment.

"Hey," Eu-meh said from behind me. I turned to see her. She was wearing a T-shirt with a picture of an angel on the front, but one in pain, with his right arm outstretched and the left thrown back behind his head. I knew the work. I remembered it from my summer of weekly MFA visits.

"Evening, the Fall of Day," I said before it occurred to me to say hello.

"What?"

"The picture on your shirt. It's 'Evening, the Fall of Day,' by William Rimmer."

She looked down at it.

"Yeah, it is. I know that," she said. When she looked up again with those beautiful eyes I didn't see any friendliness in them. What I read in them was contempt. And her voice had none of the fear I heard on the phone earlier. Lee was angry, too, but also was acting jumpy. He barely looked my way, and instead seemed focused on taking in the sites. I wondered if he felt guilty because he was the one who brought his grandfather's message to me in the first place. But no. There was something else going on. I realized that, as hot as it was, he was wearing a windbreaker over a T-shirt. And the jacket was zipped up.

"Is Lee packing?" I asked Eu-meh. She looked uneasy, almost like she didn't know what to say.

"He was insistent on carrying it."

"C'mon," I said. "We're at the monument. A really public place. Tourists come here all the time. Nobody gets killed up here."

She looked over at Lee, whose back was to us, then took in the full 360-degree view of the square, a place of brick townhouses, the public library, and the granite fortress of a high school.

"It doesn't look much different than I remember it," she said.

"I thought you didn't know Charlestown. What you said about the Prescott statue and all—"

"I said that because I was pissed. Still am pissed. This town..." she said, looking around again. "When I was small my parents took me to visit an uncle and aunt who had a laundry behind some old bread factory down near the projects. But sometimes we'd make a snack and come up here to eat."

"The laundry behind the old Bond Bread? I remember that from when I was really little. That whole area was torn down long ago. There's a school there now."

She didn't say anything so I kept talking.

"Did you think the town was okay then? Did your aunt and uncle like it?"

"They said the town was rough. A lot of the people were very nice, but they said some were troublesome and rude. Today you'd just say racist."

141

"I'm sorry," I said. I meant it.

"My auntie said that sometimes these kids—little kids—would come up and stand outside the window of the laundry and use their index finger like a toothbrush, going up and down, up and down, then laugh and run off," she said.

"Why? What was that about?"

"The little shits thought it was a way of signaling 'fuck you' in Chinese. Kind of like 'the finger.'" She laughed, then was angry again. "Why the fuck would they do that? What parents or any grown-up would teach their kids to do that?"

"I'll have to ask my mother about that. She's lived in the town for a long time."

"Ask your mother?" she said, a look of horror on her face.

"No! No! I didn't mean she would have done that," I quickly said. "Jesus, no. But she probably would have known about it. You gotta realize, my mother's a for-real Kennedy Democrat. Not just John Kennedy, but Bobby. She cried for days after Bobby was killed. Not many like that in Charlestown anymore. Not with this busing thing coming."

I told her briefly about my mother and her long-lost friend meeting up in the projects and what happened.

"Your mother sounds like a decent person," Eu-meh said. "What about you?"

"I'm not prejudiced, if that's what you're

asking," I said. "I've never done anything to a Black person."

"Right, okay. But do you have any Black friends?"

"Look around," I said, more sharply than I intended. "When you drove over here, did you see any Black people? This is Charlestown. It's White because it's always been White. Last time it had a majority of anything else it was Indians. And now and for a long time it's been Irish. If you came over here without using the expressway you'd have passed the North End. You think there are any Black people living in the North End? No. It's Italians there. Maybe with some Irish and others, just like there are Italians, Filipinos, Hispanics and some others here. But, yeah, it's pretty much all White. Are there many Black people in Chinatown? I'm guessing there aren't. Not many anyway."

"What about the high school?" she asked, nodding toward the building's upper floor and rooftop, visible from where we stood. "No Black kids from out of town?"

"None this year. There were some in the past, but never many," I said. "That'll change next year."

"So that would be a 'no' for having Black friends," she said. "And I guess you're not happy with the busing plan."

"I'm out of school. Hell, I never went to high school in the first place. But I am hoping my sister doesn't get bused. How do you expect anyone to be thrilled about being sent to a school in another town, just so that kids in that other town can be sent here?"

"I took the T after elementary and middle school to go to Boston Latin. Lee does now. Because there are no junior and senior high schools in Chinatown. The only way you're going to get to a public junior or senior high is by bus or train."

"Well, that sucks. It does. But it's really not the same thing. Your choice of school was that: a choice. And a good one, too. But what if you did have a local junior and senior high in Chinatown, but then were forced to be bused across the friggin' city just because a judge said so?"

She didn't answer right away. I could see she was thinking about it.

"If the school in Chinatown was as good or better, then I probably wouldn't like it."

"Would not liking it—even being angry about it —make you a bigot?"

After a brief pause she answered. "No."

Lee, who is still in high school, just looked at his sister.

"What?" she said.

"Some city councilor told *Yeye* a few weeks ago there's a good chance Chinatown will be left alone, but that maybe, just maybe, some Chinatown kids could be bused to the North End next year."

Eu-meh looked surprised. "But they're just middle school kids."

"Yeah. All I can say is I'm glad I'm already in high school," Lee said.

Eu-meh pursed her lips. Jesus, they looked good.

"Okay, I do see your point, Jimmy." She then looked at Lee. "I don't suppose I'd like it either."

"Would not liking it—even being angry about it—make you a bigot?" I asked.

After another pause, she answered. "No."

Lee spoke then.

"Did you have someone tag behind you for protection or did you set us up?" he asked, looking more scared that pissed. I had no idea what he was talking about and figured he had let his imagination run away with him. That kind of imagination doesn't mix well with a gun.

"What are you talking about?"

"There's some guy sitting on a bench over by the monument and he doesn't look touristy. He looks like trouble."

I didn't look directly over but moved my head enough so I could catch a glimpse. Maybe Lee didn't have that kind of imagination after all. I felt more than a little fear as I spotted Brendan Connor.

"Follow my lead, okay?" I said.

I turned to look out over the city, raising my arm out and pointing here and there.

"He's not with me and there's a good chance he is following me," I said. "Now if you guys could just nod as if we're discussing the skyline that might be a good idea."

They nodded. Eu-meh pointed in the same direction I did.

"Maybe if I point at nothing in particular this bluff might even be better?" she said.

"You want me to point, too?" Lee asked.

"Yeah," I said. "That would be a better use of your hands than reaching for that piece in your jacket. You do that and you, maybe all of us, end up in the hospital or the morgue."

"I'm not scared," he whispered.

"You fuckin' oughta be," I said, then turned to Eu-meh. "Now might be a good time to find some other place else to talk."

We all nodded—the Bobbleheads of Bunker Hill —then headed down the stairs to where Eu-meh parked her car.

We drove. Not anywhere in particular at first, but just around. I had them head down Main Street toward Sullivan Square.

"When I was little and my family came over to visit my aunt, driving under this monster terrified me," Eu-meh said.

Outside the window the steel beams of the elevated rail line shot past. A few times a year someone rammed into one of the uprights, leaving a wrecked car, wrecked bodies, but a perfectly indifferent upright.

"You don't seem too worried about them now," I said.

"Just following my grandfather's advice."

"Which was?"

"Don't hit them."

I laughed. I wasn't sure I was supposed to, but she laughed, too.

"You would not know it but my grandfather can be funny."

"Really?"

"Yes, but you've only seen his business side. He is very serious when it comes to business. And family."

I thought: Deadly serious, I bet.

From the back seat Lee asked about the "guy on the bench."

"His name is Brendan Connor," I said. "I'm pretty sure he killed my father."

"Oh, Jesus," Eu-meh said.

"Holy fuck," Lee said.

They didn't ask any questions but after laying that on them I felt I needed to give them some explanation. I gave them the *Reader's Digest* version. Basically, that there were conflicting stories about who killed my old man but that in any of the talked-about scenarios—bad cops or mob hit—Connor seemed a good fit for the trigger man.

I'm really sorry about your father, Jimmy," Eu-meh said.

"Me, too," Lee added. "Geez, man. You never mentioned that. Not ever."

I smiled, because his comment really struck me as funny. "It's not exactly lunchtime talk, is it? 'Lee, this sweet and sour shrimp is great. And did you know my father was gunned down when I was a kid? Oh, pass the noodles.' Besides, we've known each other for about two years, and in all that time it's only been at the restaurant and the talk has been about movies. Not about our families or what our life is like away from lunch hour."

"I see your point."

Eu-meh glanced at Lee, shaking her head.

"It's a damn good thing that guy didn't come near us at the monument. If you thought he was just some punk and pulled out your starter's pistol hoping to scare him off he might have killed us."

Lee's face flushed with embarrassment.

"A starter's pistol?" I said. "You brought a phony gun to Charlestown in the event you wanted to 'scare' someone?" I started laughing. "That's pretty fucking stupid, Colonel Mortimer."


We drove the rest of the way without saying much. I kept checking to make sure we weren't being followed while directing Eu-meh around Sullivan Square and back into Charlestown, to the Prison Point Bridge. We crossed into Cambridge and went on to Harvard Square. Harvard draws people from all over the world and the Square reflects that. No one would give us a second look there. We parked a block off the Square and went into a restaurant I liked.

"The Blue Parrot?" Lee asked as we walked up to

the door. He seemed to have recovered from his gun shaming. "Really?"

"Well, there is no Rick's *Cafe Americain* here," I said.

"What are you talking about?" Eu-meh said.

"Rick's. Everybody goes to Rick's," Lee answered in a perfect Peter Lorre impression.

"I get it. Movie shit," she said, and shook her head.

We ordered coffees that none of us were really interested in. The waiter had barely turned away after taking the cash I handed him when Eu-meh looked me in the eye and said, "No more movie talk. Tell us what's really going on, the important stuff going on. And how we keep my grandfather from getting jailed, beaten or killed."

For the next half hour as our coffees turned cold I went over what her grandfather had asked me to do, what I had done, and what I knew. To no great surprise, Eu-meh was at first stunned to hear that her grandfather was the one who brought me into this dangerous mess. She refused to believe it. At least until Lee confirmed it. But she refused to believe that the mystery movies were for blackmail. Worse still, that their value as blackmail was in their being porn.

Neither one accepted this as a possibility. The idea that their beloved grandfather was involved in theft, blackmail and pornography?

"No fucking way," she said.

"Then you tell me what the deal is with these movies."

She shook her head and said, "I can't. But there's no way my grandfather would be involved with porno movies or blackmail."

"Well, what does that leave?" I said. "Maybe the movies are only a part of it. Maybe there's drugs involved somehow."

"I can't believe that," Lee said. "And didn't you just tell us that one of your Townie friends opened up the film cases? And that there were no drugs in them?"

Just because Zhang was involved in drugs when he was a Tong boss doesn't mean he'd be involved in them today. And there was no good in talking about his bad old days to Lee and Eu-meh.

"First of all, the guy who has the movies is not a friend. He's a low-level but still dangerous hood with a crew. I've known him for years but he's not a friend. For fuck's sake he's already hinted more than once he'll kill me if things go bad for him."

They didn't say anything to that.

"Yeah, he found nothing except film in the cases. So I'm just speculating is all. That just maybe there's a drug connection. Somehow, that I'm not seeing."

"Okay, then. There's no evidence that these cases are carrying anything except movies. Right?" Lee said.

"Yeah, right. For that matter we still don't know what these movies are, what's on them that makes them worth stealing, and what your grandfather intends to do with them if he gets them."

Lee and Eu-meh said nothing.

Eu-meh tapped a finger on the table.

"Right now, it doesn't matter what's on the film. And it doesn't even matter, to me, if there are drugs involved," she said. "Right now, the only thing that matters is my grandfather. Whatever he's done or whatever he may be into, I'll care about that after I know all this is over and he's safe. That's the bottom line for me and Lee, and it should be for you, Jimmy."

Part of me wanted to point out that I had myself and my own family to consider, but I didn't. That might make me sound selfish or, worse still, chicken. I couldn't stand the idea she would think I was a coward.

But her bottom line forced me to confront the biggest question I had when I agreed to meet with them. What—or even whether—to tell them about Mickey's planned double-cross on the money-for-movies swap.

I didn't know which way to go on this, so I said nothing.

"Do either of you know how this started? I mean, any idea when this whole thing about the movies began and why?"

They looked at each other, found nothing there, then turned back to me.

"There's gotta be something. Did your grandfather start acting anxious, angry, strange, weird—shit! I don't know. Anything? If we know what's going on then maybe we can figure out what we do next."

Eu-meh's gaze wandered down to her ignored coffee. It came back up again.

"There was a phone call. About two weeks ago," she said. "My grandfather got a call from New York, from a friend there, Edith. I remember because the call started out very light, breezy. It was obviously someone he hadn't spoken to in a long time. He asked, teasingly, if Broadway's lights were going to be staying bright or going out. The whole area and Times Square is in the pits, apparently."

"Edith," I said, more to myself than to them.

"Yeah, like Edith Bunker," Lee said.

"No, I was just thinking. There's a couple of photos on your grandfather's wall with someone named Edith in them."

Eu-meh nodded. "I know those. In one really nice picture she's there with my grandparents and a family friend, Butterfly."

"That's right."

"Anyway," Eu-meh continued, "the conversation went like that briefly—about Broadway, Times Square looking like hell and whether the whole theater industry there was crashing. Then it turned pleasant with catch-up talk. You know, my grandfather saying 'so good to hear from you,' 'are you coming to Boston anytime soon?' 'oh, yes, the restaurant is still open and always will be' 'yes, I did read about so-and-so. Very sad.'"

Eu-meh's brow wrinkled like she was trying to solve a problem.

"Then the conversation got strange. Grandfather got very quiet. I went over to see if he was okay and he barely noticed me. His expression was very serious. I'd say intense, really. I walked away. When he spoke again his voice was low. I remember hearing him ask if he could get them. Whatever 'them' were. The answer must have been no, because he then insisted there had to be someone he could talk to. 'Give me a name,' he said 'I'll pay for them. No problem.'"

"Shit, you never said anything to me about that," Lee said. She didn't answer him.

"I don't know if he got a name, but I did hear him say 'When is this supposed to happen?' That was it, then he said 'Thank you, Edith. I will do everything I can.'"

I was picking up a different vibe from both Eu-meh and Lee now. There was no longer the anger and disdain I saw earlier. Something had shifted for the better.

"So, this Edith? What do you know about her?"

"She was in show business, I'm sure, but I have little memory of her. And when I got older I never asked about the people in the photos," Eu-meh said. She looked over to Lee, who shook his head.

"Sorry. I was never into old movies," Lee said, sounding a bit embarrassed.

"How about the other woman. Butterfly?"

"Probably another actress or something," Lee said.

"Our grandparents didn't really talk about her, except to say that she was nice."

"To tell the truth, I was so young I don't remember ever seeing her," Lee added with a laugh.

I thought about Edith. As they said, she was doubtless in show business. She's on Zhang's wall of fame, and when she calls him they talk about Broadway. It's not much of a leap to figure she put the bug in his ear about these movies. But the bigger picture, and there has to be one, is why? And why should Zhang give a shit? Blackmail? Some kind of public shaming? Hell, if it's that, then Zhang is spending a boatload of money just to embarrass someone. It would help to know who.

"Could you ask your grandfather who Edith is? If we know, that might help us figure out why this is happening and what we can or should do."

They both said no. Eu-meh said there's no way he would tell them if, in fact, she's part of this whole illegal deal. And he'd be furious if he knew she and Lee were putting their noses into it.

"Okay then. Can you smuggle that photo out of the restaurant, so I can show it to the old guy I work with? He's been dealing with movies for half a century at least."

"Are you crazy?" Eu-meh said. "Grandfather practically lives in the restaurant and nothing escapes his notice. He would certainly know if anything was removed from his personal table."

I knew she was right.

"What I can do is draw it," she said.

"Huh?"

"I can draw Edith's face to the smallest detail. No problem."

"That's right. You're an artist." I took a chance and tried to redirect the conversation. "I like your T-shirt, by the way."

"I was surprised when you recognized the drawing and even knew the artist."

I told her about my MFA summer and how I once wanted to draw comic books. I thought she'd laugh or say that sounded stupid. Instead, she asked why I didn't keep at it. I'm not sure I know myself. I just drifted away from it, which is what I told her.

"Add it to your movie-making ambitions," she said. "Do some cartoons."

"Yeah, maybe I'll do that," I said, not really seeing it happen but happy with her suggestion.

I looked at the cold coffees.

"Anyone want anything else?"

They shook their heads no.

"C'mon, I'll drive you back to Charlestown," Eu-meh said. "If you come by the restaurant before you go to work in the morning I'll give you the sketch of Edith."

"At the restaurant?" I said, surprised. "I figured I was no longer a welcome *ègùn* there now."

"A what?" she said, her eyes wide.

"An *ègùn*. You know—honored guest?"

She laughed. "*Ègùn* means bad guy, villain, you know? A douchebag."

I looked at Lee, who was studying the cold coffees again.

"Okay. Well, thanks for that, Lee."

"Sorry, Jimmy," he said, without looking up. I sensed he was smiling.

"But you're right," Eu-meh continued. "You are *persona non grata* at the restaurant. Call from the payphone by the corner. I'll meet you outside."

# CHAPTER
# ELEVEN

The next morning I called Eu-meh as instructed and by the time I got to the front door of House of Dragons she was outside sweeping off the sidewalk. She didn't say a word, but pulled a paper out from the pocket of her bib apron and handed it to me. I put it in my shirt pocket, the silence making me feel like some kind of undercover agent. I turned to leave.

"Call me when you know something," she said in a matter-of-fact tone.

I turned back around. "Yeah, okay. Here at the restaurant?"

"You kidding? No. Call my apartment. I wrote the number on the paper."

"Got it."

Work dragged. It dragged almost as badly as my own frustrated and deflated ass. Usually I'd be full of energy, looking forward to a weekend of partying and drinking, what with the Bunker Hill parade set for Sunday. Tonight should be about hitting a few bars and downing some beers with Red and Jump.

Now I felt like that old guy in the too-fucking-long Ancient Mariner poem they made us read in junior high. Stuck. Not going anywhere fast. Not even slow. Just stuck. A painted ship on a painted sea, or something like that. And I'm the old fucker with the goddamn seagull draped around his neck. No! An albatross. That's even bigger and heavier. And every film case I had to lug between the elevator, the storage area, and Turk and Ralph's work stations made me feel like Sisyphus, that other totally screwed guy we had to read about, who had to roll the same fucking rock up the same fucking hill, non-stop, for eternity.

I waited until lunchtime before asking Turk about the drawing. Ralph was in today. Sober as a judge and no evidence of a hangover. He was also talkative. Well, to Turk, anyway. Guy wouldn't shut up, it seemed. I wondered if he'd decided to give up booze and go onto speed. He seemed to be recalling every movie he ever saw and wanted to talk about them. Turk did his best, but after some two hours he retreated to saying things like "I remember that one" and "oh, yes, a classic" to uttering agreement with Ralph on whatever the born-again chatterbox said about movies or the actors.

At noon Ralph headed off to lunch and I went over to Turk's station.

"Not going to lunch, kid?" he said.

"Yeah, I'll go in a minute. Just want to show you something." I took the paper out of my pocket, unfolded it, and held it up. "You know this person?"

He looked at it closely, touching it with his finger but making no attempt to hold it. Turk laughed.

"Sure! She's in one of the pictures on Zhang's wall of fame. Did you do this? It's pretty good, kid. Now why do you have it?"

"C'mon, Turk, don't kid around. Do you know who she is? And whether she's still alive."

He looked at it again, as if he was studying it. But I had the feeling he knew exactly who she was, and was weighing whether I should know.

"Why?" he asked. "What is she to you?"

"Please, Turk. Who is she?"

If ever a guy seemed to wish he was a deaf mute it was Turk right then. He turned back toward his film editor.

"Edie Adams," he said.

I didn't say anything at first. I knew the name. I knew she was an actress and singer. But I really only knew her from those cigar commercials where she's this seductress-type, telling guys to "pick one up and smoke it sometime." But after convincing myself that knowing her identity would clue me in on what Zhang is really up to, I was disappointed. It told me nothing and I felt stupid.

"Anything else, kid?"

"Nah, nothing. Just wondered is all." I put the drawing back in my pocket. Turk got back from

159

lunch just before one. Normally I'd have taken my lunch then, but I kept working another 30 or 40 minutes as I thought about what my next step should be. I finally decided I should just go to lunch, so walked up to a Liggett's Drug Store at the corner of Boylston and Tremont. It's no House of Dragons but the lunch counter there is good enough for a sandwich when you don't want to eat in the first place. Maybe Eu-meh, once I tell her who Edith is, will remember something about her, something important. I didn't really believe that. I was trying to justify calling the restaurant and trying to talk with her. She told me not to. She'd probably be pissed. She'd hang up, for sure. I knew all that. I dropped a dime in the payphone.

"House of Dragons," someone—not Eu-meh and, luckily, not Zhang—said after two rings.

"Hello, is Eu-meh available?"

The immediate silence told me that personal calls are not expected or welcome at the restaurant.

"She is busy," the voice at the other end finally said. "She cannot take calls at this number."

"Can you give me a different number?"

"I am sorry, but no."

"Okay," I said, thinking fast. I couldn't leave my name in case this guy told Zhang. "Just tell her that Edith's friend called and I'll call her at home later, like she told me to. Okay? Edith's friend. Got it?"

"Edith, yes. Like in Edith Bunker. Good bye."

I ordered a grilled cheese and tomato sandwich

and a Coke to go and took them across to the Commons. I found a bench and had my lunch while trying to figure out my next move. In the end all I could come up with was to go back to work. Eu-meh doesn't work all day, just through the end of lunch, so she could be home by 2:00, maybe even earlier. I'd call her then. It was about 1:10 as I turned the corner to the film exchange and saw Eu-meh headed toward me. Oh, shit. Here it goes.

"Hey, I'm sorry. I shouldn't have called you at the restaurant. But I didn't give my name. I—"

"Never mind that. There's something you need to know." She looked scared.

"What's up? What is it?"

"That old guy you work with. Turk? That's what you call him, right?"

"Yeah, why?"

"My grandfather got a call a little while ago. I didn't catch everything but I did catch a few things. My grandfather called him Ahmed. But then I heard him refer to you, telling this Ahmed that you sometimes mention him when talking to Lee. My grandfather laughed then and said 'So you're still called Turk.'"

She was quiet for a moment, looking at me to see how I'd respond. I didn't want to jump to any conclusions. Zhang and Turk have known each other for years, after all.

"Anything else?" I asked.

"Edith's name came up. It sounds like Turk

called my grandfather to tell him you showed him the drawing."

"Shit!"

"Yes, something's not right here," she said. "Can you trust this Turk? Have you been talking to him about any of this stuff? Has he been feeding whatever you say back to my grandfather?"

"I know they go back a long way but I didn't think they were in regular communication. Jesus! I can't believe Turk would go back to him with anything I said. Fuck!"

"There's more," she said. "That lady, Edith. She has a book out—"

"Edie Adams," I interjected. "That's her name. That's who she is."

"The Muriel Cigar lady?" Eu-meh said, her eyes wide. "Edith is Edie Adams? Huh!"

"Okay. Turk told your grandfather about the drawing? Would your grandfather guess you drew it for me? And if he does, what then?"

"I don't know. I just don't. I finished my shift at two o'clock and raced over here to see you. I love my grandfather. I want to protect him. But I'm worried about all this. If my grandfather's in danger ... I mean, should I go to the police?"

That came out of left field.

"Hell, no," I said. "Based on what we do know, you go to the cops and the first thing they'll want to hear about is why your grandfather arranged to steal a bunch of possibly—just possibly—pornographic movies from someone in New York. And whatever answer he has won't save him from being prosecuted."

She took a minute to think about it and agreed.

"So the call with Turk. Did you catch anything else?" I asked.

"Yeah, he told my grandfather that Edith—Edie Adams—is down in Providence. Something about promoting a book."

I thought for a moment, and the next thing I knew I was telling Eu-meh I'd find out where she was in Providence and go talk with her.

"Just out of the blue? You think that's a good idea?"

"I'm done worrying about all this. Screw it. I'll find out where she's at and head down there after work. I think I can borrow a friend's car. But I'll go even if I have to thumb."

"You'd really do that? Jesus, Jimmy. Be careful," she said in a tone I welcomed.

"I will be. Listen, if Cigar Lady has someone vetting people who want to see her—like a public relations guy—I'll need to have something that will get me face to face with her."

"Like what?"

I took out the drawing.

"This, and also permission to mention you by name. To say you're my friend. Will that be all right with you?"

"She's hardly going to remember me."

163

"If she's known your grandfather this long, she certainly knows who you are, even after all this time."

"You think so?"

*You're unforgettable, for chrissakes.*

"I'm pretty sure," I said.

"Okay, you can 'drop' my name."

We both laughed, forgetting for a moment the reason for the trip: the fact her grandfather stole a bunch of movies that are now a contested prize between himself, Charlestown hood Mickey Ryan, and the murderous Whitey Bulger.

"I'll call you at your place after I talk to her" I said.

"I'll be home. Normally I'd be going out but this isn't a normal Friday and I'm not in the mood. Maybe Donna—that's my roommate—will stay in and we'll watch something on TV, drink some wine."

"That sounds like a good plan," I said. I didn't want to leave her, not for a moment, but I had to get back to work. "Talk to you tonight."

I said little to Turk. I was afraid I'd say something that would tip my hand and he'd know I was onto his little spy operation. Damn, I was pissed. But it was more than that. I liked that smart-ass, know-it-all old shit, and it hurt like hell that he'd betray me.

Ralph was back from lunch. Whatever had

gotten into him in the morning was apparently gone. Flushed out by a liquid lunch if I was any judge of alcohol-highlighted eyes. Yet, he was back at his station, threading film through the editor, rewinding it, and wrestling it back into the case. He worked like a robot: deliberate, quiet, and well-oiled to be sure.

"Ya wanna take these back and shelve 'em, Lyons?" he'd call out, and I'd walk over to collect them. He never did get back into talking movies with Turk, who seemed relieved to have the old Ralph back. In fact, Turk seemed content with the overall silence. I was a wreck. I needed to get going. I went into the men's room, dispensed a bit of the liquid soap onto my hand and drank it. God, it was awful. I wanted to barf, which was the point, but not right away. I held it down, rinsed and dried my hands and went back out.

I grabbed a film case from the back room and walked over to Ralph's station.

"You have another case to put back?"

"What? No! I didn't call you over. Jeez, you don't look well."

And then I let my resistance drop and the soap and more came back up onto the floor.

"For God's sake, Jimmy! You're sick!"

Turk was suddenly at my side, the voice of concern.

"Oh, kid, what'd you have for lunch?"

"I'll be okay," I said.

"Like hell. You get yourself home. You need a

cab? I'll pay for it."

That was tempting, but I said no, that maybe getting into the fresh air would help. Turk said I needed to get home and go back to bed. Then he whispered to me. "I'll punch you out at five, kid. Don't worry."

I was out in two minutes and heading for the T. I stopped at the payphone upstairs from the station and called Red to ask if I could borrow his car, that I had to get to Providence right away. It was important. He was agreeable. No problem. As long as he could go along for the ride.

"I'm not going down to party, Red. I've got to do an interview."

"You mean like a reporter? Or you got a job interview? Man, you leaving Charlestown?"

I told him it was a practice interview. I hoped to be able to talk with celebrities someday and there was an author down there peddling a book.

"Who?"

I figured there was no harm in telling him. I mean, he isn't much into entertainment media or gossip.

"Edie Adams."

"Shit! You mean the cigar chick? She's fucking hot, man. Can I meet her?"

We went around for a few minutes on that before he finally accepted he could not meet her. He agreed that we'd drive down in his car, but that he'd be off at a bar while I was "playing Gene Shalit."

# CHAPTER
# TWELVE

Red met me at City Square and we jumped back onto the expressway and headed off. We did the speed limit going down because Red still didn't have an inspection sticker. I figured we'd get there by 4:00, 4:30.

Once into Rhode Island we got off 95 and pulled into a gas station. I picked up a copy of *The Providence Journal* and leafed through the pages for arts and entertainment. Fortunately there was a calendar section, and I found the listing for Cigar Lady's book-signing. She was at the College Hill Bookstore on Thayer Street. I asked the counter clerk if he knew where Thayer Street was in Providence and he asked me if I was going to buy the paper. I did and then he gave me directions to take 95 to the Branch Avenue exit, then stop and ask someone else. That's what I did.

"Just follow Branch to Cypress and stay on it until you come to Hope Street," some guy shouted to me from the sidewalk after I asked. "Take a right there and go straight. Remember that. Go straight, because Hope veers off to the left. But if you stay straight, you'll be on Thayer."

As I started down Branch Red turned to me and said, "That's fucked up."

"What's fucked up?"

"The directions. Can you find any place in Boston that easy? He's probably bullshittin' us."

He wasn't. We found Thayer Street, the bookstore, and a parking space right around the corner from it. While Red went looking for a bar, I headed into the bookstore. The place was pretty busy for a Friday evening, but then it was still early. As you'd expect, given the Brown University campus sprawled all over the area, the clientele looked to be 98 percent college students and college professors. I figured me and Cigar Lady, if she was here, made up the last 2 percent.

I found her at the back of the shop, seated at a table with a pile of her books nearby. The group facing her, about twenty-five people, were forming a line to go past the table and buy an inscribed copy of the book. Most of the group were women, probably forty and older, but some men were also in the line. As her commercials and, more recently, Red made clear, Cigar Lady is hot. It was also clear that I got there just in time. Once she was done with the buyers she was bound to head off.

I fell in at the end of the line. When I was in

front of her at the table, I saw she looked quite sweet. There was humor in her eyes, very unlike the seductress of the Muriel Cigar commercials. She read my face like a book.

"Not what you were expecting?"

She smiled and I smiled back. What else to do?

"I really didn't know what to expect, Miss Adams. But, yeah, when I finally see you—yeah." My voice trailed off.

"Are you seriously interested in a book on beauty, makeup, skin care and fashion tips? You're not some weirdo kid with a fixation on me, I hope." She signaled to someone off to the side to start packing away the unsold copies of her book.

"No, Miss Adams. It's nothing like that."

"That's good. To tell you the truth, a lot of the people who came here to see me didn't want so much my book as to hear me talk about the 'old days,' Ernie, and some of the people I worked with. But I don't mind."

I took out Eu-meh's drawing and showed it to her.

"That's a lovely drawing, though a few years old. Did you want me to autograph it? I thought you said you weren't a weirdo."

"Actually, I'm a friend of Eu-Meh's. She's the granddaughter of Zhang Wei. You know. House of Dragons in Boston?"

She put her hands out, palms up. The surprise was evident.

"Are you serious? Eu-meh sent you here? Why?"

"I volunteered. She didn't send me."

"And you are who, exactly? Her boyfriend?"

"My name is Jimmy Lyons. Like I said, I'm her friend."

She looked me up and down, then directly into my eyes. She spoke slowly.

"So why are you here, Jimmy Lyons? What's with the drawing?"

"It's a detail from a photo that hangs on the wall at the restaurant. I only brought it with me to—"

She took the drawing from my hand and studied it.

"I remember that photo. Zhang, his wife, Bao, and Butterfly are in it." She smiled at the memory. "They were wonderful days."

"I came to talk to you about the films, Miss Adams. The films you called Zhang about."

The smile fled from her face and a minute later we were in a back room of the store.

"You mean he has them?"

"That's the thing. He doesn't have them. The van carrying them was hijacked. Now it's possible there could be a gang war because Zhang is not the only one who wants them."

She looked anxious, scared.

"I don't think I want to say any more." She was still holding one copy of her book. She opened it up and began writing in it. "Tell Eu-meh I'm sorry. Really."

"Eu-meh is afraid her grandfather is going to get hurt. Or worse, Miss Adams."

"I'm sorry," she said again.

I should have bitten my tongue then while figuring out a better approach. I didn't. After thinking I was onto something that would help me make sense of this, and let me know which way I should go—who to help, if anyone, and how—I found myself in Providence on what suddenly looked like a wild goose chase. I thought I had something, a sliver of a clue to help me figure everything out, and I had squat. Like I said, I wasn't diplomatic. I played the smartass. I was so busy listening to myself talk that I barely listened to her.

"Sorry I wasted your time, Miss Adams. I thought you being a longtime friend of Mr. Zhang you'd be more helpful. He's gotten himself into some real shit up in Boston. I hoped you would let me know what's really going on. Eu-meh hoped so, too."

"I'd help if I could but—"

She looked sincere. I didn't care.

"You know, I saw you in some of the photos Zhang has hanging up in the restaurant. You with Zhang and his wife. You with Jackie Gleason and a bunch of other celebrities. But you were the one who called Zhang about these films and that's why I'm here."

"As I said already, I wish I had not called him."

"So do I. But you did," I changed my tone,

making sure I sounded disappointed in her. "I wish it had been Jackie Gleason who made the call. I'll bet if he knew anything that could keep Zhang he'd say something. Hell, he'd probably do something—hire lawyers or even hire some muscle of his own to stop Zhang from getting hurt or going to prison."

I thought she would cry or tell me to piss off but she did neither. She laughed.

"Yeah, Jackie's that kind of guy. He would do that. Too bad you're not talking to him." She shrugged her shoulders. "He was a force of nature back in the day and he still is. Shit, my husband once said that 'Mr. Saturday Night' not only had enormous star power but enough mass to emit gravitational waves."

I wondered if she noticed that my initial expression was deer-in-the-headlights startled. But I quickly recovered and laughed. It was a genuine laugh, even as I told myself I was an idiot for not realizing before this that Edie Adams was the wife—make that widow—of Ernie Kovacs. I only saw one of his movies, *Sail a Crooked Ship*, but I had heard of him. He was supposedly a comic genius. The poor guy died in a car crash.

"That's funny, Miss Adams. Did he ever say that to Gleason?"

"Of course, Jackie laughed, but then asked if audiences would need a science degree to get it."

"I'm crap at science, but I got it," I said. Truth is, I would have preferred to dislike Cigar Lady because

172

I got nothing out of coming down here. But I couldn't. She seemed genuinely nice. She was just scared. I couldn't fault her for that.

I turned to go and she said to wait.

"I've not seen Eu-meh in years. Look, I know it's not much, but could you give her this for me?"

"Thanks, Miss Adams. I'll be sure to give it to her." And with that I was out the door.

Red was sitting in the car. He looked pissed.

"What happened?" I said.

"I got into an argument with the bartender over the Pats and had to leave," he said. "What an asshole! First thing he says when I told him I'm from Boston —even as I'm payin' him for the beer—is that he's lookin' forward to seein' the Pats do worse next season than they did last year, with three wins and eleven losses. Like Providence has an NFL team, y'know?"

I didn't say anything. Right then the fate of the Pats was not important.

"You didn't hit the guy, did you?"

He shook his head. "You kiddin'? I'd probably get charged and then it could screw up my enlistment. I just drank down the beer and left. Fuckin' Rhode Island, man. Place sucks."

I told him to give me a minute and I went to a payphone on the corner, threw in a dime and called Eu-meh. The operator cut in to tell me I needed another quarter for the first three minutes because, you know, long distance.

Eu-meh picked it up mid first-ring. I barely said hello before I knew she was crying.

"What is it, Eu-meh? What's happened?"

"It's Lee. He's in the hospital. Shot. Someone fucking shot him, Jimmy."

I moved my mouth but nothing came out at first.

"Lee? Shot?" I finally said. "Who did it? Who did it? Do they know?" I thought of Connor, who had seen me with Lee and Eu-meh. Would he have done it? Would Whitey have ordered it? But Whitey didn't know anything about Zhang's connection to the movies. At least, I didn't think so.

"Eu-meh, listen to me. First off, you said Lee's in the hospital? What's his condition. Is he gonna be all right?"

"I don't know. I don't know. My grandfather is there with him, at Mass General. He called to say Lee is in surgery and that I should stay here. I want to see Lee, Jimmy. I want to go."

"Not now. Do what your grandfather says. He needs to know you're safe."

I couldn't think why anyone would shoot Lee. That's not going to get the movies. That's only going to spur a bloodbath. Zhang would go old-school Tong gangster in revenge. I doubted even Whitey was ready for that.

"Did your grandfather tell you what happened, exactly?"

"No, he said there was an argument. Some customer pushed and punched one of the waiters.

Grandfather rushed over. He intervened to try and calm the customer, but the customer and his friends only got angrier. They called my grandfather horrible names. They called him Chink. They called him Uncle Ho. Then one of them pulled out a gun. And then Lee was there and he tried to knock the gun away. It went off and now he's in the hospital. Oh, God, Jimmy! I'm so scared."

"I'll be back as fast as I can. But stay there. Is your roommate home yet?"

"No. She's went off to Worcester for the weekend. But there's a guy parked out front. My grandfather sent him over."

I was relieved to hear that. I had no doubt "the guy" was packing and wouldn't hesitate to bury anyone threatening Eu-meh. I could only hope he wouldn't shoot me when I went to the door.

"Good. You stay put. Please. Try to calm down. Have a glass of wine if you think it'll help."

An automated voice cut in, asking me to deposit more money. *Fucking telephone company!*

"Eu-meh, the phone's about to disconnect. Listen. I'll be back with you as soon as I can. See if you can let the guy downstairs know I'm on the way and he shouldn't—" I was going to say shoot me, but I thought better of it. "That he should let me go see you. Okay?"

"Okay. Okay, Jimmy. Hurry back."

I slammed the receiver into the cradle and rushed to the car.

"Jesus, Jimmy, what gives. You look like you've seen a ghost."

I told him a friend, a guy from Chinatown, had been shot and was in the hospital. "You actually know someone from Chinatown? And he's shot? What the fuck is goin' on?"

"I'll fill you in tomorrow, Red. Right now, I gotta get back to Boston. Shit!"

He didn't press me for information. He put the key in the ignition and fired it up. I sat in the shotgun seat, Edie Adams' book on my lap. I looked at my watch. It was six o'clock. Most traffic would be coming out of Boston now, so we could get to the city by a little after seven if we're lucky.

"Buckle up, man. We're gonna risk being stopped 'cuz I'm gonna hit the gas once we get on 95," Red said. He pulled away from the curb and drove back the way we had come, looking for the on-ramp. I was so worried about Lee and Eu-meh that I didn't want to talk. I opened the book to look at the inscription. *To my dear Eu-meh. I hope you enjoy this book, though I doubt you need any tips to bring out your beauty. I've not seen you in years but your grandfather has at times shared photos of you and your handsome brother, Li. Love to you both and to your grandfather, Edith.*

All the way down to Providence and back. And for nothing.

We got into Boston and I had Red stop at the first payphone we saw. I called Ma and told her I was with Red and that we were going to hang out for a while then go back to his place. That I'd be staying the night. It was a call I've made any number of times. She didn't even ask me how work was. I was grateful.

On the way to Eu-meh's place I told Red that if, in the unlikely event my mother called his place later on, to tell her I was asleep, and nothing else. I also scribbled down Eu-meh's phone number.

"Call me at this number if there's an emergency. But only an emergency, okay?"

"You got it, man. You sure you don't need me to do anything else?"

"Nah, I'm good for now. Thanks, Red. Thanks for everything."

"Hey, you gonna be around for the parade Sunday?"

I could tell from the way he asked the question that it had sunk in that I was into something big and dangerous. If I said no to watching the parade it would be like firing off a distress flare and he probably wouldn't leave my side.

"Shit, yeah! It's the fucking parade."

He drove off and I looked around for the car with the Chinatown muscle. I spotted him and gave him a small wave. The guy rolled down the window.

"You're good. Go ahead."

The book tucked under my arm, I went to the front door and rang the bell to her apartment. She buzzed me in and I went up the stairs two and three at a time.

"Oh, God, Jimmy! What is happening? What are we going to do?" she said as soon as I was inside. I placed the book on the dining table and slowly, carefully took her hands in mine. I wanted to hug her but was afraid she'd take it wrong.

"It's okay, Eu-meh. Just tell me what you know. You've talked to your grandfather, right? What did he say about Lee's condition?"

She talked. It was almost stream of consciousness but I got the picture. Lee was out of surgery and resting in intensive care. But the doctor said he should be fine. The bullet went in and went out—a through-and-through—without hitting any vital organs or arteries.

I led her over to an armchair and took a seat on the sofa next to it. I was close enough that I was still able to hold her hand. She calmed down. It looked like she had pulled herself together, but then it was like the whole thing hit her square between the eyes again and she was up, pacing.

"Come and sit down again," I said. Instead, she walked to the kitchen and poured each of us healthy glasses of wine. I'd have preferred a beer. Better yet, a whiskey. But this was not the time to be picky. I took the glass and then a sip. Eu-meh kept pacing as she sipped.

"You've got to calm down. Lee will be fine. You've got to believe that."

She sat down and almost immediately got up again, pacing again.

"I'm so scared, Jimmy," she said, barely above a whisper. "What has my grandfather gotten us into?"

It was the first time she said anything indicating the old man was at fault here. I let it pass without comment.

"If my brother—"

She didn't have to complete the sentence. I stood up and went over to her.

"Shh, now. Think positive, Eu-meh," I said.

She looked into my eyes. I wondered what she saw. In hers I saw fear had replaced her usual confidence. She also looked tired. She sipped more wine.

"Do you believe in God, Jimmy Lyons? Do you pray?"

I guessed I believed in God. I mean, I never thought there wasn't one. Thing is, I'm not much of a Catholic or a church-goer. When I did pray it was by rote. Right now, it felt different. "I'll pray with you Eu-meh," I said.

"I'm so scared. So fucking scared," she said. "All I can do is imagine my life without Lee, without my brother. And think: Is my grandfather next? Will someone kill him?"

"Scared makes sense. How could you not be? But listen. You know Lee is gonna be okay. You know it wasn't some gang hit, just some racist, dickhead Texan with a gun. And no one's gonna hurt your grandfather. He's smart and it's clear to me he's one tough old bastard."

She looked at me in silence for a moment, and I was worried that I'd said the wrong thing.

"Eu-meh, I wasn't insulting your grandfather. It's just an expression."

"I know that. You think I've not heard the expression before? Or used it before?"

"I just wanted to be sure—"

"You know why I didn't go out with you when you asked me?"

That came out of nowhere.

"No. Why?"

"Because I've dated White guys before. It's mostly been disappointing."

"What do you mean? Disappointing ... how?"

She laughed and poked my chest. "Well, it's not what you're thinking if you're thinking that." She laughed again, then asked if I'd ever dated any Asian women. I told her no, which was true.

"Most White guys who've asked me out in the last year or so? I've simply said no. The last White guy who I even considered saying yes to—well, before you—I interviewed him before giving an answer. And the answer was 'no.' I didn't want to interview you, Jimmy, because I was afraid I'd have to give you a no, too. I thought it better to put you off with a lighthearted 'we're just friends' kind of excuse. Because if I didn't like your answers, we probably wouldn't stay friends."

I didn't know what to make of this. *What the hell is she talking about? Interviews?*

"Jesus! What were the questions?"

In the brief silence that followed we both sipped wine.

"I ask them about Asian food—if they like it, like it *a lot*. Or if they take Kung Fu, Taekwondo or Jujitsu lessons. Oh, you'll appreciate this one. I ask them about movies and TV shows with Asian characters, to get a sense of their thinking."

"Okay. Where does all this go? To see if they're really interested in Asian culture?"

"No. It's to get sense of whether they're really interested in me. In me, or in some image of me based on some Oriental fetish. I dated a guy once—I think for two months, which was at least six weeks longer than I should have—who always pressed me to wear 'Chinese clothes' when we went out. You know: Silk top with Chinese characters and, of course, the mandarin collar. He didn't want me. He wanted Suzie Wong."

I didn't know what to say to that. I was taken aback at the idea that other guys' fantasies made her wary of me. At the same time, I was relieved it wasn't me, personally, that was the problem. The fact is she did like me, enough that she didn't want to risk being disappointed in me. Crazy as it sounds, I took some heart in that.

"Eu-meh—"

"You don't have to say anything. Not right now,"

she said. She sounded tired. "Right now, you're the guy who went to Rhode Island for me, and who came racing back when I called. Right now, you're the guy who I want you to be and..."

She moved in close to me, then closer, raising her mouth up to mine and kissing me, lightly, tenderly, so that the kiss itself felt as sacred as any prayer could be. I touched her cheek, ran fingers down along her neck. She put her arms around me. I'd waited a long time for this, but I never imagined it would really happen, let alone in a moment like this. I slid my hand down along her back, then lower. She moved to step away and I thought for a moment I'd made a mistake. The apology was on my lips but then I saw she stepped back only to unbutton her blouse. She dropped it to the floor and reached back to undo her bra. I began taking off my shirt and she stepped back toward me for another kiss. But this time I was conscious of the taste and the smell of wine on her mouth. I looked at her face, seeing eyes glassy from the wine. There was a red flush to her cheeks. I glanced over at the wine bottle she'd poured from. It was empty. In an instant I realized she had finished off most of the bottle before I even got there. Her bra followed the T-shirt to the floor. She unbuckled her belt and slipped her thumbs into the sides of her jeans to pull them down. I could see the top of silken dark-blue panties that shimmered in the light.

"Eu-meh," I whispered.

"What, Jimmy?"

"I want you more than I've ever wanted any one or any thing. Right from the day I first saw you."

"Good, Jimmy. I'm glad." Her jeans dropped softly to the floor. She stepped out of them, took my hand and led me to her bedroom. I was only a pair of shiny, silky panties away from paradise.

"But with what's going on, especially what happened tonight with Lee. You're scared, probably confused, and you've had a few glasses of wine. Maybe more than a few."

She dropped my hand and turned to me as if I'd insulted her.

"Now you don't want me. Now you're afraid?" she asked, confused. "Jesus, Lyons! You don't think I know I'm the reason you come into the restaurant? That when you look at the menu you're wishing to God I was on it?"

"I won't deny that. It's true. Believe me, I'd rather bite off my tongue than be saying this, Eumeh, but I have to. We gotta wait until this other stuff is over." I looked at her again. "Or at least until we're clear-headed."

"That's funny," she laughed. The wine seemed to be hitting her more by the second. She sat down on the edge of her bed. "You say that, Lyons, but ... but I can see that 'little Jimmy' has a different opinion."

I didn't have to look down to know she was right.

"He doesn't always know what's right," I said. "That's why I make important decisions with the head on my shoulders. If you still want to do this after we've put this other stuff behind us, I'm there. Not only that, I won't leave your bed for a month, believe me, and I'll probably cry like a baby whenever you get out of it."

She didn't say anything, but sunk sideways onto the bed, asleep. I gently lifted her legs onto the bed, moved her to the center and covered her with a blanket. I went out into the living room and stretched out on a sofa by the bay window overlooking the street. I didn't have a clear idea of what to do about Zhang and these movies. In that moment, I just wanted Lee to recover and for Eu-meh to get a good night's sleep.

I began going over my meeting with Edie Adams. She was scared. I get that. Still, I wished she had given me *something*. I thought about my dig at her, when I said Jackie Gleason would have been a real help. What was it she said? "Yeah, Jackie is that kind of guy. He would do that. Too bad you're not talking to him. He was a force of nature back then and still is." She sounded like Gleason might know something about all this. Why? Is he in the films? How would I find that out? I doubted Gleason was anywhere in the area hawking a book. And even if he was, I seriously doubted I'd ever get within shouting distance of him. What would his connection be to Edie? I thought of Turk. I knew he'd have answers, but I could no longer trust the guy. Not a bit. So who? Who could I ask? Who knew this kind of shit?

Who was Boston's Gene Shalit? I saw a pile of magazines and newspapers by the television. The only newspaper was *The Phoenix*. I pulled out the "*Boston After Dark*" entertainment section and went through the pages. There were film reviews, but I didn't get the sense the writers would know the kind of information I was looking for. Then I decided the whole idea of talking to a reporter, even one who just wrote about movies and television, was a bad idea.

What did I know, exactly, about anything at this point? I knew that Edie called Zhang because of some movies that had her worried. Zhang bribed someone to snatch them for himself. So what do Zhang and Edie Adams have in common? Zhang's an old time Boston Chinatown gangster turned successful, legitimate businessman. Edie Adams had made some movies, she sang, she was the pretty face of Muriel Cigars, and now she had a book out. And she was in at least two photos that I saw at the restaurant.

Gleason also turned up on Zhang's wall. He'd done movies, television and live stage shows. I could see an Edie and Gleason connection because they were both from the entertainment industry. As for Gleason being interested in these stolen movies, Edie seemed to imply he would be, or maybe I misunderstood her? So I didn't even know that for a fact. But Zhang? He was the odd man out here. Aside from hosting them at his restaurant a few times, many years ago, he didn't fit into their world, even if he was in the photo with them. If he did, then there was a piece of the puzzle missing, or I was just not seeing it. I thought of the photo. When Edie looked at Eu-meh's drawing more closely, she recognized it from the photo. She also remembered that the woman named Butterfly was in it. So who was Butterfly? I wished I'd asked. That's another question I could ask Turk. If I trusted him.

Maybe in the morning, when my head was clearer, I'd figure it out. It had been a long day and I was exhausted. I glanced over once more to where Eu-meh was sleeping, then closed my eyes. I suddenly thought, *'Little Jimmy'? God, I hope not.*

I woke up a little after seven. Eu-meh was still asleep. I wondered if she'd remember what almost happened between us. And, if she did, whether she'd want to talk about it or pretend it didn't happen. I'd go along with however she wanted to deal with it. Outside, I could see Zhang's man was still parked at the curb. I hoped Zhang was sending over someone to relieve the guy.

I heard Eu-meh moving around in the bedroom. The door opened and she came out, wrapped in the blanket I'd put over her. She looked at her clothes, still in a small pile on the floor, then over at me.

"It's not what you think. We didn't—I didn't..." I said.

"It's okay. I remember. Not all of it, but I remember the important parts," she said. She scooped up the clothes with one hand while holding the blanket in place with the other, then came over and gave me a light kiss on the lips. "Thanks, Lyons. You're okay." It wasn't the passionate kiss of the night before, but it still put me on top of the world.

"How you feeling?"

"I'm doing okay, I guess," she said and headed back into the bedroom, closing the door behind her. When she came out a few minutes later she was in a bathrobe. "I'm going to jump in the shower. You can grab one when I'm done. I'll give you a towel."

I listened to the water running and I couldn't help but remember what she looked like undressed. Then I felt guilty, as if I was looking at her through a keyhole in my mind. *You're more Catholic than you thought, Lyons.* I pulled my mind's eye away from the memory and again went through the Edie-Zhang-movie connections and what they meant. I still drew a blank. But my thoughts kept going back to Eu-meh and what I could do for her. The one thing I was determined to do was to keep her safe. Lee, too. As for the Shadow King, my street sense told me he deserved whatever happened to him. Just not if I could help it.

The bathroom door opened and Eu-meh stepped out, wrapped in her robe again and with a towel around her hair. I could tell that tears as well as shower water had run down those cheeks, but she gave me a small smile. She'd be devastated if her grandfather is harmed in any way. So, yeah, I had to find a way to help him without getting myself killed or jailed. As it turned out, deciding that actually made my next step clear.

Eu-meh came back out of her room with a dry towel, which she handed to me. Then she went into her roommate's bedroom and came out with a black Creedence Clearwater Revival T-shirt. The band's name encircled a picture of a hippie chick holding up a tambourine encircled bearing the words *Mardi Gras*.

"This should fit you. I don't think Donna will mind."

# CHAPTER
## THIRTEEN

It was about 9:00 when we went downstairs. The night watch was just pulling away from the curb. His replacement was leaning against a gold Chevy Malibu. I never got a good look at the first guy, but Eu-meh's new bodyguard was built like a linebacker. Even with the over-sized sports jacket you could see there was a piece holstered under his left arm.

"Who's the brick wall?" I asked Eu-meh.

"My cousin, Chou. He's a good guy."

Eu-meh rushed to over to Chou and the two wrapped their arms around each other. They said some things in Chinese. Eu-meh nodded her head several times. Tears welled up in her eyes but she smiled. She turned to me.

"Lee's going to be okay. Chou's going to take us over to the hospital."

Eu-meh got into the passenger seat and I climbed into the back.

"Will they let me in to see him?" I asked.

"Sorry, dude, family only," Chou said. "But the boss is there and he wants to talk to you."

I didn't have to think hard to know "the boss" was Zhang. Not long before this that would have worried me. Not now. I was no longer torn between what I was expected to do and what I should do and wanted to do. My focus was on Eu-meh and Lee and, to the extent their welfare depended on their grandfather not getting killed, on Zhang. But Eu-meh and Lee were my principal concerns. As things were, I hadn't done anything to hurt Zhang's plans, just kept my mouth shut about Mickey's. The more I learned about Zhang the more convinced I was that he wouldn't hold that against me. I think he understood turf loyalty, even if it was stupid or made no sense. Not to say he wouldn't do something to me if Mickey's double cross went off as planned. But that's not something I was going to have to worry about now.

Then there was Eu-meh. The old man had to know I spent the night at her place. I'm sure the guy guarding her cleared it with Zhang before letting me go upstairs. Would the old man have issues with me on that? Is he going to assume I screwed his granddaughter, maybe against her will, and want to take revenge? Funny thing is, I didn't care now what he thought. I'd be honest. I wouldn't go into details but I'd make sure he knew that nothing happened. Hopefully, he'd believe me. If not, so what. I didn't care.

Chou took Eu-meh up to see Lee.

"Wait here, Jimmy. The boss will be right down."

About fifteen minutes later Zhang stepped off the elevator. It was obvious the old man had slept little, if at all, during the night. He walked a bit slower than he did at the restaurant and there were some small bags under his eyes. Yet he was alert and wore the same tough visage he showed when sitting at his table throne during lunch hours. He wore exhaustion better than anyone I'd met.

"How is Lee?" I asked.

"The doctors say he should make a full recovery. He slept well through the night and woke up only minutes ago. He took some juice, which is good."

"Thank God."

I wanted to ask him for details of the shooting. I also had something else to discuss. I decided to wait. He wanted to see me so there must be something particular he wanted to say.

He said he had spoken to Mickey Ryan and that they had set up an exchange.

"I don't know if this is too much to ask, Mr. Lyons, but I would like you to be there. Mr. Ryan and I agree that you've been helpful in getting things this far, even though doing so has not been easy for you. We both believe that your being there would make things go smoothly for both parties."

I was not expecting that. Jumping right back into the movies deal? Lee gets shot maybe twelve hours ago and here's Zhang, his grandfather, talking to me about getting his stolen movies back.

"First things first, Mr. Zhang. Was Lee's shooting connected in any way to these movies? Was someone trying to send you a message to back off?"

"I can see how you might think that. I certainly did. Until I learned the group was from out of state, with no connections to any Boston gang. No, it was one of those things that can happen when the drunk, the stupid or the racist mistake Chinatowns for anything-goes-towns." His voice oozed contempt. "The police tell me the group is from Texas. Tourists out for a night on the town. They thought Chinatown, thought my restaurant, was a place they could act like cowboys."

"Were they arrested?"

"Yes. The District Attorney is weighing what charges the shooter will face. I would like to see a charge of attempted murder, but I doubt the DA will do that. We'll see. None of the others were armed. They have all been booked for assault against Lee and myself."

He must have seen my next question in my eyes.

"Believe me, my first instinct was to kill the shooter. Or, rather, have him killed," he said. "Within an hour of the shooting a member of Ping On asked if I wanted it handled. I told him no."

I wondered if the offer was professional courtesy, a sign of respect for a local legend, or payback for a favor Zhang had done.

"I will let the law handle this. If my grandson died, or even if he had been seriously injured, that would be a different matter."

Nothing he said shocked me. It didn't bother me either. And since he had already brought up the meeting with Mickey, I turned the conversation back to it. I told him I wouldn't be there for the meeting.

"That's not something I'll do, Mr. Zhang. I got into this with mixed feelings in the first place. I was curious about the movies, but mostly it was the finder's fee you offered. I figured that would pay some of my tuition to film school." I didn't say anything about Eu-meh just yet.

"Nothing has changed, Mr. Lyons. I will still pay you the two thousand dollars."

I shook my head. "A lot has changed." I was warming to what I was going to say. For the first time I felt that, whatever came of this, I was the one deciding my next move and why I was making it. It felt good. "For one thing, I don't care who gets the movies. I don't care what's on them or what you or Mickey or whoever gets them does with them. It's not my business."

I didn't say anything about my trip to Providence or my chat with Edie Adams. Hell, that would make it sound like I still wanted to find out about the films. I didn't.

"I am sorry you feel that way, but I understand," he said.

"There's something else, Mr. Zhang, and this is

more important. Mickey has no intention of giving you those movies."

He listened as I spelled it out for him: how Mickey was going to take Zhang's money but hand over the films to Whitey Bulger, that the meet-up was not a swap, but a robbery. More than that, it would probably be an ambush, since Whitey was supposed to be there in person and he'd not likely want any witnesses that were not on his side.

"No honor among thieves," he said when I finished. I couldn't tell if he was making a sad observation or cracking a joke until he added with a laugh, "The criminal world has not changed all that much."

"I don't think you should be there, either," I said.

He turned a quizzical look my way. "Why are you telling me this? Shouldn't you be loyal to your own? Even if you don't like this Mickey Ryan, he is still from your town. You know him. You don't know me —not well, anyway. And he may, let us face it, hurt you should he learn you told me of his plan."

I laughed then. "Let's also face the fact that you might want to hurt me if you thought I double-crossed you."

He smiled. "Possibly."

"I'll take my chances with Mickey Ryan," I told him. "And no, I don't know you well, but I'm not about to let you walk into an ambush. Because I think Mickey's plan is only going to work if you go down right there."

"Is he capable of doing that? Is he a killer?"

"Sure he is. He's especially motivated by Whitey Bulger threatening to kill him if he doesn't turn over the films. Yeah, he'll kill you if he can. And Whitey and some of his guys are sure to be there, or at least nearby."

"Why, Mr. Lyons?"

"Why? Because Whitey is—"

"No. Why are you determined that I should not walk into an ambush and possibly be killed?"

I kept silent for a moment, wondering how this was going to go.

"Because of Eu-meh," I said.

He looked at me and shook his head.

"You care for my granddaughter?"

"Yes, I do, Mr. Zhang."

"I know you stayed over t Eu-meh's last night."

"I did. Yes."

We stared at each other. He wanted to ask the question. Me? I figured I'd wait for it.

He sighed.

"Do you really believe you and Eu-meh can be together? In our family, that is not something that..." His voice trailed off and he looked away. For a moment I wondered if he was having some kind of seizure, but then he shook his head and looked down at his hands.

"Mr. Lyons, do you intend to tell Mickey Ryan of this conversation?"

"No. I'll let him know I'm done with all this. I'll

tell him I won't be part of any meeting. But that's it."
I got up to leave. "Mr. Zhang, please don't meet with him."

I went out onto Fruit Street, down North Grove to Cambridge Street, where I found a Dunkin' Donuts. Breakfast was coffee and, what else, a couple of doughnuts: a chocolate and a honey-dipped cruller. I took the coffee with a drop of milk but skipped the sugar. With those doughnuts who needed the two-packets of white that go with a regular coffee? Once the sugar buzz kicked in, I went out to find a payphone. A dime and a minute later I had Mickey on the phone. He sounded in a chipper mood. Maybe he was already counting the $5,000 he expected to net out of his scam. Or maybe it was just because it was Bunker Hill Day weekend.

"Glad you called, Lyons. We're all set for tomorrow. I talked to the Chink and he's going to meet us down at Montego Bay at twelve-thirty. I figured that's the best time because the parade is just getting started and all the cops will be up on Bunker. Whitey will be there with a few—"

I had intended to tell Mickey as calmly as possible that I wouldn't be going to the meet-up. Though I knew the conversation would get ugly, I thought I'd start out by simply saying I wanted no part in any of it, that it wasn't my business. But then he mentioned Montego Bay as if it had no more meaning to me than, say, Wisconsin.

"Not going, Mickey. I wouldn't have gone

196

anyway, but how the fuck you thought for a second that I'd go down Terminal Street for some gangster shit is beyond me. Are you really that clueless?"

"Who do you think you're talkin' to? What's this about, Lyons? Your old man?"

"I'm just telling you that I'll have nothing to do with this shit you're pulling."

"What? You feel bad for the Chink now? Is he paying you or something?"

"I'll say this for the guy. He's no bullshit artist. He's played straight with you this whole time."

"Who really gives a shit? No one needs you there anyway. I might have thrown a few bucks your way but fuck that now. Fuck you. And fuck that snitch of a father you had. He—"

I hung up. I was so angry my hand was shaking. Or maybe it was the sugar. I needed to clear my head. I started walking. Twenty or so minutes later I was downtown, and not far from the Brattle Book Shop on West Street.

It was early but I wasn't surprised to find George already there. He was getting on in years and I thought he was looking kind of tired. His son, Ken, was taking on more of the work these days, but George was still the heart of the shop. He looked up from the book he was either reading or, more likely, appraising, and eyed me over the top of his glasses.

"Mr. Lyons. When can we expect to see your documentary about—where is it again? Somerville?"

He likes to pretend he forgets where I'm from.

"Hi, George. As soon as I finish it you'll be the first one I tell. I'll make sure you have a good seat for the premier. Maybe we can hold it over here."

He made a horrified face. "I'll pass, thank you," he said.

I headed slowly toward the stacks, looking over the books set out on the tables along the way. George's bookstore is the kind of shop that makes you feel smarter by just being there. I'd hoped when I walked in that I'd see some old book or magazine that would grab my interest and hold it for a time, something that would take my mind entirely off the last few days. But, nothing.

"What are you looking for these days?" George called over. "There's a good book down in the film section on pre-Hays Code cinema. You'd probably like it. Lots of pictures."

Only later did I appreciate the cleverness of the dig. It was damn funny. I just nodded to let him know I heard him but said nothing. He seemed to sense something was not right.

"Do you require something for nausea, Mr. Lyons? You seem out of sorts."

I walked toward the film section, browsing the books on the shelves along the way. I was going past volumes on bugs, birds and whatnot. Nothing that interested me. Ever. But my eye caught one book, on its spine a picture of a Monarch butterfly.

*Shit. You just can't get away from this mess.*

I turned and walked back to George.

"I need some information. You may not have a book that'll help but maybe you know it just because you've been around so long."

He put the book down as if he was annoyed. Maybe he really was. It's hard to tell with him sometimes.

"If only you had not come in for another ten minutes, when I'll be too busy," he said, with a hint of a smirk.

I told him I was trying to find out if there was a Chinese actress or entertainer named Butterfly who worked with Jackie Gleason or Ernie Kovacs back in the 1950s. He offered me the expression I expected for asking such an odd question so far out in left field.

"Butterfly? Is that all you have?"

"Yeah."

He looked out into the shop, scanning the rows of shelves like a teacher waiting for the student with the correct answer to raise a hand. While he was doing that I was asking myself a question: *Why can't you leave things alone, Lyons? You said you were done with this. So why keep digging for information?*

*I am done. But I can be curious, right?*

*Sure. And you know where curiosity got the cat.*

"Well, Mr. Lyons," George was saying, "the only actress I can think of named Butterfly is Butterfly McQueen."

I shook my head. "Right, but she wasn't Chinese."

199

"Nor is she now. Butterfly McQueen is still alive, Mr. Lyons. Didn't you know that?"

I had to admit, I didn't.

"I cannot think of another actress who goes by the name Butterfly. Feel free to go through the film section. You might find something."

I started back down the aisle when George called to me. He asked if I knew the Chinese word for butterfly. I didn't, and he pretended to be pleased by that. He directed me to a shelf where there was an English/Chinese dictionary. I found it and looked up butterfly. I went back his desk.

"*Húdié*," I said, then repeated the name, more for my own benefit than George's.

"Okay," George said. "Let me think. No actress by that name comes to mind. There is a Chinese filmmaker by that name. And her name, in English, was Butterfly Wu, but she has never worked in the United States. You know, you really should have come a little later when I wouldn't have time for this nonsense."

"I will. Next time. Promise." Then I remembered where I'd heard the name. It was from Turk. *Húdié* was Zhang's first love, the girl he was forced to leave behind in Los Angeles.

"Sorry. That's the best I can do," George said. He sounded disappointed, but then a light seemed to go off in his head. "You said this Butterfly or *Húdié* worked with Gleason and Kovacs, didn't you?"

"Yeah, that's right. Or at least knew them both."

He motioned me to follow him back down into the stacks, where he pulled out a book about early TV. I was never big on old-time television, though I knew a bunch of shows at least by name. He pulled out a book called *Accidental Visionary: A Biography of Allen Du Mont*.

"Why this book?"

"You said Gleason and Kovacs. You're familiar with the DuMont Television Network?"

"Vaguely. I know Gleason started *The Honeymooners* as a regular skit on a DuMont show."

"Good for you, Mr. Lyons. Well, that's where Kovacs had his show, as well. That's where their careers intersected. Take the book and look through it. If you want it, come back and pay me. If you don't, then return it—in the same condition, of course. Maybe something in there will help."

"Thanks, George."

"Go. Get out. I'm busy now. Good luck, Mr. Lyons." He sounded very pleased with himself.

It was after 10:30 when I took the chaise, a can of Coke and the book up to the roof. I was still wearing the Creedence shirt but had changed into a pair of cut-off jeans and sandals. I wanted a little time to relax and consider what to do. How could I stay clear of the Zhang's mess—not mine anymore—and still try to build a relationship with Eu-meh? Was that possible?

I looked over at the bridge that so often led the way to Revere Beach and a fun day. Now all that seemed like a long time ago. If not for Ma and Helen I'd head not for the Mystic Bridge and Revere but for the Mass Pike and head west. I'd go anywhere my thumb could get me that wasn't here.

The Du Mont bio was on my lap. I opened it to the forward, then went on to the table of contents. I began flipping through it and spotted several pages of photos about halfway through the volume. Among the first were photos of Du Mont and his cathode ray tube. There were lots of photos of his network's stars, including—no surprise—Gleason as Ralph Kramden. Art Carney was there, too, as Ed Norton. And no wonder Carney's character on *The Honeymooners* was a fan of *Captain Video*. That was one of the shows created for the DuMont network. If not for the reasons I was thumbing through it, I could actually enjoy reading this book. And there were a number of photos of Ernie Kovacs and Edie Adams. Damn! She was gorgeous.

Then I saw a photo that made me catch my breath.

*Butterfly*.

"Holy shit!" I said out loud. "Holy fucking shit."

"Shit is right, and you've made quite a pile of it, Jimmy."

I turned to the voice so fast I thought I'd get whiplash. Brendan Connor stared down at me. I froze, but then managed to utter a simple, "Huh?"

"I ask you: Whose fault is it you're in a pile of shit? Seems to me you made the pile and climbed into it. You should have minded your own business, Jimmy. Just hung out with your friends and enjoyed the weather and the carnival and the parade."

His eyes were blue ice. I couldn't read a fucking thing in that face. I only hoped my fear wasn't obvious.

"Calm down or you're gonna piss yourself. Maybe worse," he said.

I guess it was obvious.

"The way you're going, this isn't going to end well for you. You have to know that."

I felt like I couldn't breathe. My voice wouldn't kick in. After dealing with Zhang and then with Mickey, I couldn't believe the fear this guy instilled in me. I thought I'd be past that with him. I managed to find my voice, though.

"You gonna kill me? Right here?"

"Keep your voice down."

"Where's Harry Hollywood? You off him down on the Cape? No one's heard from him since you went down there."

For an instant there was a flicker of emotion. It was anger, but when he spoke it was business as usual.

"Who told you I went to see him?"

"Mary," I lied. "I ran into her at the Red Store just after you dropped her off. And like I said, no one's been able to reach Harry since the day you went down there." I wasn't about to tell him it was Helen who spoke to Mary. That could make her a potential witness in the event Harry was killed and Connor tied to it. And if she was a potential witness she'd be a likely target.

"Mary say anything else?"

"Like what?"

He cocked his head, silently pressing the question.

"No. She didn't say anything else."

He turned and walked over to the roof's edge.

"You've been following me. And my friends," I said.

"Half right. I've been following you. You know why?"

*To fucking kill me,* I thought, but I said nothing.

"Jimmy, why you want to go and get into shit and cause your Ma and Helen pain? Huh?"

*Good question. I don't know.*

He looked off into the distance, beyond the other rooftops and toward Medford Street.

"C'mere," he said.

I took a swig of Coke, put it down and walked over. I stopped about five feet from him. I chewed on the idea of turning and running, getting off the roof, but spit out the thought like a piece of moldy bread. I was damned if I was going to come off as a coward. Where could I really go? To the cops? I couldn't prove anything against Connor. He'd just bide his time and kill me anyway. Maybe Ma and Helen, too.

But why? And how does he know about what I'm involved in? What's his interest in any of this? Mickey Ryan's games would be the shit Connor would scrape off his shoe and nothing more. So what's Connor's angle?

He was talking but I wasn't catching any of it. I was thinking of Ma and Helen. In that moment I only wanted to call Ma, but that wasn't possible. I doubted that I'd be able to talk as if nothing was wrong. And even if I could, what words do you use to say goodbye without letting on that you are really, truly, no shit saying goodbye? She'd know something awful was going on, maybe even guess what was happening, and she'd start crying. No. Even if I could talk to her, I wouldn't. I couldn't let her live with that memory.

I heard Connor saying again that I was going to miss the parade because of this mess and that seemed to bring me around. I wondered if I could push him off the roof before he made me "accidentally" fall. Not likely. But it was broad daylight. He had to worry about being seen tossing me. But what if he just left it to me? Maybe told me to stand there until he left, then, after say ten or fifteen minutes, jump? That if I didn't jump, Ma and Helen were dead?

I swallowed hard. Yeah, that'd work.

He nodded toward the distance. "Montego Bay over there. Lots of shit, lots of bad shit, associated with that place."

"Yeah," I said, wondering if the sadness I heard in

his voice was real or my imagination. He turned and looked directly at me. I tried to look tough but I'm sure he saw my fear. He shook his head like I was something pathetic.

"Tell me what you know about me killing your dad?"

What was strange is that his asking me that, flat out, seemed to free me to say what I wanted.

"I always liked to believe it was a couple of dirty cops, but—"

"But what?"

"Then I remembered you coming over to our place to talk to my mother shortly after he died? You told her not to go to the cops. Yeah, I remember that. And she was scared shitless by something you whispered in her ear. Then you gave her money. She didn't want it. I could tell. But you made her take it."

He was looking at me but it seemed he was replaying that night in his own head. It was the first time I thought I could read anything in his expression. What was it? Regret? I couldn't tell. Didn't care, either. I was angry and I wanted to throw his betrayal of my father in his face.

"Okay. So, what about it?" he asked.

"I figure ... I think, I think you were the guy. The guy who did it."

"Who killed your old man?"

"Yeah," I said. "That's what I figure. You. You were supposed to be Dad's good friend, his best friend, but you fucking killed him. Some fucking gangster says kill him and you do it. So, yeah. That's what I figure."

His face was blue-eyed sphinx again. No idea what was going on behind that mask.

"A real Sherlock Holmes, aren't you, Jimmy. I gotta say—"

"You piece of shit!" I said as I stepped forward and swung at him with everything I had. He moved out of the way and I was off balance, falling toward the edge and screaming *No!* but he had me by my neck and my shirt and I could see the ground directly below me in a blur that turned clear for just an instant before he tossed me like a bag of trash away from the edge. I looked back at him but he was looking to the ground. I heard someone shout "What's goin' on up there?"

"Nothin'! Fuck off!" Connor said.

I didn't wait for him to turn back to me. I bolted for the roof door and was racing back down the stairs as fast as my shaking legs let me, thanking God that someone in the street saw what was happening and said something before Connor let me fall or helped me along the way. I shot right past my own apartment and reached the street, where I made a zigzag run through a number of buildings until I reached O'Brien Court, where I saw a bunch of laundry hanging out in the clothes yard. I grabbed the first pair of dry shorts that looked like they'd fit, then dashed into another building. No one was there so I immediately peeled off my pants and skivvies. I was still naked below the waist when an apartment door opened and a gray-haired old lady looked out.

"Jimmy Lyons! Is that you? You should be ashamed."

Jesus! I didn't know her except by sight but she obviously knew who I was. I zipped up and quickly transferred my wallet from my cut-offs to the shorts. The shorts were a bit loose but it was too late to go hunting in the clothes yard again.

"I'm sorry. I spilled Coke on my shorts and I needed to change real fast."

"Coke doesn't smell like that," she said, her face finding me guilty of some terrible moral crime. "Wait 'til I see your mother. Just you—"

I was out the door. I didn't care what she told my mother. I was alive. And I was still running for my life. I was out on Decatur Street running toward Bunker, where the parade marchers and floats would be lining up the next day. I'd been lucky so far. I knew I had only one move. I crossed to the other side of Bunker and headed up Lowney Way to City Square, where I grabbed the train into Boston.

# CHAPTER
# FOURTEEN

It felt good sitting on the stoop of Eu-meh's building on Marlborough Street. It offered the kind of calm you'd expect on a warm day surrounded by brownstones, historic churches, private clubs and upscale—very upscale—but discretely appointed retail shops. But with even modest weekly pay and a roommate or two, lots of college students have been able to make this street home. Eu-meh's building was about six blocks west of the Public Garden. Just a few blocks north, past Beacon Street and Storrow Drive, is the Esplanade, a gorgeous park of pedestrian bridges, statues, and the popular Hatch Shell concert venue —summer home for the Boston Pops. It's also the best place in the city to catch the annual Fourth of July fireworks.

I could only imagine what it's like to live there. It's not much more than a few miles from Charlestown and on a good traffic day—which doesn't exist in Boston—it's only about fifteen minutes away. But it might as well be fifteen light years. I've been all over the city, the good spots and bad. Even as a kid my friends and I would come into downtown and generally knock around. We'd run through old, run-down, abandoned buildings in the South End looking for god-knows-what. The places were wrecks. It was just the thrill of being in them. But it wasn't just the South End. Even the long, granite buildings across from historic Faneuil Hall were empty hulks for years. Now they're being renovated and developed for the upcoming Bicentennial, and will be a major tourist draw. So, yeah, it was a city I knew. I wondered what it would be like to know it differently, to know it, maybe, with Eu-meh. Now that would be an adventure. *Do you really believe you and Eu-meh can be together?* The memory of those words stung. They made me feel small. I didn't like it. Not a bit. But as I thought about his words, I realized there was one thing that would guarantee us not being able to make it together. If I kept my mouth shut about tomorrow. I had to tell Eu-meh what was going down. It would be a serious mistake for me to keep it from her until afterward, regardless of how things turned out.

The question for me was what to do about it. If I was right about Butterfly, then that changed things again. There's no way I'd walk away from Zhang.

That's what was on my mind when the familiar Malibu pulled up to the curb. Eu-meh smiled from the passenger seat before turning and saying a few words to Chou. He looked over and waved. If he was surprised, pissed, or annoyed that I was there he didn't show it. She got out of the car and stood at the curb until he drove off.

"Hey," she said. She leaned down, kissed me, and then sat by me on the step. "Lee is doing good. They're going to keep him overnight again and then see how he is tomorrow."

"That's good. Was he able to talk at all or was he out of it on painkillers?"

"He was kind of sleepy when I first got there, but then that's understandable. He had a hell of a night, didn't he? Then he perked up a lot. He said he was sore where the bullet went through but he didn't want to ask for any more meds right away. He said he was happy just to be able to talk."

"Opting for pain over medication? The guy's a Spartan."

"Yeah. Oh, he said to tell you that he's reassessing what he thinks of Westerns now."

"What?"

"My father told him the man who shot him was some Texan, so..."

That made me laugh.

"I'm sorry you couldn't go up to see him. They're pretty strict," she said.

"Not a problem. I'm just glad he's gonna be okay. I'll see him when he gets out."

Around then she took a look at what I was wearing. "What's with the shorts? You lose weight since this morning?"

"Just something I threw on without paying much attention. I was thinking of going into town and shopping for something else. Come with me?"

"Sure. I don't have any hours at the museum today and my grandfather told me to take today off from the restaurant."

So we made our way down Marlborough, through the Public Gardens, stopping for a few minutes to watch the Swan Boats, which, not surprisingly, brought back some mixed feelings for me. On the plus side, I don't think any of my friends have actually ridden them; it's one of those attractions that tourists go for more than locals. We moved on through the Boston Common, coming out by the Park Street T station. We crossed Tremont Street and headed down Winter to where it intersects with Washington Street and one of my favorite stores, Mickey Finn's. The place has everything, from jeans and jackets to sneakers to military surplus clothes and gear. I wasn't long finding a pair of jeans. I went into the changing room to put them on, and when I saw they fit without need for a belt I walked up to the counter to pay for them. There was some discussion about my still wearing them. The clerk didn't think I should have them on while he rung up the sale. Common sense prevailed. I shelled out the money and we headed out onto Washington Street.

Outside, Eu-meh asked me how things went with her grandfather in the morning.

"Yeah, that's what I need to talk to you about. We talked about a couple of things. But let's get some lunch first," I said. I hadn't eaten since my Dunkin's sugar feast. Eu-meh said she'd had a snack from a hospital vending machine but that was hours ago.

We went down Summer Street, turned right and went into the Chauncy Street Deli. We got a table toward the back and before long I was working on a ham and Swiss sandwich and Eu-meh was enjoying a Reuben. I had a coffee. She had tea.

I filled her in on most of what her grandfather and I had talked about. I skipped past the part where he said I had no future with her. What was the point? The Capulet-Montague argument could wait until this other business was over, too. I got right into the important stuff, that he'd set up a meeting with a Charlestown gangster to buy the stolen films, that I'd warned him it was a double-cross, and that he was probably walking into an ambush. I told her that I asked him not to go.

At first it was like she didn't even hear me. She just looked at me. Then she looked straight ahead, toward the door.

"What did he say? Did he say he will not go?"

"He didn't say one way or the other. But I think he still plans on doing this."

She put down her sandwich and wiped her lips with the napkin.

"We ... we need to go. I want to walk. Let's go."

I already had the receipt so I left a buck tip on the table and we walked to the register to pay. We backtracked Chauncy to Summer to Winter and into the Commons again, where she picked out a bench. We hadn't said a word since we'd left.

"Eu-meh, do you want to go down to see your grandfather? Maybe you can talk some sense into him. I'll come with you."

"I already know he won't listen to me. This is his business and nothing I can say will change his mind. I can't believe this is happening over some stupid fucking movies."

She got up then and began heading through the Commons, heading home. I got up and followed her.


She put an album on the turntable and went to the fridge as the playing arm moved over and dropped onto the first track. I recognized the guitar play instantly and knew she had put on Joni Mitchell's *Blue* album. This didn't bode well.

"You're not cracking open a bottle of wine, are you?"

She turned, a carton of chocolate ice cream in one hand and two spoons in the other. This reaction

I could support, and we were soon sharing it at the table.

"Jimmy, I know my grandfather brought you into this. I know that. But can't you do something? Anything? This gang from Charlestown? Do you know them? Can you talk to them?"

I told her that I knew the gang but had zero influence, plus the leader was himself under the gun —literally—from an even bigger gangster to do the double-cross.

"The only thing that will keep your grandfather safe is for him to just walk away," I said.

"And he won't do that."

"Isn't there anyone who could make him change his mind?"

She waved the spoon back and forth. "Nana might have been able to make him listen, but she's dead."

I reminded her that her grandfather has some history in matters like this, even if it was a long time ago.

"He could come through this okay. He is a pretty tough guy, from what I heard."

I wasn't telling her anything she didn't know, even if his gangster days did come as a recent revelation to her. I could tell from her expression she didn't like thinking about her wonderful grandfather having once been the Al Capone or Bugsy Siegel of Chinatown.

"So we can't do anything except wait to see if he's

still alive after this shit happens tomorrow?" Her voice cracked and I knew the tears would follow. How could they not? "Jimmy, I know why you told my grandfather you'd have no more part in this. And I know I sound selfish for saying this, but I was hoping you'd be able to do something."

I stepped up close to her and took her face in my hands. "Listen, Eu-meh, I can't make your grandfather not go and I can't make Mickey turn over the films to him for the cash and call it a done deal. I certainly can't do anything about Whitey Bulger. But I'm telling you now, if I'm right about what your grandfather is doing here, I'll do whatever I can to help him out. No matter what it is."

She looked at me with a mixture of confusion and hope.

"What do you mean? What do you think this is about?"

I handed her the phone. "Call your grandfather and let me talk to him. It'll just take a minute."

"You sure? You want to talk with him?"

"Go ahead. Call him."

She dialed the phone and exchanged a few words with someone in Chinese. Then she handed me the receiver.

"Mr. Zhang?"

"Yes, Mr. Lyons. Eu-meh says you have something to tell me."

I was going to feel pretty stupid and embarrassed if I was wrong.

"Anna May Wong."

There was nothing from the other end, not even breathing.

"Yes, Mr. Lyons. Anna May Wong," he finally said. "You are clever."

"Good. That's good. Thank you. I'll call you later."

He hung up.

"Anna May Wong?" Eu-meh said, the shock clear in her voice. "The actress? What's she got to do with any of this?"

"She's Butterfly."

"Oh, my God! First Edie Adams. Now Anna May Wong. I must have slept through my childhood. I mustn't have listened or asked any questions. For God's sake. How could I not recognize her in that photo?"

"C'mon. How many of us look at our parents' or grandparents' old pictures or mementos or care who their friends were? We just tune them out if they talk about 'the old days' because we figure the only things worth knowing occurred after we came along."

"Still. Anna May Wong," she said, shaking her head. "I don't know much about movies, but I know that she was the biggest Asian movie star in ... probably forever."

"I like to think I do know movies and actors from the old days," I said. "I should have recognized her in the picture at the restaurant. I didn't."

"But you'd heard of her, right?"

"Sure. I've seen a number of her movies, and I know that she was screwed over by Hollywood. As good as she was, she couldn't land a leading lady role, even if the character was Asian. Those were reserved for White actresses because there was probably a love interest with a White guy."

"Yellow Face," she said. "That I do know about. Just like they used to put shoe polish on the faces of White people to play Black roles, they'd make up Whites to look Asian."

There was no missing the contempt in her voice.

I thought of Lee J. Cobb as the Chinese war lord in the Bogart film *The Left Hand of God*, Marlon Brando as the Japanese interpreter in *The Teahouse of the August Moon*, and Mickey Rooney as I. Y. Yunioshi, the Japanese photographer in *Breakfast at Tiffany's*. Rooney's shamefully cartoonish character has to rank as one of the most racist depictions of an Asian in modern movies, a caricature in thick glasses, speaking pidgin English, who lusts after Audrey Hepburn's Holly Golightly. In Truman Capote's original story, Yunioshi is a serious, successful American magazine photographer—nothing like Rooney's buffoonish version. And what did Yellow Face casting mean for Anna May Wong and other Asian actresses looking to play lead roles? It often meant work for Myrna Loy. That is, unless the role was as a villain. Then Wong was just what the director was looking for.

"I swear, Lyons, if you ever do make a movie and

it includes any Asian characters, they goddamn better be played by Asian actors," Eu-meh said.

"I promise," I said. It was the easiest goddamn promise I ever made, and I goddamn meant it.

"Wait! These movies," Eu-meh said. "Does this mean that these movies everyone is trying to get their hands on are porn? You mean that Anna May Wong was in pornographic movies? Please don't let it be that."

I shook my head. "No. Not at all. I think your tough old grandfather, one-time Tong gangster, Chinese and American patriot, successful business-man, and friend to the stars, is trying to save some of the last and possibly most important work Anna May Wong did."

"I don't get it. What work?"

"Turns out Anna May Wong starred in a TV series called *The Gallery of Madame Liu-Tsong*. She played a detective who also happened to operate a bunch of art galleries around the world. I don't know a great deal about old-time TV, but I can safely say that her show would have been the first—and now that I think of it, the only—American TV show ever to have an Asian in the lead role."

"I never heard of it. It's embarrassing." She held her face in her hands. "Okay, but why is he saving these shows. Why risk his life to do that?"

There was no dodging the question. I told her the story I heard from Turk. I thought she might get upset that her dear old grandfather still had a place in his heart for an old girlfriend, even after years of marriage to the lovely Nana she remembered. She didn't. She found it romantic.

"So where does 'Butterfly' come into it? A pet name?"

"I don't know. You'll have to ask him. Now that you know this much, maybe he'll tell you."

"I want to love this story. It's beautiful in a way," she said. "But look at what he's done. And it's not only himself now, but other people could get killed."

"Yeah."

"You said you'd do what you can to help him now. Is it because Anna May Wong is in the films?"

"No, I'd already decided I'd try to help. I promised you that. But knowing his motivation makes it a lot easier. In fact, I like his motive."

"So what will you do? What's the plan?"

I shook my head. "I don't have one yet. I'm working on it."

# CHAPTER
# FIFTEEN

I decided that, no matter what, I would go with Zhang to the meeting. Meanwhile, I wracked my brain trying to come up with some plan that didn't end with either of us getting killed. Eu-meh had her own idea.

"Jimmy, I've been thinking. Here's what I think we should do." She was standing by the window. "If you know where and when this meeting is supposed to happen, I want you to call the police and tell them there's a drug deal going on. And I don't want you to be there."

"What?"

"It sounds too crazy to explain what it's really about. They might not even believe it," she said. "But a drug deal? Who wouldn't believe that?"

"That's a bad idea. Very bad. Cops showing up to disrupt a drug deal and arrest a bunch of people will come in armed to the teeth. Not just sidearms, but shotguns. Probably even military-type rifles. One dumb move and it'll be a free fire zone. And even if your grandfather is not killed, once he's arrested the cops and the DA will look deep into his background. His—"

"So, what of it?" she said.

"Think about it! His entire life will become an archaeological site and every illegal thing he ever did or was suspected of doing will be dug up, examined and publicized, until it erases any and all memory of the good he did."

"At least he'll be alive. I don't care what anyone says about him."

"He'll care. He's a proud guy."

The phone rang and I felt I'd been saved by the bell, at least momentarily. She picked up, said hello, then turned toward me with a dumbfounded look on her face. Without taking her eyes off me she said "Hold on, please." She held her hand over the mouthpiece.

"It's someone named Red. He says he needs to talk to you."

I took the phone. "Red? What's up?"

"Sorry to interrupt, man, but you need to call your mother. She's been calling me, asking where you are. I didn't want to give her this number—"

"Did she say what's going on? How'd she sound?"

"No, she didn't say anything. But she sounded frantic. Like I said, you better call her."

I hung up, told Eu-meh I needed to call my

mother, and tapped in the number. It felt awkward. It's like I was suddenly twelve years old. That passed as I had the terrifying thought that Mickey Ryan had done something to her or to Helen. Eu-meh was saying something, asking me what was going on and who was Red. I held the receiver away from me to give her a quick run-down, not realizing Ma had already picked up the phone.

A lot of us in Boston talk fast. We talk faster when things get tense. When I put the receiver back to my ear Ma's speech was the *rat-tat-tat* of a machine gun. *What's going on? Where are you? Who is that girl? Red lied for you last night and said you were at his place. Why? What's going on? Who is that girl.*

I told her to slow down. I told her again. Finally, I yelled into the phone. As soon as I did, I thought I must sound like an asshole to Eu-meh. What kind of guy yells at his mother? When she finally slowed down, her rapid-fire interrogation turned to tearful pleas. She begged me to come home. She said I was in danger. She said something about Uncle Barry being mixed up in bad things and that she didn't want me following in his footsteps.

"I buried your father, Jimmy. I can't go through that kind of pain again. If anything happens to you—"

"Ma, I don't know what you're talking about. Nothing's gonna happen to me." I found out the hard way that Connor knew I was into something, though how much and what his connection was to it I had no idea. But Uncle Barry? How did he come into this? "What did Uncle Barry say?"

"He said you're in trouble and that you could get hurt, or worse. He told me to warn you not to get involved with this Chinatown gangster. Oh, Jimmy, you're breaking my heart. Don't do this."

My jaw tightened at the thought of Barry scaring the shit out of Ma. If he's so fucking concerned he should come to me. And how the hell did he find out about Zhang?

"Ma, hold on. What did he say to you?"

"He said you were supposed to help a friend of his find a way to watch some old movies. Help him find a projector."

I didn't like what I was hearing. That I had planned, on my own, to approach Mickey to find out information was one thing. It was entirely another that my uncle offered me up to the dirt-bag to be a part of some criminal shit.

"A friend of his? I don't know any friend of his that I was supposed to help out. Ma, you sure that's what he said?"

She told me she understood him perfectly, that he was very clear.

"He told me he recommended you to a friend who has some old movies because you know about projectors and such. But he said you're now helping some Chinese gangster who wants to steal the movies."

Barry had done a lot for me over the years as he tried to be the father I lost. I owed him a great deal. None of that counted for anything now, and I wanted to rip out his lying, deceitful, traitorous heart.

"Ma, I think I should talk to Barry. He really is mixed up about this. Is he at home now? I'll call him."

"Are you sure? You'll call him now, Jimmy? Please call him now. I'm so scared." She started crying again.

She did her best to pull herself together after I said I couldn't call him until we hung up. When she finally stopped crying I ended the call and filled in Eu-meh about my uncle's connection to Mickey Ryan. I was pissed.

"Isn't anyone who they say they are? Turk, Uncle Barry—who's next? Am I gonna find out that my best friend, Red, works for Whitey Bulger? Christ! If there was anyone in Charlestown I thought I could trust with my life, it was my uncle."

Eu-meh had her arms around me again as I stood in the middle of the room, dazed.

"Collect your thoughts, Jimmy. Figure out what you want or need to say, and call him. Then put it behind you for the time being."

I waited about fifteen minutes before calling him. Suzie picked up. I liked her, and I had to wonder if she knew I had been played by my uncle.

Does that make her culpable? No, I decided. Her loyalty would be to him, even if he is an asshole.

"Is he there?" I asked.

"Hi, Jimmy. Yeah, he's here. I'll get him. He told me what he did. I knew he had done some kind of favor for Mickey, but I had no idea it involved you until a few hours ago. I'm sorry, Jimmy. He is, too."

"Let me speak to him," I said. I really didn't want to talk with her about it.

He got on the phone then, and I could tell he was nervous. It sounded like he had been crying. As if his tears were going to make a difference to me now.

"Feeling bad, are you, Uncle Barry?"

"Look, Jimmy, let me explain. All I did was suggest to Mickey he should ask you if you could lay your hands on a projector so he could watch some movies he got hold of. Some stupid fuck films that he thought he could sell, I think. But that's all. The next thing I know I'm hearing from Mickey that you're tight with some Chink and might be helping him."

"You don't know shit," I said. "All I told Mickey is that I didn't care who had the movies, that I wasn't gonna be part of any more bullshit. But, yeah, things have changed now."

"Don't be stupid, Jimmy. Why would you—"

"That doesn't matter now. What I want to know is why you put him on to me in the first place."

"Believe me, I wish I never mentioned you to

him. It's just that I knew he needed a good projector and I was short of money, you know. I needed a hundred bucks fast 'cuz I owed my bookie. When I said I knew who might be able to get a projector—"

"You rotten fuck. Do you know what you've done? You betray me, your own family, for a hundred bucks?"

He started crying. "I know, I know. It was wrong. It was fucked up. I ended up in the shit with Mickey over it, too. So it's not just you."

"What are you talking about? How are you any part of this?"

"Because when you couldn't get him a projector he wanted the hundred bucks back, but I didn't have it."

"So?"

"So he told me I had to pay it off by holding onto the van and those movies. I have it in the yard behind my house."

I couldn't believe what I was hearing. Barry had the movies all this time, parked in that shitty yard behind the Auburn Street house.

"Goddam it, Barry. What's wrong with you?"

"Just go home, Jimmy. Everything'll be fine. Mickey won't do anything to you. Just forget it. For God's sake, just don't help the Chink and every-thing'll be okay."

"It's too late for that," I said. "I'll help who deserves the help, and I'm gonna be there for the swap tomorrow. And you and I both know it's a fucking ambush."

"Don't. Don't you do this." He was really losing it now. He was choking on his tears and gulping for air. "I gotta be there with the van. You can't be there. Please ... I can't bear to see ... if it happens to you, too, I won't be able to live with myself. I can't live with myself if it happens again."

It was like a bomb went off in my head.

"What do you mean *happens again*?"

He said something but it was babble.

"What the fuck do you mean *again*, Uncle Barry?"

"I can't. Don't ask me that. Just don't, okay?"

"I am asking. And if you don't answer me now I'll drive the question into your head with a fucking hammer next time I see you."

He could barely form words and I thought he would just hang up. I felt something fall from my cheek and looked at the receiver. A fresh tear was running down the mouthpiece. *Great! Now you're crying.* I took a deep breath.

"Listen to me, Uncle Barry. What do you mean 'again'? Were you there? Did you see my dad murdered?" I couldn't believe I was asking that question, and to Uncle Barry of all people. His sob was an eruption and I knew the answer was yes. I never fought so hard as I did then to just stay on my feet.

"You better tell me. You tell me what happened or so help me God—"

"I'll tell you. I'll tell you, but not right now. Not like this," he said, then began to beg. "Don't take sides against Mickey. Whitey Bulger is gonna be right behind him, and he'll kill you and Mickey both to get what he wants. Just don't—"

"You watched my father die and you never said anything?"

"I'm sorry, Jimmy—"

"Did you kill him, Uncle Barry?" I was terrified of the answer.

"Fuck no! Of course not. I loved your dad. I love you, too, Jimmy. I'm so sorry. Forgive me. Please forgive me."

"But you saw him die." I thought of Brendan Connor. "You were there and watched that fucking guy pull the trigger and you did nothing? You said nothing?"

"Please. I never meant to ... I tried to be there for you ... afterward. Remember? Wasn't I there for you?"

I didn't want to say any more. I had no words. I held the phone out and just stared at it, hearing his sobs and broken words come out of the receiver, a pained ghost confessing sins from purgatory.

"I'll call you back. Don't call my mother again and don't call Mickey. Don't call anyone. You understand?"

"Okay, Jimmy. I won't. I'll stay here. I promise. I won't talk to anyone."

His voice trailed off and Suzie was back on the

line. She had also been crying. She must have been close to the phone because she talked as if she'd heard everything I said.

"I'll make sure he doesn't call anyone. If anyone does call, I'll pick up and say he's not here. He'll fuckin' listen to me now, or I swear I'll put him in the ground myself. We'll wait to hear from you. God bless you, Jimmy." She hung up.

I put the phone down. Eu-meh was next to me. She hadn't heard Barry but she'd heard every word I said. Tears ran down her cheeks.

"I ... that was my Uncle Barry..."

She nodded. "I heard. I heard the things you said. Oh, God, Jimmy, I'm so sorry." And she had her arms around me and I never felt so sick, so down and, at the same time, so grateful for her touch. We moved to the bedroom and lay there, just holding each other. Maybe a half hour passed as my mind raced back and forth, replaying Dad's killing at Montego Bay more than a decade ago and envisioning my own there tomorrow. *Is this it? Has it been coming to this all along? No, stupid! Get your head out of your ass and think of something. There's always something!* One crazy idea after another popped into my head. It didn't matter how stupid, at least it pulled me away from thoughts of my own death at Montego Bay. *Will I be left for the flies and maggots like Dad was? Will I be tossed into the Oilies?* The Oilies. What a place to end up.

Then I had an idea, one idea, that I thought could work.

When we untangled, I slowly got to my feet, looked at Eu-meh and smiled. "I don't know what I would have done if you weren't—"

"You were there for me. I'm here for you."

I straightened up.

"Right. And we've got to be there for your grandfather."

She shook her head. "Your mother is worried sick about you. It's okay to walk away from this. It's what you told my grandfather to do. It's good advice. It's the right thing to do."

"No. I can't do that."

"If it's because of us, that's okay. I'm not going to have my life choices dictated by anyone, not even my grandfather."

I loved hearing those words. If I wasn't worried about scaring her off I'd have told her then and there that I loved her. Too soon. Even I was smart enough to know that. It would have to wait.

"Glad to hear that. I don't want to lose you."

She got up from the bed and kissed me. It was delicious and I could have melted into her.

"Here's the thing," I said when the kiss ended. "I'm calling my uncle back. We're gonna talk and I'm going to see if he'll help us. Maybe he'll see that he owes me. Shit. He owes me big time."

"So you have a plan?"

"Yeah, get rid of the thing that everyone seems to want—"

"So that everyone goes away unhappy? But at least they go away?"

"Yeah, basically."

She said she liked the idea, but didn't believe a guy like Whitey Bulger would just go away. He'd want someone to pay in blood, she said.

"You're right. But if we can pull it off, do it right, it'll be Mickey Ryan who gets the blame. I'll be honest. I really don't care if Whitey goes after Mickey."

"Now that I know what those films are, I know it'll break my grandfather's heart to lose them. But I only care that he's alive when this is over."

"Yeah, I know."

Eu-meh left me in her bedroom to gather my thoughts before I called my uncle back.

Suzie picked up the phone on the first ring. She must have been right by it.

"Here's what we're gonna do," I said after Barry came on. "You're supposed to be driving the van with the films down there, right?"

"Yeah, Jimmy."

"Well, when you get there you're going to roll in like you're Mario Andretti on acid and—"

"Wait. What? I come in speeding like that and somebody's gonna shoot up the van. I can't—"

"Barry, listen to me. I don't give a shit. And you better not give a shit. After what I learned today—" I had to pause a second. "I don't wanna hear what you can't do. You understand me?"

He sniffled. I told him not to cry.

"Okay, whatever you say. Whatever you want, Jimmy."

"You're gonna make it seem like you can't control the van, and you're gonna drive it right into the water."

"Jesus, Jimmy. Into the fuckin' Oilies?"

"Yeah, into the Oilies. And you're gonna make sure the back door's rigged to open up because I want everyone to see those movies going into the water. That's the only way this is gonna end."

"What if I can't get out of the van? What if I bang my head and pass out?"

"Then I'll tell my mother you died a hero."

He got quiet for a moment.

"You sure there's not another way?"

"No. This is it. And if you don't drive that van into the Oilies, I'll do it myself. And if things go bad you'll have me on your fucking conscience, too."

Suzie was suddenly on the phone. "He'll do it," she said. "Count on it, Jimmy. I'll make sure he does."

"Thanks, Suzie. You're better than he deserves?"

She sighed. "Yeah, I know. But he's okay. Leastways, he will be if he does this."

"Good. Okay, put him back on the phone. I need to let him know how this has to go."

He listened. He didn't whine or sniffle or say

how sorry he was. He just listened, which gave me some hope. I was satisfied that he would do it.

I hung up the phone and then called Red.

"So what the fuck is going on, man? I'm hearing the craziest shit about you."

I told him I didn't know what he was hearing, so couldn't say what was true or not, but admitted that I was in deep shit.

"You gonna be able to get out of it or do you have to leave town? Come into the Army with me, why don't ya?"

"I don't wanna leave town. At least, I don't want to leave Boston," I said.

"Cuz of your Chinese friend? The guy who got shot?"

"No," I said. "His sister."

"Man, your life might be fucked up, but it sounds a lot more interesting than mine. How'd that happen?"

"Just did, I guess. Listen, Red, I need your help, and it could be dangerous. Like getting killed kind of dangerous."

I told him what was happening and what I wanted to do.

"Whatever. I'm bringing a gun, though, pal. I ain't walking into shit naked. And that goes for you, too. I'm bringing one for you."

"Sure, why not. Listen, I need you to meet me at my place in a little while, after my mother and Helen go out. And could you swing by and pick up my uncle on the way?"

"Yeah, sure."

"Okay, I'll call you back in a few minutes with the time."

So it was time to call Ma. I lied through my teeth. I told her I had a great talk with Barry and that he agreed he misunderstood what I was doing about those movies. I told her Barry and I would spend Bunker Hill Day at the corner of Bunker and Auburn. She was skeptical at first but came around. Finally, she got to the question she wouldn't let go of.

"Who's that girl you were talking to?"

Eu-meh walked back into the room and I looked at her as I answered.

"Her name is Eu-meh."

Eu-meh was close enough to hear Ma's voice.

"That sounds Chinese."

Eu-meh smiled.

"Yes, it's a Chinese name."

"Is she nice?"

"She is very nice," I said.

"Okay, well maybe you can bring her by sometime. I'd like to meet her."

"I'm sure she would like that. Listen, are you and Helen going to do the usual Bunker Hill Day eve at the carnival? Maybe we could see you there."

Ma sounded downright excited at the idea.

"You know, I think we will. I wasn't going to go

out tonight because I was so upset earlier, but I think we will. It would be wonderful if you came and brought your friend along."

"Okay, we'll try to do that. What time are you guys going down there?"

"After supper. We'll go down about five-thirty or so."

"That sounds good, Ma. Love you."

"I love you, too, Jimmy."

When I hung up the phone, Eu-meh was eyeing me like I was crazy. "We're going to a carnival? With all that's going on?"

"No. My mother and Helen are going to the carnival. I'm meeting Red at the apartment and I don't want either of them there."

"What about me?" she said.

"There's already talk going around about me working with a Chinese gangster against a Townie gangster. So it's not a good idea for you to be in Charlestown at the moment, especially the projects."

She laughed. "You think?"

"Call Chou and ask him to come pick you up and take you to Chinatown. See if your grandfather will tell you the whole story, now that you know the truth about these films and who's in them."

"Yeah, those are both good ideas."

I stepped close to her and kissed her. I didn't want to leave her, not for a minute.

"I'll call you here, later, with any news. But if

you're not here and it's urgent, I'll risk calls to the restaurant and your grandfather's place."

I called Red back with the meet-up time.


I was already in the apartment when Red and Barry arrived. Jump was with them, and I didn't think that was smart. It never occurred to me to tell Red not to bring him along. I just figured it was a no-brainer. Jump wants to be a cop, and here I was mixed up in criminal activity and getting Red involved in it. Sure, I might believe we're on the side of the angels, but the law wouldn't see it that way.

I gave a quick and dirty run-down of my plan so that Jump knew what he'd be getting into.

"But Jump, you know it's not a good idea for you to be involved. You know that, right?"

"Me?" he said. "You're on some kind of court probation or whatever and Red's supposed to be staying out of trouble so he can join the Army. If you guys can risk screwing yourselves, so can I, you know?"

We all laughed. "Okay, if you're sure," I said.

"Yeah, it'll be fine," he said. "I figure I think I can be a big help with some of it."

"Like what?"

"The parts that don't involve me being at the scene where you crazy fucks become targets of Townie, Southie and Chinatown gangsters," he laughed. "I'll help rig the van so that the movies fly out the doors like they're supposed to, and then I'll call the police to report a van going into the Oilies at Montego Bay."

That confused me.

"Look, you want the bad guys, whoever they are, to clear out of there fast, right?" he said. "Well, seconds after the van goes into the water you'll want to hear police sirens coming your way. You don't want to give Mickey, Whitey or the Chink time to wonder what's really going on."

I hated that word but I held my tongue. He was willing to help and his idea was a good one. Red seemed to pick up on what I was thinking though.

"Jump, *ix-nay* the *ink-chay* talk. Not cool."

Jump acted like he'd been smacked in the head. "What? You mean *Chink*? I can't say that now, either? Jesus, Lyons, this gotta be you. What's going on? I listen to you I'm liable to turn into a liberal."

"Not true, Jump. Maybe just the really, really good cop you want to be."

He seemed taken aback, unsure whether I was insulting him or praising him.

"Ah, you guys are fucked up," he said. "Let's get this show on the road."

A few minutes later we were all up at Barry's, where I again went over the plan, making sure everyone knew their part. Afterward, Barry and Jump went down to the yard to rig the van for the film dump. Red pulled a beer from the fridge and cracked it open. I wanted one, but I needed to make some calls first.

I called Ma and apologized for not getting to the carnival. She was a little miffed until I told her I was with Uncle Barry and that I'd be staying up at his place for the night.

"That's nice, Jimmy. But, umm, where's your friend, Eu-meh? She's not staying—"

"No, Ma! Of course not. It's just a guys' night. Red and Jump are here, too."

She was really pleased with that. She'd have a stroke if she knew what was really going on. I could only hope nothing would happen later that would bring one on.

Next, I called Eu-meh to let her know I'd definitely be there when her grandfather came to Charlestown to meet with Mickey. I didn't go into all the details but did say we had a plan. I told her I'd see her when it was over.

"What if I don't hear from you. What should I do? What should I think?"

"Just don't panic," I said. "It could mean things didn't go as planned, but you shouldn't assume the worst."

I asked her if her grandfather had said anything about the meeting. All she got from him is that he was going to have Chou and another man get to the meeting place very early. They'd stake it out from some hidden spot and watch to see what kind of trap might be laid.

We both got quiet for a few minutes, so I changed the topic, asking about Lee.

"He's doing really good. Chou and I went to see him. He's still a little tender around the wound but he'll be okay. His arm is in a sling, just like the guys in those Westerns he likes. So he's got that going for him. We think he'll be home in the morning."

"And your grandfather. How's he doing?"

She sighed. "He's got this energy about him, like something I've never seen. Knowing that Lee will be okay has lifted a great burden from him. But he's so focused on these films. He's determined to get them."

"Did he tell you anything about Anna May Wong?"

She laughed at that. "He said he knew her when they were both kids or, you know, teenagers, out in L.A., and that he wanted to stay there to be with her. But he couldn't disobey his parents and so came to Boston and married Nana."

"But he still carried a torch for Annie?" I joked.

"He said she always had a place in his heart, but that he did come to love Nana, and respect her. He said he never did anything to disrespect her or break the vows they took."

I told her that sounded equal parts sad and happy, but she disagreed.

"It is a good love story. He said Anna May was a rare beauty and a wonderful actress who deserved better than Hollywood gave her. Which is what you said. He saw those TV shows when they were on in the early '50s. He says the production sets were not super elaborate, but that Anna May's talent and dignity were evident even in—what did he call it —kinescope."

I was floored when she said that, recalling one of my earlier conversations with Zhang, when we talked about the kind of projector needed to view the films. He had to know that kinescope was 16-millimeter, and I'd told him that's what I had. He never said a word. He just smiled. The Shadow King wasn't giving anything away.

"Kinescope," I said. "Yeah, all those old, live-broadcast TV shows were recorded onto 16-millimeter film using a camera focused on a video monitor. Those were the copies sent out to stations around the country for rebroadcast. Ha! Sixteen-millimeter."

"Is that a big deal?"

I thought about it. Only for an instant.

"Not really. Just interesting."

We were quiet again. She reminded me that I said I would contact her as soon as possible when every-thing was over.

"Will do," I said. "Don't worry. Your grandfather will be fine." I could tell she was scared.

"You, too?"

"Me, too. Yeah."

# CHAPTER
# SIXTEEN

It was parade day, but my mind was hardly on the celebration. The morning dragged as we waited. We all went through the plan again.

"And the back of the van is all set to spill the movies?"

"Yeah, your uncle here did a good job. Especially good," Jump said. Uncle Barry shrugged, seemingly embarrassed by the flattery. "You're gonna love it. It's gonna work like a charm."

I don't know about the others, but I threw in a few hundred silent Hail Marys for good measure.

There was no question but that we were nervous. All of us, even future-cop Jump, had done some crimes in the past, but never anything like this. We headed out—me and Red to his Hell Trap II, Jump to his car, and Barry to the van.

"I was just thinking," Jump said before climbing into his Chevy Camaro. "Usually, we'd all be across from the Lexie gym about now, getting ready to watch the parade."

The parade had slipped my mind. From the look on Red's face, it had slipped his, too. The general silence told me that we all saw the possibility that everything could go haywire. Jump was anxious, not for himself, since he'd be waiting by a pay phone at Tully's Garage to call the police, but for the three of us who might shortly be in the middle of a gunfight.

"All set?" I asked. "Anyone got any questions? Now's the time to ask."

Silence.

"Anyone want to say a prayer?" Jump asked. He was serious.

"Yeah," Barry said. "In the words of Alan Shepard, 'Dear Lord, please don't let me fuck up.'"

"Works for me," Red said. "Let's go."


Our small convoy—Barry in the van, Jump in his car, and me and Red in the Hell Trap II—drove down Bunker Hill Street, which soon would be closed to traffic. For the last few days residents and store owners had been hanging out flags and streaming red, white and blue bunting across their windows. Today the national colors were in full bloom everywhere. People were setting up for the parade. Lots of little kids sitting on the curb, their parents and grandparents in beach chairs behind them. Teenagers milling about or walking up and down the street greeting family and friends they saw every day as if they hadn't been together in years. And even though it was Sunday and all the packies were closed, there was plenty of beer and booze around.

We turned left onto Polk Street and drove to the end, to Medford Street. That's where Barry pulled the van over. He'd park there until it was time to make his appearance at Montego Bay. I told him to start out at 12:40, ten minutes after the meeting time. I was hoping a little delay might put people off their game, so that when the van went into the water they'd just want to clear out. Barry looked scared but determined. Our two-car convoy turned left and a short distance down the street Jump pulled into Tully's. From there he'd see Barry drive past, wait three minutes and then call the cops. I was sure that whatever was going to happen would happen by then.

Red and I continued on until turning right onto Terminal Street. It was surreal. I couldn't believe I was going down there. I didn't want to, but there was no other way. I couldn't live with myself if I didn't try to pull this off.

It was 12:15 so we were early. We didn't spot Mickey or anyone from his crew. No sign yet of Whitey and his boys, either. I wondered where Zhang's guys were. We parked by the seawall. Barry would use our car it as a marker for where he should take the van over. We killed the engine and got out to wait. No one around as far as we could tell. It was Bunker Hill Day after all. Every right-minded Townie was getting set to watch the parade.

Then I heard my name called.

"Jimmy! Dude! You actually came."

I turned to see Chou and another guy heading our way. Red turned to me.

"Should I be worried? Are they on our side or, like, are we on theirs?"

I nodded. "Yeah, we're fine."

I introduced Chou and Red to each other and Chou introduced the two of us to Kang. Kang was a tall, rail-thin guy with a wispy moustache and goatee. If he was here, I knew he had to be formidable muscle. If I saw him on the street anywhere else, I'd guess he was a jazz saxophonist. Who knows. Maybe he's that, too.

"You been here long?"

"Couple of hours," Kang said. "Pretty sure we're the first at the party."

"Did you get dropped off or you got a car hidden somewhere?" Red asked.

"We got a lift here. Depending on how things go we might need a lift out, though. Can you oblige?" Chou said.

"Not a problem." Red told him.

Kang looked us up and down and asked if we were packing. We nodded.

"Good," he said, then laughed. "I mean, it's good as long as you're pointing them in the same direction we are if the shooting starts."

Another minute passed in silence, then I asked Chou whether Zhang would be coming or was he letting him handle the deal.

"He'll be here. But we all know this is not a genuine deal, right?" he said.

"Yeah, unfortunately," I said.

The minutes dragged, but at last my watch showed nearly 12:30. At the sound of approaching cars we looked back down Terminal Road.

"Well, here's *our* parade," Red said. "Only two cars."

They pulled in at odd angles, neither of them by the water or close to Red's car. Mickey got out of the front passenger seat of a red and black Dodge Challenger driven by Muggles. Walter climbed out from the back seat. Whitey arrived in a black, four-door Olds Cutless. Cautious and smart, he rode in the back but wanted his own door. He also had two people with him. Both looked experienced in all things criminal. If they gave off any vibe, it was cruelty, a characteristic Whitey was said to appreciate.

Mickey took one look at me and Red and shook his head.

"Fuck, Lyons! I thought you didn't wanna be here."

Whitey looked disgusted and impatient. "Hey,

Ryan, I thought you said the deal was that China-town was only gonna have two guys plus this Shadow King boss, or whatever the fuck he's called."

Chou and Kang looked at me, Chou mouthing the question *Shadow King? Later,* I mouthed back, and saw Chou and Kang exchange smiles.

"That's what we agreed to," Mickey said. "This ain't my doin'."

Red and me being there made everyone except Chou and Kang antsy. Mickey and his crew knew us, of course, so they knew we weren't Wise Guys or even farm-team gangsters like themselves. I think Mickey was more worried that Red and I being there made him look bad in front of Whitey. The Southie gangster wouldn't know us, so he might assume we were people to worry about. Or maybe he quickly sized me and Red up as novices. Which could be a good thing, I thought, because if things went bad he'd probably target everyone else first.

"Who are you?" Chou asked Whitey. He knew Whitey was going to be there, of course, but he was supposed to not know.

"I'm just an interested party. I was hoping to talk to your boss about buying these films off him." Whitey was trying to sound tough, yet friendly. Maybe he can do that in parts of Southie, where some still think he's Robin Hood. It didn't come across here.

"My boss has no interest in selling them, Mister

..." Kang said, leaving an opening for the Southie gangster to offer a name.

"You can call me Whitey," he said, then waited, as if to see how Chou and Kang reacted. When they didn't even blink, Bulger continued. "Nothing to lose hearing my offer, right?"

"The Shadow King will not be hearing any offers today," Chou said. "He made that very clear to us."

I couldn't believe Chou called Zhang the Shadow King. If this wasn't deadly serious, I'd have bust out laughing.

Whitey opened his mouth to speak but stopped at the sound of music. Not just any music. It was *Stars and Stripes Forever* and it was coming from the Oilies. I turned to see a sharp-looking boat all decked out in red, white and blue bunting and pennants, with a large American flag jutting out from the tail. It was headed our way, and as it got closer its unseen sailor DJ cranked up the music even louder.

"What the fuck!" Mickey said. He looked as dumb-struck as I'm sure I did. Whitey and his people were even more uneasy now but none of them raised a gun. We all watched the boat come toward us, waiting to see what would happen next. Well, not all of us. After stealing a glance at the boat Chou and Kang turned their eyes back on the other gangster crews. I knew then that this was not in any way linked to Bunker Hill Day. This was Zhang in his bridge-cruiser.

"This is funny," Red said. "A parade float that's really afloat."

"No, man," I said. "It's him. The Shadow King."

The boat was close to us now, maybe only fifty feet from the seawall. A guy dressed as Uncle Sam, complete with top hat, blue swallowtail coat, and red-and-white-striped pants—but with a full Santa Clause beard instead of chin whiskers—stood atop the roof, waving a small American flag with one hand and a Charlestown flag with the other. I didn't see Zhang anywhere. I looked at my watch. It was now five minutes to Barry. I had a sudden, panicked thought: Did Zhang find out I was going to have the films dumped into the Oilies? Is that why the boat? He was going to try and snatch them from the sinking van?

Mickey called to the boat. "Who the fuck are you?"

Uncle Sam signaled to someone and the music ended.

"What did you say?"

"I said, who the fuck are you?"

"Who do I look like? I'm Uncle Sam! Don't you know it's Bunker Hill Day!" The voice was familiar, but not in a reassuring way.

"Get the fuck out of here, asshole!" This, from Whitey. His guys took that as their cue to raise their guns to their chests, making sure everyone could see them.

From the boat's bridge, someone stepped onto

the deck wearing a brightly painted opera mask, the kind you'd find in Chinatown gift shops. I knew it was Zhang. The mask boasted a fierce face, much of it green.

"Hello, Mr. Whitey Bulger," he said, dropping any pretense that Bulger's presence was a surprise. "My original deal with Mr. Ryan, an exchange of cash for the films, will go down as previously agreed. It is not in your interest to interfere."

Bulger laughed. "I'm not interfering with anything. Like I told your boys, I just want a chance to buy the movies—after Ryan turns them over to you, of course." Whitey looked over at Mickey. You could see the contempt on his face. "So where are the fucking movies, Ryan?"

Mickey offered a shrug and put on a brave face.

"My guy is on the way with 'em," he said, not even trying to keep his voice down. "Don't worry. Screw the Chinks. We can take 'em all out if we hafta'."

Whitey shook his head. "How the fuck did you get this far in the business? You're an embarrassment," he said, turning to his crew. "Are we doing Affirmative Action for fuckin' morons now?" His guys laughed. Mickey's crew bit their tongues to not join in. But on the boat? In those few seconds of gang-related insult and distraction Uncle Sam went prone on the deck and pulled aside a tarp revealing a belt-fed machine gun that he aimed at Whitey and his crew. The laughing abruptly stopped and Zhang brought the boat up to the seawall.

"What the fuck is this?" Whitey shouted. His men didn't dare to move.

"When the films arrive, Mr. Ryan, you will have your men load them onto the boat," Zhang said. "Then I will toss you your money. Do with it what you wish. Take it, share it with your friend, Mr. Bulger, or give it all to him. I don't care. But interfere with me and you and your men, along with his men, will be dead."

As Mickey and Whitey considered their response there was a sudden and repeated blaring of a car horn. Barry was heading our way. *Don't fuck this up, Barry.* He was moving as fast as he could while throwing in a few swerves left and right, as if he couldn't control the steering.

"What the fuck!" Mickey said.

Everyone had a gun in hand now. Barry was yelling out the window. No one could pick up the words but it made for a good show, maybe even causing some shooters to hold off, at least for a few seconds. Then it turned toward the water.

"Stop that fucking van," Whitey said. But still no one fired. Not even Whitey. I couldn't see Barry in the cabin as the van came to a sudden, screeching halt only feet from the water. For an instant no one moved or said anything. I couldn't take my eyes off the van. *What the fuck! It's supposed to be in the fucking water. Goddam it, Barry!*

Barry jumped from the van, hitting the ground hard. "Don't shoot!" he said.. He waved his hands wildly in the air. "The van's gonna blow!" seemed to

The words were barely out of his mouth when the van burst into flames, its rear doors flying open and reels of burning film spilling out. Barry crawled further from the now fully engulfed van. "Don't shoot! Don't shoot!" he kept shouting.

I took a step and Red grabbed me by the arm. "You out of your mind? He's dead, man. I'm sorry but he's dead. These fucks aren't gonna let him live. And you go to him, you'll be dead too."

"It's Barry, Red. Jesus, man, he's my uncle."

"That was your man, Ryan. This is on you," Whitey shouted. Next came the sounds of car doors slamming as the Southie mobster and his guys made ready to roll. Whitey rolled down his window and called to Mickey. "On you, you stupid fuck! But don't worry. We'll catch up later."

The blood drained from Mickey's face.

And me? I was trying to keep myself together, waiting for a chance to get to Barry. I saw him moving again, trying to stand, and cradling his left arm.

"I'm sorry, Mickey," Barry shouted, "When I turned the corner back there, I smelled gasoline inside the van. I looked around and I saw something in the back, something that looked like a bomb. I panicked. I'm sorry."

I don't know if Mickey believed the van was

sabotaged or guessed that he'd been betrayed. At that point I don't think he cared. He pointed his gun at Barry, fired, and missed.

"You're dead, you motherfucker," Mickey shouted. Barry was crawling, trying to make his way to the opposite side of the van, out of the line of fire. Mickey went to fire again and my own gun hand was up and pointed at Mickey. I'd never shot anyone. My hand shook but I fired. I felt the kick but I'm not sure I even heard the report, as its sound was lost in a sudden burst of machine-gun fire. Mickey's arms flailed and he spun, pieces of him flying off before he collapsed in pooling blood. I turned toward the boat in time to see Zhang signaling to Chou and Kang to get to the seawall.

"Affirmative action for morons," Uncle Sam shouted from the deck holding the machine gun. "That was a good one!" He then tossed the gun onto his shoulder, turned and retreated quickly toward the rear of the boat. Zhang, standing again at the front of the boat, watched the burning reels of film. His mask was in his hand now. He looked crushed. After a moment he turned and went to the bridge.

Chou and Kang hadn't moved to the seawall yet. Chou asked me what I wanted to do with Muggles and Walter, who had dropped their guns and now stood with their arms spread and hands wide open.

"You guys finished with this? You gonna forget what happened here?" I asked, hoping they'd say yes.

"No problem, Lyons," Muggles said. "Mickey fucked this thing up big-time."

"Yeah, we're good," Walter said.

I told Chou to let them go, and he waved them off with his gun hand.

"You change your mind and we'll come for you," Kang warned them.

We all could hear sirens in the distance. Chou and Kang jumped aboard the boat, which quickly turned and headed out into the channel under full power. Muggles and Walter grabbed up their guns, jumped into their car, and sped off, leaving Mickey where he fell. Red slapped me on the shoulder. "Wipe the guns and toss 'em out as far as you can," he said, already in his best pitcher's stance. I looked at the gun.

"Can it be traced to you?"

"No, man, but there's a chance we could be picked up before we get out of here. If you got him with that one shot you fired, and that bullet is matched to the gun you're carrying, you'll be charged with that asshole's murder. No matter how many rounds Uncle Sam put in him."

I put the safety on and stuck the gun in my belt. Red shook his head but said nothing. We hustled Barry to the car and stretched him across the back seat. Seconds later we were screeching back onto Medford Street. I looked back at Barry. "Just lay there till we say it's okay to get up, okay?"

He grunted an okay of some sort, coughed a few

times, then sucked in a bunch of air. He continued to cradle his arm, which looked badly burned. "Fire was better, Jimmy. Drowned movies can sometimes be cleaned up."

I looked at him in the back seat, surprised by what he'd done. "Thanks, Uncle Barry."

Mickey's dead. One down, one to go. Or maybe not.

# CHAPTER
## SEVENTEEN

The parade had not yet reached the top of Bunker Hill Street when the ambulance arrived for Barry. Since Mickey's shot missed him, the only injuries he had were from the van fire. No need to anonymously drop him off at Boston City Hospital or Mass General. We figured the burns on his arm, which didn't look all that serious now, could be explained as a fireworks accident.

I left the gun in the car, which we parked on Medford Street behind the Bunker Hill pool park. We helped Barry up the stone steps and across the park to Bunker Hill Street. Then, Red stayed with him while I rushed to a corner store at Chappie Street to call an ambulance.

But not before I called Eu-meh. No answer at her place, so I called her grandfather's. I doubted she'd be doing a shift at the restaurant today.

She picked up on the first ring. "*Nǐ hǎo.*"

"*Nǐ hǎo,*" I said back. "It's me, Eu-meh. Your grandfather, Chou and Kang are all okay."

She took a deep breath. "Jimmy! Oh, God, I'm so glad you called. I was so worried. Chou called from the harbor to say it was all over and that everyone's safe, but when I didn't hear from you..."

"I'm okay. Me and my friends are all good. The van caught fire and my uncle got burned a little, and so I've got to call an ambulance for him, but I wanted to call you—"

"Oh, no! Chou didn't mention that! Okay, look—call the ambulance! I'll be fine, knowing you're alright now. Call me later or just come over as soon as you can. My grandfather and the others will be here any moment. Thank you, Jimmy. Thank you for doing this."

Being thanked surprised me. I wasn't sure what to say, so I just said, "Okay, see you soon," then hung up, plugged another dime into the phone and called police emergency.

The cops who showed up with the ambulance said nothing that suggested they thought Barry's injury was related to a burned-out van or a dead man on Terminal Street. It had just happened, so they might not even know about it yet. Later, some detective might try to put them together, but there'd be no proof that the burns were anything more than the consequences of a stupid fireworks accident.

"Aren't you a little old to be playing with fireworks," one of the cops said to Barry.

"It's Bunker Hill Day, officer," Barry said, then coughed. The crowd that had gathered to watch the scene laughed. Barry's answer seemed to satisfy the cop, though the police don't expect a straight answer from anyone in Charlestown anyway. A few minutes later the EMTs helped Barry into the ambulance and they were off to Boston City, sirens wailing and lights flashing. The cops went back to parade duty.

Red turned to me. "So, what's with holding onto the piece, Jimmy? You're asking for trouble you keep it."

"Maybe, but I might still need it." I wasn't sure what I should tell Red, but then decided he deserved an explanation. He'd stood with me every step of the way so far. "There's someone else coming after me, and—"

"Man, Mickey's fuckin' dead and his guys are scared shitless. And the Chinese gang seems to be on your side. By the way, I liked those guys. So, who's left to come after you?"

That, I didn't want to say. If I told him he'd feel obliged to stick with me and I didn't want that. He'd done more than enough already. Whitey Bulger was bad enough, but he wasn't someone Red was likely to run into on any given day in Charlestown. Someone like Connor.

"Never mind. Maybe I'm just paranoid. I'll hang onto the piece for little longer, then get rid of it."

I knew he was thinking it over, brainstorming

what he should say, or if he should say anything at all.

"Okay, if that's what you want," he mumbled, sounding guilty, as if he was doing something wrong. "I'm gonna go find Jump. I won't say anything about this shit, but I'll fill him in on what happened with Mickey. He'll keep that to himself."

Red kept talking, not knowing how to break off and walk away. I felt for him.

"I gotta get going, Red. I gotta find my mother and tell her about Barry's accident. Then I'm gonna go to Chinatown. Okay if I take your car?"

He nodded. "Yeah, no problem. Tell your Ma and Helen I said hello. Maybe you, me and Jump can meet up later or something."

"Right. That'd be good."

"Cool. And when you're done with the car, clean it out for me, would ya? Smells like burning rubbish in there now." He started walking away but turned back and stepped in close. "Listen, if you gotta use that gun, you use it. No fuckin' games. No talkin' or speeches like in the movies. Whoever it is, just drop 'em. No words."

For the first time, I wondered if, at some time in the past, Red had actually done just that. It didn't matter.

"I will. Thanks, man."

After he left I stood at the curb, one of thousands of people lined up along both sides of Bunker waiting for the parade to pass by. I could hear the drums and brass of the bands now. There'd be a Navy band for sure, and also an Army band. And the local brass, of course—the Majestic Knights.

Before long, the parade was moving past me. The military bands, floats from the local Boys and Girls clubs, the town's historical association, its merchants' association, local, state and federal politicians waving for votes in the next election. Some walked, others rode in convertibles. Then there were the Revolutionary War reenactors, marching in period uniforms, firing powder-loaded muskets into the air, and veterans of Vietnam, of Korea, of World War II. Locals wearing every kind of costume, from Frankenstein's monster and cave men to the Jolly Green Giant, the Pillsbury Doughboy and other commercial mascots marched and waved, cheering on the Townies cheering them. Hell, there were even belly dancers. A guy dressed as Uncle Sam and walking on stilts snapped me back to reality.

I left the crowd and headed back to the car. By now the entire parade must have passed the corner of Bunker and Monument streets, where Ma would have watched it. Helen was probably with her friends and, hopefully, staying out of trouble. Now was as good a time as any to face Ma and, well, lie about pretty much everything.

Back in the projects, people were already continuing the day's celebration by drinking out on the building stoops or on the steps around the incinerators. Lots of guys were walking along with a beer or

Solo cup-filled drink in their hands. Bunker Hill Day is always a great time, even if sometimes things can get out of hand as the day's partying spills into night.

I parked the car and went up to the apartment. I heard some voices inside. I took a breath, readying myself for my big song and dance. I opened the door and walked inside like nothing was wrong. That fake casualness lasted all of one step in the door, when I saw Ma and Helen on the sofa and Mary Connor in one of the armchairs.

"Mary?" I said, and looked from her to Helen and Ma. "What's going on?"

"Good to see you, Jimmy," Mary said. "Happy Bunker Hill Day."

"Thank God you're home," Ma said, her voice cracking slightly. Her eyes were red and some tears were still fresh. I glanced at Helen again. She had Ma's eyes. "What the hell's going on?"

"In a minute. One more person needs to be here," Ma said. No sooner had she spoken than I heard the toilet flush, the sink run and then the bathroom door open down the hall. Brendan Conner stepped into the living room. I could feel the gun tucked into my belt at the small of my back. It was covered by my shirt but I thought I could get it out fast if I needed to. I looked directly at Connor, right into his eyes, then looked down, seeing the red-and-white-striped pants. In an instant I knew I wasn't going to have to reach for the gun after all.

"Hi, Jimmy. How's it going?" the legendary killer said.

I looked at him, seeing a face I'd long known but now saw differently.

"Good. Surprisingly good," I said. I pointed to his head. "Where's your hat?"

He laughed. "I think I lost it in all the excitement of the parade." He stepped over to the kitchen, where he and Mary probably sat when they first arrived. When people in Charlestown go visiting, most tend to sit around the kitchen table. Sometimes that's where the whole visit will take place. There was a small bag on the table and Connor reached into it. "I have a hat for you, though." He pulled out an old, shamrock green porkpie hat. "I've had this for a long time. I think you should have it."

My head was swimming. I looked over at Ma and Helen again, and this time saw their tears were not from fear. Mary was crying, too.

"I think I know what happened," I said to Connor.

"You figuring stuff out again," he said, a smile on his lips. It was weird. I didn't think he could smile.

"Yeah. But if it's okay with you, let's talk about it out in the hall or up on the roof."

He looked around the room at Mary, Ma and Helen, as if asking their permission.

"I think that's probably best," Ma said. "Come back in when you're done."

Up on the roof I looked at the hat again. I felt Connor's eyes on me.

"You don't look scared and you don't sound angry," he said. "So what have you figured out?"

"Just now, when I realized that was you on Zhang's boat, and that you took out Mickey—not me or Red or Barry—I figured you never intended to kill me. The last time we were up on this roof together, I thought you were going to toss me off it? I guess I was wrong."

He laughed out loud, a single, unexpected act that seemed to exorcise the cold indifference I saw in his face on so many occasions on the street. "You bet your ass you were wrong. But the way I came across, I can see how you'd have thought otherwise. I was talking and acting like an asshole instead of just talking to you straight. Sorry about that."

"Why didn't you?"

"I don't know," he said, shaking his head. "Some things you keep silent about for so long that it doesn't occur to you to reevaluate the need for secrecy. It took everything that's happened in the past few days to make me see that. So ... sorry about that, too, kiddo."

I looked across the rooftops. Other people were sitting out, as well, sharing drinks, bullshitting and enjoying the hell out of what, to Townies, is like a holy day.

"It was Mary, wasn't it." It wasn't really a question. "That's why she tried to talk to me all those times in the past, when you told her not to, and why you made clear I wasn't supposed to talk to her. She was—" My own voice started to fail at the ugly imagery. "Mary was the girl raped down at Montego Bay. Dad went there to give money to a couple of detectives. And he saw what was happening and tried to stop it, and—"

"One detective, actually. Yeah, and he killed your old man," Connor said. "Your Dad saved my little girl's life. I'm sure the bastard would have killed her otherwise. But she got away."

"Why did you keep this secret? I don't get it. Me and Ma and Helen have lived for years with stories that dad was a snitch or tried to steal money from Punchy. And believe me, the story that he died trying to save some girl from being raped? That's the last thing people were likely to believe."

He sighed another surrender. "That's my fuck up again. Mary was near catatonic when I found her back home. Her clothes were all ripped. She was bleeding fr—" he stopped for a moment. "I don't need to paint a picture for you, do I? No." After taking a breath he went on. "I took her to the hospital. I knew most of the doctors and nurses at Boston City and they took good care of her. I was so out of my head with hate for whoever did this that I wanted to find him—or them, maybe. I didn't know who or how many at the time. But I wanted revenge in the worst possible way. And I thought, I stupidly thought ... I didn't want what happened to Mary to be put in a police report. In a public record." He was silent for a moment. "How fucked up is that? I investigated rapes as a cop. I told victims how important it was to find and prosecute the scumbags who raped them. But here I was doing the opposite. Jesus, kiddo, I've made a lot of mistakes."

I didn't say anything. He was on a roll.

"It was another day before Mary was able to talk. And when she did, she couldn't get past a few words before breaking down and crying. And that went on for hours. Little by little it came out. I knew about your dad being killed but it never occurred to me it had anything to do with what happened to Mary. Then she told me. Your old man was like family to us. Mary called him Uncle Ray. She told me Uncle Ray rescued her, but that he got shot."

I didn't realize I was crying until Connor handed me a hanky.

"Don't worry, it's clean."

"Sorry."

"Don't be. Even after all these years I ..."

We were quiet for another moment.

"She tell you about Uncle Barry?" I said.

"So you know about that. Yeah. She saw him in your dad's car as she was running by."

I told him how Barry broke down and told me about it.

"But he never said the girl was Mary, or anything about you."

"Not surprised. I told him I'd put him in the

hospital or the morgue if he ever spoke about it. Anyway, I got hold of him and made him tell me what happened. Not the friendliest of conversations. I punched out two of his teeth, dotted both eyes and maybe fractured a rib or two before I was satisfied that he was telling me everything."

"Did he know who the guy was?"

"Uh-huh, he did. Someone I'd known for years, even before I got on the force. I won't even mention his name. I haven't in all these years."

I thought about my next question for at least a minute before asking it. "What happened to him?"

"He went off to the Cape the weekend after all this went down. Ended up eating a bullet from his own gun in a motel room."

"What?"

"Yeah, happens with cops sometimes."

The silence that followed told me, or confirmed, what I suspected. I'll be honest. It's what I would have expected of Brendan Connor, badge or no badge.

"A few weeks after that I left the force," Connor said. I knew from his tone he'd say no more about that.

I then asked the question I'd wanted answered for years. I asked him what he said to my mother that night he came over and gave her an envelope full of cash.

"I told her what happened. That a cop raped my daughter, a girl your Ma loved like she was her own, that her husband died trying to protect Mary, and that her dear brother witnessed the murder and did nothing but keep his head down and stay in the car. Jesus, when I think about it—hearing all this in the course of a minute or two—I don't know how she stayed on her feet."

"So she knew? All these years, she knew?" I didn't know how to feel about that. Angry? I ought to have been. But then I thought of what an awful hell it must have been to live for years with those stories of her husband, and not be able to tell what she knew. I let it go. Just like that. She was Ma.

"I asked her not to go to the cops because I was gonna take care of it," Connor said.

"And the money?"

"I took it off Barry. It was the cash your dad was supposed to give to that animal. When your dad saw what was going on, even before he knew it was my Mary, he jumped out of the car. Flaherty must have forgot about it, too, after killing your dad. He took off without looking in your old man's car— which is probably why Barry is alive today. Anyway, I knew your Ma was gonna need cash so I gave it to her."

Connor looked at the porkpie hat I was holding.

"Your Dad left his hat in the car, too," he said. "After I got through talking to your uncle, I took the money and the hat from him. I wanted to keep this stupid hat. A reminder of a good friend. The man who saved by little girl. After all this today, I want you to have it. Along with the truth about what happened."

"And Barry? Did you ever do anything more—"

"No. Well, yes. That is, I laid down the law to him. My law. I told him he needed to step up and be there for you, your sister and your mother. But especially you, because being a boy you'd be more likely to get into shit. Tell the truth, I think it did as much good for him as for you. He straightened his own life out some. Well, until recently maybe. But he took his new responsibilities seriously. Made sure to get all those things you needed, or thought you did. The boxing lessons were my idea. I insisted on that. Give him some credit, though. When regular school became a problem for you, it was his idea to step in as your official tutor of record or whatever ... teaching you high school-level math and English, and dragging you around to museums and historic places. How he pulled that off with the city, I don't know, but he did."

"Well, I think I can appreciate that now more than ever."

"When he told me you were interested in movies I was able to pick up some equipment for you on the cheap. For a while, one of my beats had included the theater district and I had some good connections with a lot of them. Also, with the exchanges, film supply people and whatnot."

I looked up like I'd had cold water dumped on my head.

"For fuck's sake!"

"What?"

"Did you get me that job at Empire? Do you know Turk? And Zhang?" I asked. "Jesus Christ! I breezed into a job at the Arte House in Cambridge last year. Was that your doing, too? Have I been under surveillance my whole fuckin' life?" The idea that so much had been done for me without me knowing? I didn't know what to feel. Was it all manipulation? Should I be pissed? Or grateful that a couple of people who felt bad about my father's murder were looking out for me?

Connor shook his head. "You know, I thought this—what we're doing here now—would be a long overdue talk that would make us both feel better. I don't know about you, but I feel like I'm learning what a real shit I am."

That made me laugh. Connor continued.

"Okay, I made sure you heard about the summer job at Empire, and I put in a word with Turk to recommend you to his boss. I didn't have to ask for you to be rehired there. They liked you. Turk especially. He says you're a good worker. As for the Arte, I asked a cop friend who knows the owner if he could help out. He did. The only fuck-up there was that your boss forgot to tell *you* during the interview that it was only a six-month gig. He told my friend that."

"How about Zhang?"

"I know Zhang a bit. I haven't been in touch

with him for years, but when Turk told me what was going on I asked to meet with him. Turk arranged it. He's an interesting guy, Zhang is. Colorful background to say the least. Anyway, once I convinced him that I was only out to keep you safe, but would do whatever was necessary to keep him and his people safe, too, he brought me into his plan."

"But a machine gun?"

"Wasn't mine. Zhang had some connections that could lay their hands on an M-60, but none of his guys knew how to use it. I didn't need an instruction manual."

I told him that Mickey was left on the ground when everyone split, and asked him if there was much the cops would get out of examining the body or the overall scene. He just shrugged.

"Unless Ryan had a note in his pocket saying he was going to a meeting of gangsters and named everyone who was gonna be there, I don't think they'll find anything that links any of us to what happened." He paused for a moment, shook a cigarette loose from a pack of Camels and lit it up. "Tell you the truth, I don't think they're gonna care much."

It may sound cold but I was glad to hear that. I was finally out from under Ryan's ugly, vindictive, double-crossing thumb in every way. The only thing better than that was feeling the shame and hurt I'd been carrying since I was a boy fall way, expunged like a wrongful conviction.

"Any other questions?" Connor asked.

"Yeah. Harry Hollywood. I'm guessing you didn't kill him after all. So what's the deal? Is he okay?"

"Ah, Harry's fine. He's not really a bad sort. I've helped him get some of those movie jobs he loves so much, and he was good enough to call me when he heard Mickey had roped you into his bullshit scheme."

"So why the rush to the Cape? All I could think was—"

He put his hand up. "I know what you thought. I went down because Harry stupidly opened his mouth about the films to a guy he was sucking up to, so he could get his brother a job on the set. That guy took the information to one of the production company's lawyers, who dragged Harry in for a talk, then made some phone calls. The lawyer figured out what these films were and who wanted them back, then started putting pressure on Mickey for them."

"Mickey told me about the lawyer. He said he wasn't going to give him anything."

"I wouldn't think so, not with Whitey breathing down his neck for them. But my concern was you. I didn't want the police sniffing around this as long as you were involved, so I went down to have a conversation with the lawyer."

"How'd that go?"

"You never heard any more about the lawyer, did you?"

"No. Nothing."

"Then I guess it went okay."

I decided I'd simply accept that Connor talked the lawyer out of trying to get the films.

"Okay, one more thing about Harry. Why wasn't Mickey able to get in touch with him all those times?"

Connor let cigarette smoke out through his nose, then chuckled.

"Because Harry was fed up with his shit. Just didn't want to talk to him."

We started heading for the hall stairs when Connor tapped me on the shoulder.

"Why don't you give me that piece tucked away at your back and I'll get rid of it for you."

Back downstairs all eyes were on me as we came through the door. There were no tears now. Ma, Helen and Mary looked relaxed. They looked happy. As if this were a normal Bunker Hill Day—maybe the best one for all of us in years.

"You had the talk?" Mary asked her dad. He nodded and she turned to me. "All those years? First when I seemed to be stalking you? And then just embarrassed you with some, I don't know, over the top hellos maybe? I'm sorry about all that."

"That's okay, Mary. It was nothing. I guess I did blush sometimes and my friends liked to rib me about it, but..."

"So many times I wanted to tell you, to let you and Helen know what happened. So you'd know your dad was a hero." Her face was wet with tears again as she got up and walked over to Helen, bent and kissed her on top of her head. "Thank you for your dad," she said. Then she came over to me and kissed me on the cheek. "Thank you for your dad."

To say I was stunned would be an understatement. I was that and more. I was afraid to speak. I was proud of my Dad and ashamed at what I had thought of him for so many years.

Helen rushed over and hugged me. "Did you hear that? Daddy was a hero," she said before going into full balling mode. I was afraid I was going to follow. Nothing is worse than seeing your baby sister cry. No matter the reason.

I put my hand out to Connor.

"Thank you, Mr. Connor," I managed to say.

"You're welcome, Jimmy. You call me Brendan now that you know I'm not going to toss you off a roof."

"What's that?" Ma said.

"Nothing, Ma. A joke between me and Dad's best friend."

The talk became easy and light. Connor told stories about my dad from the old days. Funny stories. Not even a misdemeanor came up.

After a while I called Eu-meh from the phone extension in Helen's room. When I didn't get an answer I called Zhang's apartment. No answer there, either. The restaurant was the only other place I could think of and so that's where I called next. It rang twice and Lee picked up. He sounded good, and I'm sure part of that was seeing his grandfather, Chou and Kang all come back from Charlestown in one piece. He sounded quite pumped about what happened but he kept his voice down, as if he didn't want anyone to hear him.

"What did you think of the boat, man?" he asked.

"The Uncle Sam boat?"

"Yeah," he said, and gave a stealthy laugh. "That was my idea. I told *Yeye* that if he did up the boat all patriotic-like they'd get closer to the seawall before anyone got wise that they were up to something. Kang said it worked really well."

"It did. But with all the guns and the possibility of a bloodbath it was hard to appreciate the tactic at the time. Is Eu-meh there? Can I speak with her?"

Lee's tone changed. "This isn't a good time, Jimmy. We're all together, the family, I mean, and a bunch of friends. I gotta tell you, my grandfather's not too happy with you. He told us what happened to the movies."

"Yeah, right. I can explain that. Is Eu-meh there?"

"Like I said, now's not a good time."

"Don't give me that," I said. "Tell her I'm on the phone and need to talk to her."

There was the rattle of the receiver finding the cradle, then silence.

Fuck that!

．．．

Within minutes I was in Red's car, headed up Lowney Way toward City Square. It was all I could do not to gun it. Being stopped for speeding would only be the start of trouble. Never mind not having an inspections sticker. One whiff of the inside of the car and I'd be sitting in a police station waiting for a public defender.

I was soon on the expressway. Traffic was light so I made at the Chinatown exit in good time. I got off the ramp and a few turns later I was parked outside House of Dragons. The place was not open for business yet. Too early. I rapped on the door. No response. Okay, rap again. The fourth time was the charm. None other than Chou opened the door. He nodded a hello.

"Didn't expect to see you over here, dude. Lee said he talked to you on the phone and told you to hold off on coming by for a while."

"Chou, this is bullshit. After everything that's happened, after what we did today, basically together, you guys are gonna keep me out? You know how fucked up that is?"

He stepped outside and closed the door behind him. "Look, man, I'm sorry about this, but my uncle made it clear that you're not welcome here. Not today and not ... not for some time. Sorry."

I knew my chances of pushing Chou out of the way and getting through the door before he picked me up and hurled me into the street were between zero and no-way.

"How about Eu-meh? She doesn't want me here either? At least let her know I'm out here."

Chou nodded. "I can do that. If she wants to come out, that's fine with me. I have no problem with you, dude. You showed yourself loyal to Uncle Zhang today, even if he doesn't know it yet. Loyal to me and Kang, too. Hang tight a minute." Then he was gone back inside. I knew that when Zhang laid eyes on me it would be uncomfortable at first, but that wouldn't last. Not once I explained things. The problem was getting in to see him. Crap. This was supposed to be the easy part.

It was probably just a few minutes since Chou went back inside but it seemed longer. I walked over to the car and popped the trunk. Man, it smelled.

The restaurant door opened again and Eu-meh came out and ran over to me. The kiss was sweet. The kiss was welcome.

"Thank God you're okay," she said.

"I tried to call you but Lee—"

"I know. He told me. I told him he's on my shit list now."

"I need to see your grandfather."

She shook her head. "Absolutely not. We're going to have a special dinner in a little while and use that time to relax and get past what happened today. You coming in now would be—" She stopped and waved her hand in front of her face. "Your car smells like bad barbecue! What is that?"

I gave her my best smile. "Among other things, Uncle Barry and burning sands."

"You're weird, Lyons."

"I've heard that, yeah."

When we stepped into the restaurant all eyes turned to us. Well, mostly to me—the uninvited skeleton at the feast. Even people who hadn't seen me before seemed to know who I was. My reputation preceded me, I guess, and if they got it from Zhang it wasn't a good one. I spied Lee looking very pissed, Chou looking amused, and Kang whose eyes moved from me to the kitchen, looking concerned. It was like a scene from some Western movie, and I was the guy walking into a saloon where he's not wanted. All that was missing was festive music from a tinny piano coming to a dead stop.

Zhang was nowhere to be seen at first. Then he came out from the kitchen. He was wearing a full-length apron and carrying a tray of appetizers. I could only think he was doing some of the cooking himself as a way to get his mind off what happened in Charlestown. If he was curious as to why the room fell silent so quickly it was only for an instant. He saw me and quickly but quietly placed the tray on the nearest table.

"Mr. Lyons," he said. After drilling me with his eyes he turned to Eu-meh. I had no idea what was going to happen next and wasn't going to wait and find out. I held up a single-reel film case I took from the trunk of the car.

"Mr. Zhang, this is *"Burning Sands,"* the fifth episode of *The Gallery of Madame Liu-Tsong.*"

Zhang sat down at the table. I'd seen him calm, angry, determined and, when the van exploded into flames, despondent almost to the point of broken. Now I was seeing him confused.

"You saved one, Mr. Lyons?"

"No, sir. All of them. The rest are out in the car."

Zhang stood up. He looked around the room at everyone, then said something in Chinese. I caught only 'Anna Mae Wong' and 'Liu-Tsong' but that was enough so that I got the gist. There was a general gasp and sudden applause, and maybe for the first time I didn't feel like an idiot or a bum in front of Zhang. I caught Chou's eye and motioned him to come over. He did, and I passed him my car keys. I told him there were another nine film cases in the trunk, if he wouldn't mind bringing them in. I also asked him if there was a safe place off the street to park the car, because it smelled like a fire sale and didn't have an inspection sticker.

"It's really ripe to be towed and Red might have to answer some serious questions," I said.

Chou laughed, then signaled to Kang and two other guys and they all headed out.

I looked back at Zhang to see him staring, waiting to get my attention. He said something in Chinese to me.

"What? I don't understand."

"He says, 'young man, you're full of surprises.'" The voice came from behind me. I turned to see Turk.

"I'm not the only one," I said when I found my voice again. "There's so much to talk about, Turk. I never knew—" I stopped, and started again. "I'm sorry for what I thought of you. I thought—"

He cut me off with a wave. "Relax, kid, we're fine. If the situation was reversed I'd have thought the same thing. I might even have asked Zhang to have you whacked before learning I was mistaken."

"What?"

"Just kidding," he said and smiled. "You did good, Jimmy, real good. This night is yours now as much as Zhang's."

"Thanks, Turk."

"Sure thing. Don't be late for work tomorrow, okay?"

When everything was ready to be served I was given a seat next to Zhang. I felt like I'd been invited to the Round Table with Arthur. Eu-meh was next to me on the other side and Lee—now officially *off* her shit list—next to her. Chou, Kang and Turk were directly across from us. There was no menu but there were dishes I'd never seen before, dishes that most non-Chinese wouldn't even know to ask for. This was Chinese New Year, Christmas, Thanksgiving and Bunker Hill Day all in one.

When the dinner was over Zhang led me, Eu-meh, Lee and Turk over to his personal table, where he asked me to tell him how I saved the Anna May Wong films from the fire. He had seen the burning film reels spill out of the van.

"I had Red, Jump and my uncle meet me over at my apartment yesterday, when my mother and sister were out at the Charlestown carnival. We grabbed up a dozen or so reels of my own film, brought them to Barry's place, and swapped them out for the Anna May Wong films. I was able to eyeball the titles using a magnifying glass, so I wrote the name of each episode on its film case."

"I don't know what to say, except thank you, Mr. Lyons. I am truly grateful."

Eu-meh put her hand on my shoulder.

"You mean you sacrificed some of your documentary footage? Jimmy, I—"

"It's fine, Eu-meh. The bridge, the projects, the Bunker Hill Monument and the El tracks are all still there. The El for at least another year, I think. I can reshoot them. But those," I said, nodding to the film cases stacked on a nearby table. "I couldn't let them be lost. I was glad to do it. I'm glad your grandfather rescued them in the first place."

We all looked at Zhang, who raised his hand to indicate the wall photo that included Edie Adams.

"Edith called two weeks ago to tell me these shows, and every other reel of film in the DuMont archive in New York, were in danger of being lost. She said the company was being sold, yet no one wanted to bear the costs associated with keeping and maintaining the film library. A lawyer, she was told, assured everyone involved in the negotiations that he would 'take care of it."

Turk shook his head. "When a corporate lawyer says he'll take care of something..."

Heads nodded around the table and Zhang picked up his story.

"The night I had these rescued, as Mr. Lyons aptly put it, they were scheduled, along with more than twenty thousand hours of other programs, to be hauled by tractor trailers to a dock in New Jersey, loaded onto a barge and taken out past the Statue of Liberty and dumped into the bay. But I arranged to have *Húdié*'s series smuggled out of the building in unmarked cases before that happened."

"So everything else produced for DuMont is gone?" I said.

"Jackie Gleason secured copies of his own show, probably long before this criminal destruction was planned," Zhang said. "He was always able to read the tea leaves. There may be others who rescued their work, as well, but I don't know."

"Why would the company dump all those shows? It makes no sense," Lee piped in.

"It does if you're only interested in the money and not the culture or history," Turk said.

"Assholes," Lee said, a remark that brought a quick rebuke in Chinese from Zhang.

"*Duìbùqǐ, yéyé,*" Lee said.

281

I know an apology when I hear one.

Zhang made a small motion to Chou, who nodded, turned and rounded up several volunteers to follow him into the kitchen. They returned with trays of champagne-filled glasses and made the rounds to ensure that everyone in the room who wanted one had one. Then Zhang went over to the center of the room and raised his glass.

"To Jimmy Lyons, his Uncle Barry, Red Whelan and Billy Jumper—good men of Charlestown who saved the wonderful work of Wong Liu-Tsong—Anna May Wong," he said. Our names were repeated and everyone drank.

"To Anna May Wong," Eu-meh said as she raised her glass.

Lee, all of sixteen, raised his glass then.

"To the Shadow King of Chinatown!" There was dead silence. I looked around quickly. Some people were visibly uncomfortable, a few perplexed, but a good number were smiling. Every eye turned to Zhang, who nodded to his grandson and smiled. "Thank you, Mr. Van Cleef."

Eu-meh was right. The old guy did have a sense of humor.

Zhang came over to me. He was smiling. "A private word, Mr. Lyons." He'd already thanked me for the films, so all I could think was that he wanted to talk about Eu-meh. It wasn't a discussion I wanted to have then. Everything was going well and I didn't want to ruin it with a debate over whether I could see her or not. Turns out, it wasn't that.

"I want you to know that I intend to honor our arrangement," he said. "I am going to give you the two thousand I promised for information that led me to recover the films. In addition, since you actually rescued and brought them to me, I am going to give you another five thousand."

"I don't know what to say, Mr. Zhang. And to tell the truth, I don't feel right taking the money from you. It's not about that anymore." Still, one voice in my head was telling me to take the cash while another was making it clear I didn't want to come across as a mercenary in doing something for Eumeh's grandfather.

"Whatever it is about, and I suspect I know, accept this as a heartfelt gift. I would be honored if you will do so. A good film school will be expensive, Mr. Lyons."

And so I accepted with a simple thank you.

At some point Chou hung a sign on the door outside, stating the restaurant would be closed all day and evening. I called Ma to let her know not to expect me home until the morning. She didn't ask a single question. I think she was still walking on air after more than a decade of pain she could never speak about. I also called Red to let him know the Hell Trap II was safely stored and that I'd get it back to him tomorrow, all freshly cleaned.

"What about that other thing you thought you might have to do?" he said.

"It's all good, man. It's better than I could ever have imagined. I'll fill you in tomorrow."

The time passed quickly, too quickly. I don't know how many times I was asked to retell the story about swapping out the movies. But it was a lot, I know that. The restaurant shades were down and the curtains drawn. But I could sense it was twilight. I looked at my watch. It was after 8:30. The sun would be down by 9:00. Zhang told me I would be a guest at his home for the night. Who was I to say no? Eu-meh was staying, too, but I was under no illusions that Zhang was going to look the other way if we tried to stay together. That was fine. For now.

I took a seat by the window while Eu-meh was having her own private chat with her grandfather. I pulled aside the curtain and pulled the shade away from the window so I could look down the street. Being Sunday, it was generally quiet, though other restaurants were open up as well as a grocery store. It occurred to me that I don't know *squat* about anyone in my family beyond a grandparent or two and some family names I'd heard mentioned now and then when I was a kid. Now, knowing that the Irish were among the parade of ethnic groups who made this section of Boston its own at one time, I wondered if any of my people—the Brodericks, Hurleys, Allens, Breens, and others lived here before finding their way to Charlestown. Perhaps. It made

Chinatown different for me now. It made it a living, breathing place where generation after generation of people from Europe, the Middle East and Asia found a home and work after arriving in the country with little or nothing. Turk proved a great teacher of local history. I looked out onto Beach Street and wondered which of the old buildings might have housed some ancestor. *Geez, Lyons, are you feeling something profound or is the beer, champagne and that baijiu stuff Zhang served up?* Whatever it was, I knew I was feeling better than I had in a long time.

I thought of Ma, realizing how happy she must be now. With all that weight off her shoulders because Helen and I at last knew the truth about Dad. He was never a perfect guy, but no one is. He broke some laws now and then but, then again, who hasn't? And he died saving Mary. Even knowing the truth about Barry was easy to get past now. Even if he did have some early encouragement from Brendon Connor to watch out for me, he did it. And he went above and beyond today when he risked his life to make sure our deception succeeded. And all things considered, he did a pretty good job.

I wished he, Red and Jump were with me at the restaurant. They'd have loved it. In a few months Red would be in the Army and Jump at the Boston Police Academy. And Barry? Probably back behind the bar at The Brig and, if he's lucky, still with Suzie. I hope so. It occurred to me that, with all this behind him now, he might be a different person. Maybe he'll do something with that degree. Whatever, those guys stood by me under circumstances that a lot of people would have taken a pass on. When things were about to be at their worst, believing they were getting into something that could put them on the business side of Whitey Bulger's gunmen, they didn't balk. Sure, Jump put some physical distance between himself and the ill-fated Montego Bay money-for-movies swap-and-shooting-match, but that didn't change the fact he helped out. If he can get his head out of ass and also keep it out of a white hood he'll be a good and decent cop. The town can use a few. People might even start talking to them. And Red? There's never been a more loyal friend. Charlestown's loss— my loss—will be the Army's gain. Well, the commercial says *Today's Army wants to join you*. Maybe Red will end up running it.

I wondered, too, if Harry Hollywood got his brother a job on the Cape film lot. Doubtful. And a bummed-out Potato Head will probably look for sympathy from Helen. Better be all he looks for. Hopefully, Harry's loose lips didn't sink his own periodic gigs with visiting film productions. I read in *Variety* not long ago that there's talk of a new movie about the 1950 Brinks heist in the North End. That'd be a film he'd love to get in on. I thought about Mickey, too, but not for long. Whitey was right about one thing: Mickey climbing up the crime ladder as far as he did was nothing short of a miracle. Muggles, who's a lot smarter than his now dead boss, will probably take over Mickey's drug business and crew, or maybe look for a better boss elsewhere. I have no doubt that Walter will follow where Muggles leads.

I finished off another shot of *baijiu* and was pondering getting another when Eu-meh sat down next to me.

"Hello, shweetheart," I said.

"A little drunk?"

"Nah, I was doing my Bogart impression."

"Ah, okay. I think you're gonna have to work on that one." She smiled and my whole world lit up.

"You've been in deep conversation with your grandfather. Anything I should know?"

"Yes," she said. "I found out why he called Anna May Wong Butterfly." I could tell by her voice that she was in tease mode. She knew what I wanted to talk about but wasn't going there yet.

"Turns out that her birth name was Wong Liu-Tsong."

"Yeah, the same as her TV character. I only learned that when your grandfather made the toast. She must have been an incredible lady."

"Definitely," Eu-meh said. "It also turns out her birth name was interpreted to mean Second Daughter Yellow Butterfly. Grandfather, young and in love as he was, simply decided to call her butterfly, which in Chinese is *húdié.*"

"I can't say I understand how the interpretation works—with *húdié* not being part of her given name

—but I love it anyway," I said. "So, you got any other news?"

"Like?"

"How did it go with your grandfather? After today, or tonight I guess, will he still like me? More importantly, is he going to insist I look elsewhere for a girlfriend?"

She laughed. "To be honest, he has his doubts that we'll last. He says the cultural and racial differences will prove too big a hurdle for us. But he won't interfere."

"I don't want anything to come between us."

She gave me a kiss on the cheek, which was as intimate as it was going to get at the moment, and smiled again. "Then we're on the same page."

"What I did today, and everything that's happened this past week? I'd go through it all again in a heartbeat. It was all worth it to be here with you now, and to know your grandfather is okay with us being together."

"I would have kept seeing you anyway, but I'm glad to have his blessing. And you did help him, so—"

"I don't think that's why he's okay with us seeing each other."

"Then what?"

I looked over at the bar. "Hold on one second," I said and got up. I went over and came back with two more shots of *baijiu*. I handed one to Eu-meh.

"I think that what happened this week reminded

him what it was like to be young and in love, only to be ordered across the country to marry someone else because of culture, of tradition."

"You think so?"

"You said it yourself. It's a story you want to love because it's romantic."

I raised my shot glass. "To Anna May Wong."

"You really are okay, Lyons," she said, and raised her glass. "To Butterfly."

# ABOUT BRYANT JORDAN

Bryant Jordan spent more than 35 years writing non-fiction. As a journalist, he covered cops, courts, government and business for newspapers and magazines in Massachusetts and New Hampshire. For nearly two decades he wrote about the military, first as a reporter for the Military Times newspapers, then as an associate editor/reporter for Military.com, where his beat included the Pentagon, Capitol Hill and the White House.

He grew up in the Boston's Charlestown neighborhood, the setting for this, his first novel. Today he lives in Ireland with his wife, Linda.